Sophie
Flakes Out

Also by Nancy Rue

You! A Christian Girl's Guide to Growing Up
Girl Politics
Everyone Tells Me to Be Myself ... but I Don't Know Who I Am

Sophie's World Series
Meet Sophie (Book One)
Sophie Steps Up (Book Two)
Sophie and Friends (Book Three)
Sophie's Friendship Fiasco (Book Four)
Sophie Flakes Out (Book Five)
Sophie's Drama (Book Six)

The Lucy Series
Lucy Doesn't Wear Pink (Book One)
Lucy Out of Bounds (Book Two)
Lucy's Perfect Summer (Book Three)
Lucy Finds Her Way (Book Four)

Other books in the growing Faithgirlz!™ library

Bibles
The Faithgirlz! Bible
NIV Faithgirlz! Backpack Bible

Faithgirlz! Bible Studies
Secret Power of Love
Secret Power of Joy
Secret Power of Goodness
Secret Power of Grace

Fiction

From Sadie's Sketchbook
Shades of Truth (Book One)
Flickering Hope (Book Two)
Waves of Light (Book Three)
Brilliant Hues (Book Four)

The Girls of Harbor View
Girl Power (Book One)
Take Charge (Book Two)
Raising Faith (Book Three)
Secret Admirer (Book Four)

Boarding School Mysteries
Vanished (Book One)
Betrayed (Book Two)
Burned (Book Three)
Poisoned (Book Four)

Nonfiction

Faithgirlz! Handbook
Faithgirlz Journal
Food, Faith, and Fun! Faithgirlz Cookbook
No Boys Allowed
What's a Girl to Do?
Girlz Rock
Chick Chat
Real Girls of the Bible
My Beautiful Daughter
Whatever!

Check out www.faithgirlz.com

faiThGirLz!™
the beauty of believing

Sophie
Flakes Out

2 BOOKS IN 1
Includes *Sophie Flakes Out*
and *Sophie Loves Jimmy*

Nancy Rue

ZONDERkidz

ZONDERKIDZ

www.zonderkidz.com

Sophie Flakes Out
Copyright © 2006, 2013 by Nancy Rue

Sophie Loves Jimmy
Copyright © 2006 by Nancy Rue

This title is also available as a Zondervan ebook.
Visit www.zondervan.com/ebooks

Requests for information should be addressed to:

Zonderkidz, 3900 Sparks Drive SE, Grand Rapids, Michigan 49546

ISBN 978-0310-73854-1

Published in association with the literary agency of Alive Communications, Inc., 7680 Goddard Street, Suite 200, Colorado Springs, CO 80920. www.alivecommunucations.com

Zonderkidz is a trademark of Zondervan.

Interior art direction and design: Sarah Molegraaf
Cover illustrator: Steve James

So we fix our eyes not on what is seen,
but on what is unseen.
For what is seen is temporary,
but what is unseen is eternal.

—2 Corinthians 4:18

Sophie Flakes Out

One

"Dad-dy!" Sophie LaCroix closed her brown eyes behind her glasses so she wouldn't narrow them at her father or, worse, roll them at him. Daddy didn't like eye-rolling.

"Look, Soph," Daddy said. "I can't break it down for you any further. The answer is no. End of discussion."

Sophie wailed anyway, pipsqueak voice rising to the kitchen ceiling. "I'll be the only one in the whole entire *school* who doesn't get to see the movie."

Daddy squinted at her as he shrugged into his black NASA jacket. He didn't like whining either. "I'm sure there are other parents who don't want their twelve-year-olds seeing a PG–13 movie about gangs."

"It's a documentary!" Sophie said. "It's about real life."

Daddy's dark eyebrows shot up. "That makes it okay?" He picked up his laptop case and ran his other hand down the back of his spiky hair. "Drive-by shootings and foul language are not a part of *your* real life, and I'd like to keep it that way."

"What do I tell Mrs. Clayton and Ms. Hess?"

"Tell them I'll be calling your principal with a full explanation."

When Sophie opened her mouth, Daddy closed it with a black look. He didn't like arguing more than he didn't like anything.

He's calling Mr. Bentley? Sophie thought as she hoisted her backpack over her shoulder. *That is the most humiliating thing I can think of.*

It was probably worse than humiliating. She'd have to ask her best friend Fiona Bunting, the walking dictionary, for a word to describe feeling like a kindergartner in a seventh-grade body.

"Don't forget, it's your day to watch Zeke after school," Daddy said from the doorway. "Walk you to the bus stop, Baby Girl?"

How about NO! Sophie wanted to shriek. But she didn't even want to find out how much Daddy didn't like shrieking.

As she trudged to the corner, Sophie felt as if she had a chain attached to her ankle, and for somebody as small for a twelve-year-old as she was, that was not a good thing. She could almost imagine it clanking on the sidewalk. But, then, she could imagine almost anything.

But I don't have to imagine how heinous this situation is! she told herself. It wasn't just having to babysit her six-year-old brother while her mom, who was going to have LaCroix Kid Number Four in a few months, cooked dinner. Zeke wasn't even that bad since he'd figured out New Baby Girl wasn't going to wipe out life as he knew it. And it wasn't just that Daddy wouldn't let her go to the movie that everybody in the entire school was seeing that day—except her.

It's just all of it, Sophie thought.

She climbed aboard the bus and slumped into her usual seat behind Harley and Gill, the two soccer-playing girls Sophie and her friends (the Corn Flakes) referred to as the Wheaties.

"Hi, you guys," she said.

But they only nodded at her vaguely. Their eyes were glued to the other side of the bus, a few rows back.

"Dude," Gill said, her green eyes wide. "Cell phones?" She shook her head so that two lanky tendrils of reddish hair fell out from under her wool, billed cap.

As usual, husky Harley just grunted.

Sophie swiveled around to catch sight of two girls sitting on the reserved-for-eighth-graders-only side. The very blonde one with even blonder highlights had a phone pressed to her ear, and her striking blue eyes were dancing a reply to the person on the other end. She pulled her hair up in a handful and let it fall like a fountain of blondeness to her shoulders as she laughed.

"It's only eight o'clock in the morning," Sophie whispered. "Who could she be talking to?"

"Probably the girl next to her," Gill said.

The talker's seatmate was a slender girl with a wispy cut to her honey brown hair that made her look like a stylish elf. Her lips were moving, but she seemed to be chatting to nobody.

"Where's her phone?" Sophie said to Gill.

"In her ear," Gill said. "See the wire coming down?"

Just then the girl glanced their way, and Gill and Harley turned in their seats like they were about to be shot. But although there was an unspoken rule that seventh graders didn't stare at eighth graders, just like they didn't even venture into the eighth-grade halls, Sophie couldn't pull her eyes from the girl's golden brown ones as she raised her teen-magazine eyebrows at Sophie. Even though they'd been riding the same bus for three months, it was the first time she seemed to notice Sophie. Being seen by a girl who looked so together was like being under a spell.

The girl spread out her palms as if to say, "Well?"

"Sorry," Sophie said. She shriveled back into her seventh-grade world.

"I can't believe they're taking cell phones to school," Gill whispered over the back of the seat.

"I'll never even own one 'til I'm out of college or something," Sophie whispered back. Even her fourteen-year-old sister, Lacie, didn't have one, and she was in high school.

Sophie scooted closer to the bus window and gazed out through her glasses as Poquoson, Virginia, went by in a November mist. *I'll never even get a phone in my* room, she thought. *My conversations with my friends might as well be on the six o'clock news.*

Not to mention the whole rest of her life. In less than an hour, everybody in her section at school would know that her parents didn't think she could handle a PG–13 movie.

They're way overprotective, Sophie thought. And then she squirmed a little. Back in October, when Mama and Daddy had come to the school to stand up for her, she had liked them being her guardian angels. But this was way different, she decided—and way confusing.

She ran her hand over the top of her very-short-but-shiny light brown hair like she always did when she was confused, and she closed her eyes. Time to imagine Jesus. And of course, there he was, with his kind eyes, waiting for her questions.

Okay, so what is WITH Mama and Daddy lately? she murmured to him in her mind. *The baby that hasn't even been born yet has more privacy than I do!*

Sophie opened her eyes and squirmed some more. It didn't feel exactly right to be complaining to Jesus about her parents. There was that whole "honor your father and mother" thing to consider.

She was still pondering it when she got to her locker. Most of the other Corn Flakes were waiting for her. That was the name they'd given themselves when the Corn Pops, the wickedly popular girls, had said they were "flakes." To the Corn Flakes, that meant they were free to be themselves and never put down other people the way the Corn Pops did.

"How come you weren't online last night?" Fiona tucked back the wayward strand of golden-brown hair that was always creeping over one magic-gray eye. "I wanted to IM you. I tried emailing, but you didn't answer."

"Guess," Sophie said. She dropped her backpack and went after her combination lock.

"Lacie had another paper to write," said Darbie O'Grady. She swept both sides of her reddish bob behind her ears. "I bet you were up to ninety."

In Darbie's Irish slang, that meant Sophie was ready to explode. Sophie nodded and yanked her locker open.

"You're so lucky you're an only child, Darbie," she said. "You too, Mags."

"Huh." The sound that came out of Maggie LaQuita was as square and solid as everything else about her, including the blunt cut of her Cuban-dark hair.

"You don't have other siblings reading your emails and getting into your stuff," Fiona said. "Not like Sophie and I do."

"But my mother is the only other person in my house," Maggie said. "If I close the door to my room, she says I'm shutting her out."

Sophie looked up, her literature book poised in midair. "Really?" she said. "I thought you and your mom got along really well. She makes all your clothes and everything."

"Huh," Maggie said again. She looked down at the bright turquoise-and-orange poncho that covered her chest. "She hasn't figured out that we don't have the same tastes anymore."

"And does she say you're giving her cheek when you complain?" Darbie said.

15

Maggie frowned. "You mean like I'm talking back to her?"

"Yeah."

Maggie's dark eyes answered for her.

"I have the same problem," Darbie said. She leaned against the bank of lockers opposite Sophie's. "When I first came here, I liked it that Aunt Emily and Uncle Patrick were always protecting me from scary things. But I've adjusted—"

"You're practically American now," Fiona added.

"But they still turn the channel every time someone says a cross word on the telly, and they look at me like I might go mental."

Sophie gave her locker door another shove and smiled at all of them.

"What?" Fiona said.

"I'm glad we all have parent problems," she said. "I mean, I'm not glad about the problems, but I'm glad at least we all understand what we're going through."

"So we can empathize," Fiona said.

"Define," Maggie said.

"It's better than sympathizing, where you just think you know how somebody feels. When you empathize, you really *do* know how the other person feels."

"That's why we're the Corn Flakes, isn't it?" Darbie said.

"Is empathizing part of the Corn Flake Code?" Maggie said.

Fiona counted off on her fingers. "Never put anybody down even though they do it to you. Don't fight back or give in to bullies; just take back your power to be yourself. Talk to Jesus about everything because he gives you the power to be who he made you to be."

"I didn't hear anything about empathizing," Maggie said, words thudding.

"It's got to be in there somewhere," Darbie said.

"We can add it," Sophie said. "Corn Flakes are totally loyal to each other and will always empathize."

"I love it," Fiona said. "And a Corn Flake will help you with the things your parents can't help you with." Her pink bow of a mouth went into a grin. "Like dealing with *them!*"

"Who are we dealing with?" another voice chimed in.

Sophie shoved her shoulder against her locker door, which still wouldn't close, as Willoughby Wiley joined them. Her wildly curly brown hair was springing out of a messy bun in just the right way, and her hazel eyes were shining. Sophie always thought you didn't have to see the red, white, and blue Great Marsh Middle School pom-poms sticking out of her backpack to know she was a cheerleader.

"We were talking about parents," Fiona said.

"And I'm talking about you getting away from my locker so I can get in it—please."

That came from Julia Cummings, the tall, auburn-haired leader of the Corn Pops, who had trailed in behind Willoughby with her fellow Pops at her heels. On the chubby-side B.J. Schneider nearly plowed into the back of Julia as she glared at Willoughby.

Cheerleader envy, Sophie thought. The Corn Pops were still mad that they had been kicked off the seventh-grade cheerleading squad while Willoughby, a former Corn Pop herself, was now captain. *But they don't dare do anything about it or they're toast*, Sophie added to herself. They'd gotten into enough trouble for harassing the Flakes to last them until graduation.

Which was probably why, Sophie decided, Julia gave Darbie an icy smile as Darbie said, "Oh, sorry," and stepped away from Julia's locker. Pale, thin Corn Pop Anne-Stuart sniffed at Darbie as she moved, but, then, Anne-Stuart was always sniffing. Sophie had never known her not to be in dire need of a box of tissues.

"You're not supposed to touch other people's lockers," Cassie said to Darbie. She tossed her very long, almost-too-blonde hair as if she were adding punctuation. Cassie was the newest of the Corn Pops. It seemed to Sophie that she was always trying to prove herself, especially to Julia.

Willoughby turned her back on them completely and widened her eyes at the Flakes. "What about parents?" she said. "You all looked bummed."

Darbie groaned and Maggie filled her in, with Fiona adding details. Sophie listened while she fought with her locker door, which was now jammed half open and half closed.

"You know what?" Willoughby said. "Maybe it's because I just have a dad and not a mom, but I have way a lot of freedom. Y'all can escape to my house anytime."

The bell rang. "How about now?" Fiona said. "I don't really want to go see that lame gang movie." She gave Sophie a sympathetic — or maybe empathetic — look.

"You better come on," Maggie said to Sophie as they all hurried toward the hall.

"You all go ahead," Sophie said. "I have to get this thing open so I can close it."

"That makes total sense," Julia muttered as she and the Corn Pops sailed away.

"Makes sense to us," Fiona said. Although there wasn't time for the official Corn Flake pinky promise shake, she held up her little finger and wiggled it, and the rest of the girls did the same.

I would LOVE to escape to Willoughby's, like, tonight! Sophie thought as she put one foot up on the locker below hers to brace herself for one more tug. But then she felt a pang of guilt. *I want to escape from my own house?*

She pulled on the locker with both hands, but her fingers slipped off and she dropped to her seat on the floor. At the end of the row of lockers, feet rushed past, and she was sure she heard Colton Messik say, "Oops, Soapy, you fell. Too bad."

He was one of the absurd little creep boys the Corn Flakes had named the Fruit Loops. At least there were only two of them now, since Eddie Wornom was no longer around.

Two too many, Sophie thought as she got to her feet and readjusted her glasses. *I need to escape from them too.*

Actually, she thought, as she gave up on getting the locker open and shoved at it with her backpack to get it closed, she didn't really need to go to Willoughby's or anywhere else to shut it all out. Escape was never more than a dream character away.

And do I need one now or what? Sophie thought. *Hello!*

She stopped pushing and headed for the hall. Somebody who could protect the right of kids to grow up—that's what she saw taking shape in her dream-mind. Maybe the leader of a good gang.

What could her name be? Goodie?

Nah, too sappy.

My name will be revealed on a need-to-know basis, thought the tough little woman with the smooth muscles that made her T-shirt sleeves curve outward. I don't tell it to just any punk who shoves me in a crowd, she told herself as she dodged passing elbows like a championship boxer. They can see that I can't be pushed around.

But though she was tough, she didn't swagger. It was sheer confidence that drove her straight into the thick of the danger on the street—

"Sophie LaCroix—do you want to tell me what you're doing down here?"

Sophie blinked and found herself standing in the middle of an eighth-grade hall.

TWO

"Sophie?" The voice of Miss Imes, Sophie's math teacher, was as pointy as her dark eyebrows that shot like arrowheads toward her almost-white hair.

"What are you doing way down here?"

"I don't know," Sophie said.

"Why doesn't that surprise me?" Miss Imes looked over Sophie's head at the students surging past. "Slow it down. You'll all get a seat."

Nobody talked back. *Even eighth graders don't mess with her*, Sophie thought. Rumor had it that eighth graders really didn't take orders from anybody. She'd never had a chance to check that out firsthand. She'd never even been in an eighth-grade hall.

"You'd best get yourself to class before you're marked tardy," Miss Imes said to her. "I don't want you getting into any trouble that will keep you out of the new Film Club project."

"What new project?" Sophie could feel her eyes popping.

"You'll find out at lunch," Miss Imes said. "It's exciting."

Nothing actually sounded exciting when it came dryly out of Miss Imes' mouth. After all, she was a math teacher. But if she said it was, it was.

"No tardies," Miss Imes said.

Sophie turned and followed the throng toward the main hall where she could cross to seventh-grade territory.

And the sooner the better, she thought.

It was different down here. There were boy-girl couples holding hands and girls striding as if they were going down a fashion show runway and guys spewing out language Sophie hadn't heard since Eddie Wornom had been sent away to military school.

But even all that didn't dampen the promise of a new project. Sophie went into a higher gear. No way was she going to be late and mess up being able to participate.

Not only that, she thought as she ducked around a hugging couple, *I don't want to get kicked off Round Table either.*

Round Table was the handpicked council of students and faculty members who figured out how to help kids who got in trouble and needed to change more than they needed punishment.

The tough little good-gang leader quickened her steps. There was so much work to be done. The more punk-wannabes she could get out of trouble, the better.

Sophie was three long leaps from her first-period-classroom door when the final bell rang. She slipped in just as it was closing—one of the few benefits of being the smallest kid in the seventh grade. Inside, everybody was standing up, yelling "Here!" as Ms. Hess, the younger of the two English/History block teachers, called out their names so they could head to the gym for the movie.

Fiona grabbed Sophie's arm. "I answered for you. There's so much confusion in here Ms. Hess didn't even notice."

"I'm glad it wasn't Mrs. Clayton," Sophie said. Not only was the other teacher older and sharper, she was the head of the Round Table.

"Wish you were coming with," Darbie said as Ms. Hess herded the class out.

Sophie nodded miserably and stepped aside so Julia and Anne-Stuart could pass.

"What are you hanging back for?" Anne-Stuart said through her nose.

"Not going," Sophie said.

Anne-Stuart exchanged glances with Julia, and they both curled their lips.

"Oh," Julia said. "I get it."

No, you do not "get it," Sophie thought as they gave her a final smirk and exited. She was pretty sure they didn't know what *empathize* meant. She was grateful for the pinky fingers Darbie and Fiona wiggled at her as they left.

But Sophie still felt like a loser as she went up to Mrs. Clayton's desk. "My dad wouldn't sign my permission slip," she said to the top of Mrs. Clayton's cement-like helmet of yellowy-blonde hair. "He thinks it's too violent."

Mrs. Clayton bulleted a long look at her before she said in her trumpet voice, "I'll write you a library pass for first and second periods." At least she added, "I can trust you."

That didn't make Sophie feel any less out of it. But when she walked into the library, she could feel a smile spreading from ear to ear.

"Kitty!" she said.

"Shhh!" the librarian said.

Sophie hurried over to the set of shelves where her friend Kitty Munford, the final Corn Flake, was flipping listlessly through a book. Her face, pale and puffy, seemed to fill with light when she saw Sophie.

It was hard to hug somebody who was sitting in a wheel-chair, but Sophie managed. She'd just seen Kitty on Sunday, but now that Kitty was being homeschooled while she was having chemotherapy for her leukemia, Sophie missed being with her every day.

"What are you doing here?" Sophie whispered as she squatted beside the chair Kitty used when she got too weak to walk.

"My mom's talking to somebody in the office," Kitty said. "I'm supposed to be checking out some books, but I'm sick of reading."

Sophie nodded. She hoped she looked empathetic, since she had never been as sick as Kitty was and had no idea what it must be like. From the tired look in Kitty's blue eyes and the lack of hair under her pink-and-black-tweed hat, Sophie knew it must be pretty awful. The hair was the only thing she *could* empathize with, since she'd shaved her head at the beginning of the year so Kitty wouldn't have to be bald alone. Sophie's was growing back in. Kitty's wasn't.

Kitty folded her fingers weakly around Sophie's arm. "Are you doing another Corn Flakes production soon?"

"Yes!" Sophie said. "Miss Imes says it's going to be something special."

"Can I please, *please* be in it? I'm going nutso being at home."

"Of course you can!" Sophie said. "You're a Corn Flake."

"My mom is driving me bonkers, Sophie. She 'protects' me every single minute!"

Sophie nodded. She was sure she was empathizing now. "I hear you. We *all* hear you. Just about everybody's parents are, like, smothering them."

Kitty tugged at her hat. "Mom's totally in my space all the time."

"Don't worry," Sophie said. "We'll make a part in the film for you."

"You're saving my life," Kitty said.

When Kitty's mother bustled into the library looking like she expected to find Kitty passed out on the floor, Sophie was sure Kitty hadn't been exaggerating.

"Mom, Sophie says I can be in the next movie!" Kitty said.

"Shhh!" the librarian said.

"We'll see," Mrs. Munford said.

When she'd pushed Kitty out the door, with Kitty grabbing at the wheels of her chair and saying, "Mom—I can do it!" Sophie found a corner and began to see...

The good-gang leader still did not expose her name to the world. But she did reveal what she was about. With her gang of good-hearted members gathered around her, hanging on every tough-love word that came from her lips, she explained to them how they needed to protect the right of every kid on the streets to grow up to be independent and unafraid. "It's a jungle out there," she told them, eyes intense beneath the bill of her ball cap. "Everyone is telling them who to be, but we can't let them get tangled up—"

By the time the bell rang for third period, Good-Something was fully formed. Sophie dashed to PE ready to reveal her to the Flakes in the locker room.

Marching forward on her short but muscular legs, she could feel the desperate kids following her. They were waiting for their street orders, and she was ready to deliver them, just as soon as she got through this crowd of unruly boys who obviously didn't need protection and support as much as they needed somebody to teach them some manners. They were spilling out from a clogged doorway, blocking her path, but Good-Something lowered her head and plowed right through them. Oh, but her spirit was mightier than her body, and she felt herself going down—until a large hand seemed to come down from the heavens and lift her up—

"Little Bit, you want to get yourself trampled?"

Sophie felt her feet hit solid ground again as Coach Nanini, the boys' PE teacher, set her down in the hallway, apart from the mob of boys pushing into the locker room.

"I must have lost my head," Sophie said. She grinned at him. He grinned back, his one big eyebrow crumpling down over his eyes. He always reminded her of a big happy gorilla with no hair. To her, he was Coach Virile.

"You're going to lose worse than your head if you get under those animals' feet," he said. He handed Sophie her glasses, which he'd obviously rescued.

"I'll lose *worse* if I don't get to roll call on time," Sophie said as she put them back on.

"You got that right." Coach Virile leaned down and lowered his high-pitched-for-a-huge-guy voice. "I wouldn't cross Coach Yates today. She's a little grumpy."

More than usual? Sophie wanted to say. The girls' PE teacher yelled more than Sophie's father did when he was watching the Dallas Cowboys on TV. Sophie hurried into the locker room. Fiona, Darbie, and Maggie were already there changing.

"You are so lucky you missed that movie, Soph," Fiona said instead of hello.

Darbie nodded through the neck hole of her T-shirt as she poked her head in. "I nearly went mental with boredom."

"Our films are a lot better," Maggie said.

Sophie knew they were all lying, but she appreciated it. Besides, they'd reminded her of what Miss Imes had said about a new Film Club project. She was explaining when Willoughby dashed in, backpack flying out behind her.

"You're gonna be late for roll call," Maggie said, voice matter-of-fact.

"I know!" Willoughby said. She tried to slide her backpack off, but the strap caught on her sweater.

"Stop before you hurt yourself," Fiona said. "Come on, guys."

The Corn Flakes went into action, Maggie and Darbie stripping off Willoughby's backpack, sweater, tank top, and jeans, while Sophie and Fiona pulled on her sweatshirt and track pants as soon as there was a place to put them.

"Give me your arm," Sophie said, holding out the sleeve of the sweatshirt.

But Fiona had Willoughby focused on shoving her foot into a tennis shoe, so Sophie took the arm herself.

Willoughby yelped. She was always shrieking in a voice that reminded Sophie of a poodle, but this was different. Willoughby pulled back her arm and cradled it.

"Did I grab you too hard?" Sophie said.

"No," Willoughby said. "I hurt it last night. I was practicing a new cheer and I fell over the coffee table." She did give her poodle-laugh then. "I'm such a klutz."

"You guys carry her while I get this other shoe on her," Fiona said.

They made it to the line in time for roll call, but not without a stony stare from Coach Yates. Her graying ponytail seemed to pinch her face even tighter than usual, and Sophie decided Coach Virile had been right.

By the time she got through PE and Miss Imes' fourth-period math class, Sophie was sure she would unzip and come right out of her skin if she didn't find out what the special film project was. All the Film Club members met in Miss Imes' classroom at lunch. That included the Corn Flakes and the boys they thought of as the Lucky Charms—because they never acted heinous the way the Fruit Loops did and were actually fun sometimes. When Mr. Stires, their other adviser and also their science teacher, arrived, Miss Imes, as Willoughby put it, dished.

"There is going to be a film festival in one month," she said. "Schools from three counties have been invited to participate. Each entry is to follow the theme 'Bringing History to Life Today.'"

Sophie squealed. Could that have been any more perfect? The Corn Flakes had been making movies about history for a whole year. And Jimmy, Nathan, and Vincent were such huge history buffs, they had their own swords and swashbuckler boots.

Even now, Vincent, who was skinny and had a big, loose grin that filled up most of his face, was waving his arm.

"Did you want to say something, Vincent?" Mr. Stires said with the usual chuckle. He thought just about everything students did was amusing. Even his toothbrush mustache always looked cheerful.

"Seeing that movie this morning made me think of this," Vincent said. His voice cracked, which it did a lot. Whenever Vincent's voice cracked, Nathan's face turned red. But, then, Nathan's face was always turning red.

"No offense, Vincent," Fiona said, "but I don't think gangs are history."

Vincent wiggled his eyebrows. "1920s gangs are."

There was a thinking-silence.

"You mean, like gangsters and Al Capone and tommy guns?" Jimmy said. He was quieter than the other two Charms, but when he said something, everybody listened. The Corn Pops, Sophie had noticed, listened because Jimmy was also blond and tanned and had muscles from being in gymnastics.

"I know about the twenties," Darbie said. "They did the Charleston and swallowed goldfish back then."

"I'm not doing that," Maggie said.

"We could have some really good characters," Vincent said. "Guys with names like Bugsy—"

"Goodsy!" Sophie said.

Nathan cocked his curly head, topped as always with a Redskins ball cap. "I don't remember a gangster named Goodsy." He reddened.

"I think she's talking about a new character," Fiona said. She leaned into Sophie. "What have you got, Soph?"

Sophie launched into Goodsy—Goodsy Malone—and the rest of the group listened. Vincent added ideas, and his voice cracked more with each one, which meant he was excited. Jimmy nodded. Maggie pulled out the Corn Flakes Treasure Book to take notes. Nathan turned a happier red, and Willoughby was already designing twenties hairdos on binder paper.

"I think it's our best idea yet," Fiona said.

"A lot of people are going to see this," Miss Imes said, "so you want it to be the best you can do."

"It will be," Sophie promised her.

"Let's all take a vow to give it 200 percent," Fiona said.

"I think it only goes up to 100," Vincent said.

"I'm in," Jimmy said. Everybody else agreed. Then they all looked at Sophie. She was always the director.

"Okay," she said. "We start doing research today after school. Meet in the library—"

"I can't," Willoughby said. "I have cheerleading practice."

"That's not 100 percent," Maggie said.

But Sophie put her hand up. "We already knew Willoughby has practice every school day. You can meet other times, right?"

Willoughby nodded until her curls bounced like springs.

"Let's cut her some slack," Sophie said. She was sure that was something the tough but bighearted—and definitely empathetic—Goodsy Malone would say.

Three

Right after sixth period, Sophie ran for the pay phone near the gym to call Mama before the after-school line formed. Her mother's voice was thin when she answered.

"I need to stay after, okay?" Sophie said. "We have a new Film Club project—we're going to be in a *festival*—wait 'til I tell you about it—"

"Soph—"

"I can take the late bus—"

"Sophie." Mama's voice stretched like a rubber band. "You have to watch Zeke, remember?"

Sophie didn't mean for the impatient, "Aw, man," to slip out, but it did.

"I'm sorry," Mama said, "but I'm feeling really tired. I'm afraid Zeke will try to Spider-Man his way up the side of the house if nobody's watching him."

Mama tried to laugh. Sophie didn't.

"Things are going to be a lot easier after this little one is born, Dream Girl," Mama said.

But even Mama's pet name for her—the one that always showed she really did understand who Sophie was—added a link to the imaginary chain around her ankle.

"Z-Boy won't be home for half an hour," Mama said. "That gives you a little time with your friends."

If the bus wasn't leaving, like, right this minute, Sophie wanted to say. As it was, there was barely time to sprint to the library to deliver the bad news to the club and race to the front of the school. When she finally got there, panting like a dog, the bus was already leaving.

"No!" she called after it. Her voice squeaked up.

"Miss your bus?" said an all-too-familiar voice. The expected sniff followed.

"What'll you do now?" B.J. chimed in.

"I'd call a cab," Julia said. "But that's just me."

Cassie gave her stringy tresses a toss. "Use your cell phone. Oh, wait—you don't have one!"

Only the Corn Flake Code kept Sophie from rolling her eyes at all of them. She turned away and Willoughby popped up, curls dancing in the wind.

"I have a cell phone, Soph," she said. "You want to call your mom?"

"Since when did *you* get a cell phone, Willoughby?" B.J. said.

Julia snapped the Pops away with her fingers. Willoughby produced a pink phone from the pocket of her track pants, flipped it open, and pulled up the antenna with her teeth.

"Where did you get this?" Sophie said.

"My dad. He spoils me." Willoughby poised a finger over the tiny buttons. "I already have your number programmed in."

"Can we call the high school instead?" Sophie said. "I need to find Lacie."

It took a while to leave a message, then wait for Lacie to call back. Willoughby stood first on one foot and then the other and glanced at her watch every seven seconds. Sophie was afraid she'd have to give her back the phone and let her go where she was obviously dying to get to. But it burst into a tinny version of "It's a Small World," and Willoughby shrieked, "Answer it!"

"Whose phone do you have?" Lacie said when Sophie said hello.

"I need you to take my Zeke duty today," Sophie said. "Please? It's vital."

"Yeah, I'm sure it's a matter of life and death." There was a pause. "You are so going to owe me for this."

"Thank you!" Sophie cried. She knew she sounded like Willoughby, who looked like she was about to let out a poodle-yelp herself if she didn't get to wherever. Sophie hung up before Lacie could elaborate on just *how* she was going to owe her.

Whatever it was, it was worth it, Sophie decided when she was deep into research in the library. The 1920s were, in Fiona's words, "positively scintillating."

"Does that mean it gives you chills?" Sophie said.

"Precisely," Fiona said.

Maggie grunted from behind a book called *Fashions of the Jazz Age* where she was getting ideas for her mom to make their costumes. "I don't feel any chills," she said.

But all of it made goose bumps chase across Sophie's skin.

The girls of the twenties, called flappers, bobbed their hair and shortened their skirts to be free of the shackles of Victorian corsets and gowns.

The college boys in oversize fur coats sat on top of flag-poles and swallowed goldfish, just because they could.

The good people of Chicago tried to reclaim their city from the corruption of mob leaders like Al Capone. That was what made Sophie suggest that Goodsy Malone should be a police officer instead of a gang leader.

"They didn't have female cops back then," Vincent said. He squinted at the computer screen. "Women had barely gotten the right to vote."

31

"So I'll play a boy," Sophie said. She ran a hand over her head. "I've got the hair for it."

Jimmy jabbed a thumb toward the computer. "This says girls made a lot of advances in the twenties. Maybe we could make it like Goodsy is a girl, but she's pretending to be a guy so she can be a cop." He shrugged his big gymnast's shoulders. "It's just an idea."

"It's brilliant," Fiona said.

Goodsy Malone pulled her fedora low over her eyes the way the other plainclothes detectives did and was grateful for her bobbed hair. For once it was even a good thing to be the flattest-chested woman in America. There wasn't a chance anyone would guess her secret, and with Al Capone's mob pumping out bullets with their tommy guns all over town, the Chicago coppers needed all the help they could get —

"You didn't hear any of that, did you, Sophie?" Maggie said. She closed the Treasure Book.

Sophie peeked out from under the bill of her newsboy cap and shook her head.

"Vincent's going to email us with more information tonight," Fiona said. "Then we can finish the outline."

"This is going to be brilliant," Darbie said.

"It's gonna be swell," Nathan said. His face went radish-colored as they all stared at him. "I was looking up slang. They said 'swell' instead of 'cool.'"

"Let's all start saying that," Sophie said.

She said it in her head all the way to the late bus. The word fit Goodsy's lips as if it were made for them.

Taking the bus is a swell way to spy on the mob, Goodsy told herself as she scanned the passing city with trained eyes. They'll never think of it, and they'll let their guard down. Maybe she would see them attempt one of the drive-by shootings. That would be really swell.

Even as the thought appeared, so did a long black car with darkly tinted windows. It slowed to a crawl in front of a small grocery store, and Goodsy watched as the glass in the back opened and the barrel of a gun inched its way out. Before Goodsy could shout for the driver to stop the bus, she heard the shots rat-a-tat-tatting in rapid succession.

"Everybody down!" she shouted—and dived under the seat. Around her the crowd roared—

With laughter.

"Hey," one of the eighth-grade boys said. "There's a chick freaking out back here."

Gill's face appeared upside down under Sophie's seat. "What did you think that was?" she said.

"Gunshots," Sophie whispered.

"Dude, it was that eighth grader's cell phone. She has it on vibrate, but you can hear it all over."

"Oh," Sophie said. She crept out from under the seat and turned to the window to avoid the okay-she's-whacko looks being cast her way. "Uh-oh," she said.

"Wasn't that your stop back there?" Gill said.

Harley grunted. So did Sophie.

She got off at the next corner and ran back to Odd Road as if Al Capone himself were chasing her—

Which he was. Goodsy could hear the soles of his Italian leather shoes slapping the sidewalk as he gained on her, but she hadn't been through vigorous police training for nothing. She veered sharply to the left, leaving the sidewalk as if she were about to dart across the street. The footsteps grew closer as Goodsy ducked between two parked cars.

As soon as she heard the fancy shoes hit grass, she zipped back to the right, leaped over the sidewalk, and ducked behind a pile of leaves. The powerful Al Capone stood bewildered in the middle of the street, head whipping from side to side until he threw up his hands, diamond rings glinting in the sun, and snapped his fingers for the long black car.

Goodsy smiled smugly to herself as the car pulled away with the confused gangster inside. He's never come up against a tough woman before, she thought as she slipped, unnoticed, the rest of the way back to police headquarters. And the beauty of it is, he doesn't even know he has. That was swell.

Goodsy was still feeling pleased with herself when she entered headquarters. That was, until something heavy and warm was suddenly on her back.

"I'm Spider-Man," a six-year-old voice chirped in her ear. "You're goin' down."

"He's all yours," said Lacie, head in the refrigerator. "I'm cooking dinner and Mom's asleep." She pulled her dark head out and waved a bag of shredded cheese in Sophie's direction. "Like I said, you owe me."

"That ain't no problem for me," Sophie said.

Lacie blinked her Daddy-like eyes at Sophie. "It 'ain't'?"

"Matter of fact, it'll be swell." Sophie looked at her brother. "Come on, Z-Boy. I need your help. You're very good with shadows."

Zeke shook his head of unruly dark hair that was looking more like Daddy's every day. "I'm Spider-Man," he said.

"Swell. Good code name, fella. Capone will never guess it."

Lacie turned back to the counter, ponytail swinging. "I don't even want to know," she said.

Dinner was, as Fiona would have said, nontraditional. They had nachos, the only thing Lacie knew how to make, with celery sticks and peanut butter on the side because Mama had given Lacie instructions to be sure they had a vegetable and some protein. Sophie was sure if Daddy had been there, he would have ordered Anna's Pizza. But he was working late, and it was just the three of them at the snack bar. Sophie got Zeke to eat by promising they'd continue to play "Spider-Man and Goodsy Malone Clean Up Chicago" when he was through.

It was a promise she regretted an hour later when Daddy still wasn't home and Lacie was locked in her room with her algebra book. Every time Sophie pounded on the door for Zeke relief, Lacie just said, "You owe me."

As Sophie tried to do her own math homework, so she wouldn't fall below a B and lose video camera privileges, Zeke climbed up her closet door. Sophie was sure she had paid Lacie back at least twelve times. When Lacie came to the door and said the phone was for Sophie, Sophie tried to pawn Zeke off on her. Then she could at least have a conversation that didn't include peeling him off the shower curtain rod. But Lacie just said, "My meter is still running," and went back to her room.

"Can you hold, please?" Sophie said into the phone. She tucked it under her arm and told Zeke that Al Capone had her locked in the closet. Then she shut the door and barricaded herself behind the clothes.

"I have two minutes, tops," she whispered into the phone.

"That's all I need." The voice on the other end cracked.

"Vincent?" Sophie said.

"I just emailed you a bunch more stuff about Capone," he said. "We have to take him down in our movie. He and his organization killed all these people and made, like, six million dollars selling illegal alcohol, and the cops couldn't nab him for any of it."

Sophie could feel Goodsy flexing her muscles.

"I'm thinking Jimmy should play him," Vincent said. "He's got the body to be tough, but we'll have to work on the attitude."

Sophie giggled. She had a life-size picture in her mind of Jimmy glowering and chewing on a cigar. The giggles faded as she heard something scraping all the way down the door.

"I'll save you, Goodsy!" a voice chirped. "Even if I have to cut through—"

"No, don't!" Sophie cried.

"Don't what?" Vincent said.

"Nothing." Sophie shoved the door open just in time to snatch a pair of kindergarten scissors out of Zeke's hand. "I'll check my email," she said into the phone.

Yeah, good luck with that, Sophie thought as she hurried downstairs to Daddy's study with Spider-Man crawling down the banister behind her. *I bet Daddy is hiding out at work on purpose.* She gave a Harley-style grunt. *I wish I had a place to hide.*

At least Lacie wasn't on the computer. Sophie gave Zeke a black marker and told him to write a warning letter to Al Capone. Since he was only in first grade and couldn't actually spell anything, she figured that could take a while.

There were emails from Darbie, Fiona, and Willoughby, but Sophie checked Brainchild first. That was Vincent's screen name.

He hadn't been kidding when he said he had more information on Al Capone. There were two pages of facts before Vincent even got to his ideas for scenes.

There was one scene where Capone shot somebody going to worship and left bullet holes in the church wall.

Then he suggested another scene where Goodsy got into the Lexington Hotel and heard Capone planning his next move on the O'Banyon gang. "We'll have to rig up a chair with a bulletproof back," Vincent had written.

The scene that captured Sophie the most was the one where Capone held Goodsy at gunpoint, and she never even swallowed hard. Sophie could see that one in her mind.

"Gun," Zeke said.

Sophie jumped. She hadn't noticed him scooting onto the chair beside her. He pointed at the screen with a chubby finger, black with marker ink.

"I thought you were writing a letter," Sophie said.

"I'm done." Zeke held up a piece of paper, filled with BAD, EVUL, and even a sentence: SPIDERMAN WIL GET YUO.

"I didn't even know you could spell!" Sophie said.

"Hello," Zeke said. One eyebrow shot up into a where-have-YOU-been position. He poked at Vincent's message on the screen again. " 'He will shoot you but o-on-only in the leg.' "

"That's not in the first-grade reader, I can tell you that."

Sophie whipped her head around to see Daddy in the doorway. Zeke bolted for him and clung to his pants.

"Have you had a bath?" Daddy said to him.

"I don't wanna take a bath."

"Then I guess you won't be needing this." Daddy pulled a small Spider-Man action figure out from behind his back. Zeke clattered up the stairs with it before Sophie could even sign off the Internet.

"A little light reading for your baby brother, Soph?" Daddy said. He kissed Sophie on top of the head.

"It's just for our new film project," Sophie said. "It's about the twenties mobsters, and we're taking it to a festival. It's gonna be swell—"

"It's going to be violent from the sounds of it."

As Daddy pulled off his NASA jacket, Sophie stifled a groan, which Daddy also didn't like. *Here we go again*, she thought. Her eyes ached to roll right up into her head.

Four

Daddy folded his arms across his big chest. That was never a good sign.

"What is it with you kids and your fascination with violence?" he said.

"The movie's about fighting *against* violence," Sophie said. "It's going to be scintillating."

Daddy's mouth twitched. "I smell Fiona in this."

"It's our whole Film Club. We're doing it for this really cool—really *swell*—festival—"

Daddy put up his hand. "Seriously, Soph, I'm concerned. I don't want all this stuff about guns and gangs in your head."

"It's only a movie, Daddy," Sophie said.

"It's never 'only a movie' with you, Sophie. The next thing I know you'll be staging gun battles in the upstairs hall with Zeke."

"We already did that," Sophie said. Then she wanted to bite her tongue off. *Why do I always have to be so honest?* she thought.

Daddy ran a hand down the back of his head. That was never a good sign either. "I'm going to have a talk with Miss Imes and Mr. Stires before this goes any further," he said.

Sophie felt her mouth drop open, but she couldn't even squeak out a protest.

"I'm not trying to shut down your film," Daddy went on. "I just want to call a time-out so I can see what direction it's taking."

He put his hand on her shoulder. As far as Sophie was concerned, it was part of that shackle around her ankle.

When she climbed into bed later, Sophie dragged the imaginary chain with her. Jesus was there in her mind before she even closed her eyes.

This is heinous! her thoughts cried out to him. *You heard that, I know—Daddy's going to talk to my teachers. Like I'm some first grader! Zeke gets an action figure, and I get a ball and chain.*

Sophie let her eyes fly open. Just like last time, she wasn't sure this was right, complaining to Jesus about her parents.

Dr. Peter says I can tell Jesus anything, she thought. And then she sighed into a purple pillow. She was going to see Dr. Peter the next day at Bible study. Not only was he the most amazing teacher in the entire galaxy, but he had been special to her ever since he'd been her therapist last year. He would know how she should handle this. He always did.

It was hard telling the rest of the Film Club the next morning before school what Daddy planned to do, since they were all so excited about Vincent's ideas.

But Darbie said, "We won't let him make a bags of our project, Sophie," pronouncing it Soophie like she always did. "We're all going to help each other with these eejit parents, remember?"

"And how!"

They all looked at Nathan, who was already going strawberry-colored.

"That means 'you got that right,'" he said. He held up a bunch of papers. "I got a whole list of twenties slang off the Internet."

Sophie grinned. "That's swell, Nathan."

"And how!" Fiona said.

Using phrases like "Says you!" for "You're totally wrong" and "Bushwa!" for "That's a bunch of bunk" almost made Sophie forget about Daddy. Her favorites on the list were the expressions for things that were even better than swell. Like "That's the bee's knees!" or "the cat's pajamas!" The girls were speaking twenties slang like a second language by the time they got to third-period PE.

In the locker room, they filled Willoughby in as much as they could before Coach Yates started bellowing—louder than usual—for them to hurry up.

"Okay, here's the deal," Fiona said as they all headed for roll call. "We need more time with you, Will, to get you caught up, so let's do a sleepover at my house Friday night."

"And we'll see if Kitty can come," Sophie said. "It'll be swell."

"I can't make it."

They all looked at Willoughby, who was twirling a curl around her finger.

"Says you!" Fiona said.

"I have a cheerleading thing."

"Practice is only after school," Maggie said, words coming out in fact blocks.

"It isn't exactly practice," Willoughby said. She was still twirling the curl, so tightly that the end of her finger was turning purple. "Well, it's kind of like practice, only not like regular practice—it's sort of practice for practice."

Fiona blinked. "That made absolutely no sense at all."

Sophie wasn't sure it did to Willoughby either. Willoughby's forehead was pulled into folds, and she seemed relieved when Coach Yates yelled for them all to line up for basketball drills.

That was only one of the things on Sophie's mind when they got to Bible study class that afternoon. In spite of the fun they were having with "the cat's pajamas," she hadn't forgotten completely about Daddy pushing himself right into the middle of her business.

That was the good—*swell*—thing about Dr. Peter. He could make Bible study about any problem the girls—Fiona, Sophie, Maggie, Darbie, Gill, and Harley—brought in. There was nothing they'd faced yet in middle school that Dr. Peter couldn't find in the Bible somewhere. Sophie was convinced he had the whole thing memorized.

The second-best thing about Dr. Peter's Bible study was the fact that he had different-colored beanbag chairs with matching Bible covers, and there was always some kind of "sumptuous snack treat," as Fiona put it. Today it was sub sandwiches on big hunky wheat rolls cut into girl-size slices.

But the best was Dr. Peter himself. He was a much smaller man than Sophie's father, but he seemed to fill up a room with his sparkle. Blue eyes twinkled behind his glasses, and there was always a smile on his face and a zany gel-gleam to his short, curly hair.

As they selected their mini-sandwiches from the tray, he rubbed his hands together the way he always did when he was excited to get started.

"Whatcha got for me today?" he said.

Each one of them got a turn, between bites, to talk about the stuff they'd had to deal with since last Wednesday. Everybody, including Harley and Gill, complained about parents and brothers and sisters and the total lack of privacy in the seventh-grade world.

When they were all finished whining, and half the sandwiches had been wolfed down, Dr. Peter worked his glasses up by wrinkling his nose, like he always did.

"I think I have a story for you," he said.

"Swell," Sophie said.

"That's the bee's knees, Dr. P.," Fiona said.

"The cat's pajamas," Darbie put in.

"Let me guess," Dr. Peter said, "you're working on a twenties film." His eyes did their twinkle-thing. "That's the elephant's eyebrows."

Sophie saw Maggie jot that down.

Dr. Peter told them all to settle back in their beanbags and close their eyes. "I'm going to read Matthew 12, verses 1 through 8," he said. "So get ready to imagine."

Sophie never had to do much getting ready. She loved this way of studying the Bible.

"Jesus has been teaching for awhile now," Dr. Peter said. "People are starting to believe what he's telling them, and that doesn't make the Pharisees happy."

I hope we don't have to imagine we're one of them, Sophie thought. The Pharisees were the ones who were always trying to make everybody follow a bunch of strict rules and badmouthing Jesus.

"Pretend in your mind that you are one of the disciples," Dr. Peter said.

Sophie grinned to herself. *Now you're talkin'*, she thought. Nathan would be pleased that she was using his list.

"'At that time Jesus went through the grainfields on the Sabbath,'" Dr. Peter read. "'His disciples were hungry and began to pick some heads of grain and eat them.'"

Although Sophie would rather have dreamed up a hot order of fries, she tried to imagine herself plucking the top off a stalk of wheat and munching away as she hurried to get up closer to Jesus. She didn't want to miss a word he said, and her stomach was rumbling so loud she was afraid she would. She couldn't crunch the grain in her mouth fast enough.

" 'When the Pharisees saw this, they said to him, "Look! Your disciples are doing what is unlawful on the Sabbath." ' "

Sophie/disciple scowled as she chewed. Why were those pinch-faced men always coming around messing things up? She glanced anxiously at Jesus. The only time he really got angry was when he was talking to them, and it wasn't pretty. Besides, the Pharisees always made her feel like she'd done something wrong, even when she hadn't. She inched closer to Jesus and waited for the explosion.

" 'He answered, "Haven't you read what David did when he and his companions were hungry? He entered the house of God, and he and his companions ate the consecrated bread—which was not lawful for them to do, but only for the priests." ' "

"They ate what kind of bread?" Maggie said.

Sophie sighed. It was hard to stay in Bible-character with facts-only Maggie around.

"Consecrated," Dr. Peter said. "Every Sabbath, like our Sunday, the priests had to set twelve fresh loaves of bread on a table in the Holy Place. That bread was set aside as an offering to God."

"Okay, go on," Maggie said.

Sophie slipped back into disciple mode.

"Wait," Fiona said. Sophie groaned silently. "Why did David do that if it wasn't allowed?"

"He was running away from Saul, who was trying to kill him," Dr. Peter said. "He had no food, he was hungry, and he

43

needed strength for the things he'd have to do. So the priests gave him and his friends the consecrated bread." His eyes twinkled. "Let me read on, and you'll see what this is about."

Sophie's disciple was all but tapping his sandaled toe.

"Jesus goes on to say," Dr. Peter said, " ' "Or haven't you read in the Law that on the Sabbath the priests in the temple desecrate the day and yet are innocent?" ' "

Yeah, Sophie/disciple wanted to say to the frowning Pharisees, *haven't you read that?*

Come to think of it, had *she* even read that? She stuffed another handful of grain into her mouth and crept even closer to Jesus. She hoped he would explain.

But it was Dr. Peter who was talking now. "Nobody was supposed to do their customary work on the Sabbath," he was saying, "except the priests. They had to perform the special Sabbath sacrifices, which was their work in the temple. So technically they desecrated the day—disobeyed the commandment about the Sabbath—but they were innocent because that was what they were supposed to do." Dr. Peter's voice went back into his Jesus tone. " ' "I tell you that one greater than the temple is here. If you had known what these words mean, 'I desire mercy, not sacrifice,' you would not have condemned the innocent. For the Son of Man is Lord of the Sabbath." ' "

Sophie/disciple wasn't sure what all that meant, but her chest swelled proudly. *You tell 'em, Jesus*, she thought. *Put those Pharisees in their place.*

"I don't get it," Maggie said.

Sophie sighed again and abandoned the disciple. Everyone else's eyes were open too. Dr. Peter's were twinkly again.

"As usual, the Pharisees were all about the rules of the Sabbath," he said. "But they didn't understand what it really meant to keep the Sabbath day holy. If they had been in the temple when David and his men came in there practically starving, they would have said, 'Too bad. Come back tomorrow and we'll feed you.'"

"They could have been dead by then!" Darbie said.

"Exactly!"

Dr. Peter was rubbing his hands together again, as if he had been there. That always made Sophie wish she'd been there too.

"Jesus was saying that it's always lawful to do good and save life, no matter what day it is. The Sabbath was a day about God, and doing good is always about God."

Sophie closed her eyes again, and she could see her kind-eyed Jesus handing out hunks of wheat bread. She could feel a smile wisping across her face.

"Talk to us, Soph," Dr. Peter said.

"I think I get it," Sophie said. "Jesus was like a priest doing his job, only his job was different."

"How so?"

Sophie chewed on that for a second. "He wasn't there to bake loaves of bread for God. He was there to love people and feed them."

"And he was allowed to do that on the Sabbath because he was like a priest," Fiona said.

"Bingo," Dr. Peter said. "And we all can, because we're all priests in a way. We're all ministers for God."

"That's a relief," Maggie said.

Dr. Peter grinned. "Why, Maggie?"

"Because I would get pretty hungry if I couldn't make a sandwich on a Sunday."

"You got any more of those?" Gill said. "This is making *me* hungry."

45

While Dr. Peter passed the tray around again, Sophie flipped back to the story in her mind.

I don't get what that has to do with us and our parents, she thought. But she still liked the feeling she got whenever Jesus stood up to those razor-faced Pharisees and changed the rules on them.

Sophie wasn't sure if that was what she was supposed to do with Daddy or not. But it sure sounded good.

Five

Daddy had to work late again that night, which meant Sophie had to live through an evening of agony, wondering if he had actually called Miss Imes or Mr. Stires. She had plenty of time to think about how she might stand up to Daddy about a rule that needed to be changed. And that's all she did think about during games of Goodsy Malone and Spider-Man, and homework, and scrubbing the pot Lacie burned the tomato soup in. But even she, the daydream queen, had trouble imagining herself toe to toe with Daddy, saying things like, "If you had known what these words mean," and "I tell you one greater than your rules is here." The one thing she could picture was being grounded for life.

When Zeke was finally in bed, Sophie decided to go back to the Bible story to see if she was missing some magic sentence that would transform her father into a reasonable human being. She was sprawled across her bed, reaching for her Bible, when there was a light tap on the door. Mama poked her curly head in.

"Do you have a minute, Soph?" she said.

Sophie nodded and patted a spot on the bed beside her. Mama made her way across the room, swaying a little from side to side the way Sophie had seen ducks at the park do. Being pregnant made almost everything about Mama different. Her usually elfin face looked more like a chubby cherub's now, and there were soft little puffs of skin under her eyes that Sophie hadn't seen there before. Sophie had only been six when Zeke was born, and she didn't remember a roly-poly mother then.

Mama grabbed a bedpost and hoisted herself up, sinking onto the pink bedspread with a sigh. She sank back into the pile of purple and pink and pale green pillows so that her ponytail of highlighted brown curls tumbled down the side of her face. People always said how much Sophie and Mama looked alike, but Sophie was sure that was definitely not true now.

"I don't know how I'm going to make it all the way to March," Mama said. "It's only November, and I already feel like Humpty Dumpty."

"You want me to make you a cup of hot chocolate or anything?" Sophie said. "I have some Smarties—I'll give you all the green ones."

Mama shook her head, eyes closed. "No. I just want you. Tell me everything about what's going on in your life. I feel like I'm missing it."

Sophie had the sudden urge to curl up beside Mama and rest her head on her belly so she could feel her baby sister swimming around, and to spin out the stories of the last few days so they would last all night. But Mama was still stretching herself into first one position and then another, so Sophie sat cross-legged in front of her.

"Want me to rub your feet?" Sophie said.

"I would love to have you rub my feet," Mama said.

With Mama's puffed-up toes between her kneading hands, Sophie flipped through her memory deck for where to start.

The Film Club—Mama didn't know all about the festival yet.

But Daddy had probably told her about that, and how violent it was, and how he was going to snatch Sophie out of that the way he had with the school movie. Sophie decided not to go there.

The Flakes. Mama always liked to hear what was going on with the girls.

But what was going on with them, besides the film, was all their problems with their parents. Just like hers. Another topic to stay away from.

"I've never seen you at a loss for something to tell me," Mama said. Her eyes looked droopy.

Sophie felt a pang and grabbed for the next thing that came to her mind. "We're a little annoyed with Willoughby right now," she said. That was probably safe.

"Oh?"

"She's way involved in cheerleading, and she's missing a lot of rehearsals for our new film."

"A new film!" Mama said.

Sophie could almost hear the trap she'd landed in snapping shut.

Mama sat up a little straighter against the pillow pile. "So what's it about?"

"Daddy didn't tell you?" Sophie said.

"By the time Daddy gets home I'm already asleep," Mama said. "You probably talk to him more than I do these days."

Unfortunately, Sophie thought.

"Soph?" Mama had her head cocked to the side. "Something wrong between you and Daddy?"

Sophie pretended to concentrate on Mama's instep. This was a place she *definitely* didn't want to go. She didn't even want to drive by.

"Daddy tells me you girls have been such a help," Mama said. "But if you have a problem you need to talk about, don't think we're not here to help *you*." She patted her tummy. "If it's private, your baby sister won't tell."

For an instant, Sophie considered it. Mama was the one who always got her, the one who could make it better with a touch on the cheek or a batch of double-fudge brownies. The one who really could help.

But she'd said "*We're* here to help you." Daddy and Mama hardly ever disagreed when it came to something about the kids, at least not that she and Lacie and Zeke knew about. If Daddy thought telling Miss Imes their film project was too violent was "helping," Mama was sure to go along with it.

And I don't need that kind of help, Sophie thought.

"I'll go get some lotion to rub on your feet," she said.

When she came back from the bathroom, Mama had already drifted off to sleep.

A lot of things have changed with us, Sophie thought as she watched Mama's middle lift and sink with her breathing. It was a sad feeling.

But sad turned to mad the next day at lunch when Sophie and the Flakes arrived in the science room for Film Club. There was Daddy, sitting casually in a student desk, chatting it up with Mr. Stires.

"What in the *world*?" Fiona said, and with good reason.

Boppa, Fiona's balding grandfather, was on the other side of Daddy. Next to him was Darbie's Aunt Emily, nervously clacking her manicured nails. She spoke in low tones to a woman whose face was turning redder with every word. That had to be Nathan's mother.

And the tall man with faded blond hair and arm muscles that showed under his sweater had to be Jimmy's father.

50

"What is the deal?" Sophie heard Jimmy mutter beside her.

Sophie was sure they all would have stood there, gawking in the doorway, as Darbie put it, if Miss Imes hadn't hurried in behind them and ushered them all to seats. As Fiona sank into the one next to Sophie, she murmured, "Tell your father thanks a lot."

"You tell him," Sophie whispered back. "I don't think I'm speaking to him."

Miss Imes had the parents introduce themselves, and when they got to Aunt Emily, she said she was representing Senora LaQuita, Maggie's mom, too. Willoughby looked at them all sympathetically. It occurred to Sophie that Willoughby and Vincent were the only ones who didn't have an adult there ready to make up their minds for them. Fiona scratched a note to her: *This proves what I've always suspected: Vincent doesn't have parents. He's an adult living in a kid's body.*

Any other time that would have been funny. Right now, nothing was funny.

Miss Imes turned to the kids. "Before you all go completely into shock," she said, "let me explain that I invited your parents here because there has been some question about the content of your new film project."

Guess who asked the question, Sophie thought. So far she hadn't been able to look at her father. She was afraid she would roll her eyes up into her head and never find them again.

"Rather than simply put the kibosh on the entire project," Miss Imes was saying, "I thought it would be more of a learning experience if we all had a voice in setting the limits on the language and violence in the movie. How does that sound to everyone?"

"It sounds like you're going to end up telling us what we can and can't do anyway, so why waste the time?" Fiona said.

Nathan's face turned crimson. So did his mother's. Boppa drew his black, caterpillar eyebrows together the way he always did when Fiona had just embarrassed him to death.

Miss Imes' eyebrows, on the other hand, were stabbing at her hairline. "That is not my intention at all," she said. "In fact, I would like to hear from you students first. Perhaps there is less for your parents to be concerned about than they think. Who would like to start?"

They all looked at Sophie. *I hope I remember to thank them later for putting this whole thing on me,* Sophie thought. This definitely didn't qualify as "the cat's pajamas." Her mind raced, and she was sure she wouldn't squeak out a single thing that made sense—until somebody else stepped in ...

With her fedora dipped over one eye, Goodsy said, "All right, here's the thing." She hoped her voice was coming out low and rough, because this was no time to have her true identity revealed, not with the entire city council sitting before her. "This is the real world we're living in. We can't pussyfoot around the facts no more, see? There's killing in the streets. There's deals being made behind closed doors that are filling our city with booze and drugs, see? And innocent people are being robbed of their life savings, all in broad daylight. There ain't no way to paint a pretty picture of that. It's real, and we can't deny it, see? It's as plain as the rings on Al Capone's fingers."

"That certainly gives us a sense of the film's flavor," Miss Imes said dryly.

Sophie glanced at Daddy. He had his don't-think-I-don't-know-what-just-happened look on his face.

"I get all that," Aunt Emily said. Her silky Southern accent was a little ruffled. "But how real does it have to be?"

"How real do you think it should be?" Miss Imes said.

Beside Sophie, Fiona stiffened, and Sophie squeezed her wrist so she wouldn't fly out of the seat. But she felt like bursting out with something herself. Something like: *you might as well just let them write the whole thing for us if you're going to do this.*

"No cusswords," Nathan's mother said.

Boppa nodded. "Only as much physical stuff as it takes to suggest violence."

"No actual bloodshed on camera," Daddy put in.

The adults all laughed. Sophie didn't see what was funny.

"I'd like to see more of the problems being solved than see the problems themselves," Jimmy's father said. "Fewer shooting scenes and more discussion of how to fix the situation."

Sophie held on to Fiona with two hands.

There was a long pause. Sophie was sure Miss Imes was deciding which parent to turn the writing of the script over to. But finally Miss Imes nodded at Mr. Stires and said to the kids, "You heard all of that. Can you take that into consideration as you put your film together?"

"That's it?" Fiona said.

"Yes!" Sophie said, squeezing Fiona's wrist until she clamped her mouth shut. "We can definitely do that."

"That'll be swell," Darbie said.

Film Club heads bobbed. Sophie couldn't wait to get out of there and celebrate. *This wouldn't be so bad*, she thought. A surprise victory.

Until Miss Imes said, "All right then. And when the script has been completed, I will email it to each of the parents for approval. I'll contact those who couldn't be here today and let them know." She turned to the students, who all looked to Sophie like birthday balloons three days after the party. "Why don't you go on and get to work, and we'll wrap up here?"

Sophie didn't look at Daddy at all as she led the group out into the hall.

"We're right back where we started," Fiona said almost before the door was closed.

"And how," Vincent said. There was no big sloppy grin. "We can write whatever we want, but if they don't like it, we don't get to do it."

"I bet your parents aren't like ours," Darbie said to him.

"No," Vincent said. "Mine are worse. The only reason they aren't here is because they're out of town. I'm surprised my father didn't have himself patched in by satellite."

Wow, Sophie thought. *These guys are empathizing all over the place.* "I didn't know boys had these kinds of problems too," she said.

Jimmy nodded shyly, and Nathan turned red.

"Does the phrase 'house arrest' mean anything to you?" Vincent said. "That's the way I feel 99 percent of the time."

Willoughby put one arm around Sophie's shoulders and the other around Darbie's. "My offer is still open," she said. "Y'all can come to my house anytime you need to escape."

"We don't have time to escape," Fiona said. "We have a film to do. Only I don't see how it's going to be anything close to real now. We might as well do 'The Three Little Pigs' or something."

For the second time that day, they all looked at Sophie. She could feel Goodsy Malone giving her mind a shove. "No," Sophie said. "We just have to stick together and help each other through this."

"Corn Flake Code," Darbie said.

"Huh?" Nathan said.

Fiona gave Darbie a poke. "It's a girl thing," she said to Nathan. And then she turned to Sophie. "You think we can make it real and still follow all their rules?"

Something tickled at the back of Sophie's mind. The image of pinch-faced Pharisees saying, "Look! What you're doing is unlawful!"

"Yes, I do," Sophie said. "And maybe we can convince them that the rules have changed."

They all met after school that day and Friday—all except Willoughby, of course—and tried to recapture the fun they'd been having with Goodsy and the gangsters before the Parent Patrol came in.

But trying to "suggest" a raid on a suspected gang meeting and just "discussing" the bullet holes in the church wall instead of showing how they got there left the group feeling like deflated balloons again.

Six

The only thing that gave the girls their bounce back was their sleepover at Fiona's Friday night. Kitty was there.

"I can't believe my mom even let me come," she said.

Sophie couldn't either. Kitty's mother had made Miss Odetta, Boppa's new wife, promise to call her if Kitty so much as hiccupped. Miss Odetta, who was one of Fiona's former nannies (the one who had given demerits for breaking the tiniest rules) was now officially part of the Parent Patrol. Everyone started to sag.

"Okay," Sophie said, "I have an idea."

"Unless it's deadly dull, we probably can't use it," Fiona said.

"No!" Sophie squatted in front of Kitty's wheelchair. "We can show how heinous the gangsters were without really being violent. We'll show them kidnapping a poor sick helpless girl in a wheelchair and holding her hostage—but not hurting her."

"I can play helpless!" Kitty said.

A slow smile smoothed the frown from Fiona's face. "Now that is the ant's underwear," she said.

When the Lucky Charms and Willoughby arrived Saturday morning, they gave the official "Swell" to the idea, and they all started to work. They discovered along the way that if they used Nathan's twenties slang whenever something rough was called for, and said it out the sides of their mouths, it worked just as well as swearing. Words like *lousy* and *rotten* took on a whole new meaning. "Bushwa!" and "Gadzooks!" were by far the best.

By the time Boppa offered to treat them all to ice cream, they had an entire parent-safe script written.

"Y'know," Darbie said when they'd all piled into the big Ford Expedition, "I think it would be the bee's knees if we used our new language in our emails and IMs."

"Did you just say 'the bee's knees'?" Boppa said from the driver's seat. He smiled his soft Boppa-smile. "My father used to say that."

"Rats," Fiona whispered as they pulled into the Baskin Robbins parking lot. Out loud she said, before he could open the locks, "Boppa, why don't you just give me the money, and I'll bring yours out to you?"

There was a tiny pause before the locks clicked and doors flew open. Sophie caught a glimpse of Boppa's caterpillar eyebrows in the rearview mirror. They had a sad droop to them.

"I feel kind of bad leaving him in the car," Sophie said to Fiona as they hurried across the parking lot. "I mean, he's Boppa!"

"How else are we ever going to have a private conversation?" Fiona said. She stopped at the door, a wad of Boppa's money rolled up in her hand. "Nobody on the Parent Patrol is going to *let* us grow up. We just have to *do* it."

Sophie held back as Fiona went inside, and she imagined the kind eyes.

We aren't doing something wrong, are we? she said silently. *Don't the rules have to change so we can grow up?*

There was no answer. But for a crazy moment, Sophie thought she saw Jesus' eyebrows drooping.

When Sophie, Darbie, and Fiona got to first period Monday morning, Mrs. Clayton was standing in the hallway with Jimmy, bullet eyes looking ready to fire. For a second, Sophie wondered if Jimmy had tried "bushwa" on her already.

"Sophie," Mrs. Clayton said, "I need to talk to you too." She nodded to Darbie and Fiona to go on into the room. "Round Table tomorrow during lunch," she continued when Fiona had craned her neck as long as she could and disappeared through the doorway. "We have an interesting case this time."

"Gadzooks!" Sophie said.

"Excuse me?" Mrs. Clayton said.

Jimmy shuffled his feet. "She means—"

"I think I know what she means. I'm just not sure it's—well, whatever."

Mrs. Clayton was still shaking her cement hair-helmet as Sophie and Jimmy went inside.

"It works," Sophie whispered.

"And how," Jimmy whispered back.

"Don't forget, you two," Mrs. Clayton said from behind them. "Don't listen to any rumors about this case."

There were definitely plenty of them not to listen to. By the time Sophie got to third period, she'd heard everything from somebody stealing a teacher's grade book to someone tossing a substitute out a second-story window. The Corn Pops were responsible for most of that, Sophie was sure. They passed notes all through the two-hour English/History block.

The only story Sophie believed came from Willoughby. She cornered Sophie when Coach Yates sent them to the closet for basketballs.

"I know who's going to Round Table," Willoughby said. "They're my friends, and I need you to help them."

She was twirling a curl so tightly around her finger this time, Sophie was sure the end would pop off.

"What friends?" Sophie said. "None of the Flakes—"

"Not y'all," Willoughby said. She pulled Sophie farther into the closet by her sweatshirt sleeve. "It's two of my cheerleader friends. I really need you to make sure they don't get any after-school punishment, or they'll get suspended from the squad for missing practice. Will you—please?"

"What did they do?" Sophie said.

Willoughby spread her hands like fans. "They didn't do anything—"

She stopped, and her eyes widened at something over Sophie's shoulder. When Sophie turned to look, two heads disappeared from the doorway, but not before Sophie saw that they belonged to the two eighth-grade girls on her bus—the ones with the cell phones. Sophie whipped back around to Willoughby, whose eyes were practically begging.

"Them?" Sophie said.

"Victoria and Ginger," Willoughby said. "They're really nice, and there's no way they did anything wrong. Mr. Bentley's just too strict. He doesn't understand anything." Willoughby narrowed her eyes. "He's worse than any of y'all's parents."

Sophie's stomach squirmed. Mr. Bentley had never sent anybody to Round Table unless he was really sure they needed help with their attitude or something. But Willoughby looked convinced—

"Will you help?" Willoughby said. "I told them we could count on you."

"Where did you go for those basketballs, the factory?"

Sophie had never been glad to hear Coach Yates' voice before, or happy to see her ponytail-pinched face scowling at her.

"Sorry," Sophie said. She grabbed a bag of balls.

She headed for the closet door, dragging the bag. Willoughby tried to follow with another one, but Coach Yates said, "I need to talk to you, Wiley."

Willoughby's face snapped into a smile as if someone were about to take her picture.

"Go start handing those out, LaCroix." Coach Yates waited until Sophie was out of hearing range before she turned to Willoughby, who was still wearing a smile as fake as the Corn Pops'.

There was no time to tell the other Flakes about any of that before lunchtime, not with Miss Imes' math test fourth period. And Sophie needed to talk to them before her stomach tied into a square knot.

But when the bell rang for lunch, Willoughby was waiting in the doorway to the cafeteria. She hooked her arm around Sophie's and towed her inside — but not toward the Corn Flakes' usual table. Willoughby dragged her past the entire seventh-grade section with Fiona calling, "Gadzooks! Where are you going?" in the background.

"Here she is!" Willoughby said, and thrust Sophie into a chair. She was surrounded by eighth-grade girls, but the only two Sophie really saw were the Cell Phone Twins.

"You must be Sophie," said the very blonde one with the striking blue eyes. "I'm Victoria."

"Oh," Sophie said. She could feel her whole self turning into a very large sore thumb.

"I'm Ginger," said the one who looked like an elf. She put out a thin hand toward Sophie. Sophie stared at it for a long, embarrassing minute before she realized Ginger wanted her to shake it. When she did, it felt like a feather in her palm.

"Haven't I seen you around?" Victoria said. She nudged a cardboard tray of nachos toward Sophie. "Have one."

"You ride my bus," Sophie said. "Or I ride your bus—or something."

"That's it." Victoria smiled with the ease of a star on a talk show. "Do you know you have the cutest haircut?"

Ginger nodded as if she were going to grab scissors immediately and try to copy Sophie's 'do on herself.

"She used to be bald," Willoughby said. "She shaved her head for our friend who has cancer."

Sophie waited for the curled lips that usually came after that announcement, but Victoria and Ginger both nodded as if they were in awe.

"When you said she'd do anything for a friend," Ginger said to Willoughby, "you weren't kidding."

Her voice was low and throaty, and nothing much on her moved when she talked. It made Sophie feel like she herself was going to do something spastic any minute. She was afraid to even reach for a nacho.

Victoria leaned forward, so that her blonde hair slipped silkily onto her chest. "Listen," she said. Her blue eyes were serious, like a grown-up's. It occurred to Sophie that she seemed even older than Lacie. "Thanks for helping us tomorrow. We thought once Mr. Bentley got us on his hate list, there was nothing we could do."

"'Til Willoughby told us about you," Ginger said. She put both slender arms, clad tightly in pink, around Willoughby. "We love her."

Willoughby smiled until tears sparkled in her eyes. Sophie could feel the knot in her stomach making another loop.

I haven't said I'd help yet! Sophie wanted to scream. *I don't even know what they did. Or didn't do. Or anything!*

61

But Willoughby was gazing at her as if Sophie had just offered to give her a lifesaving kidney.

"We need to celebrate," Victoria said. She leaned in, and everyone else leaned too. "There's no school Thursday or Friday, so let's have a party Wednesday night."

And then, like someone had just given them a cue, the entire table looked at Willoughby.

"Okay," Willoughby said. "We're out of soda, though."

"Oh, we'll definitely bring more over," Ginger said.

The party's going to be at Willoughby's? Sophie thought. She couldn't have been more confused.

"You come too, Stephi," Victoria said.

"Sophie!" Willoughby said, with a half-poodle-shriek.

"You don't have to bring your own drinks, though," Victoria said to Sophie. She gave her a you're-in-on-the-secret smile. "I figure it's the least we can do."

"You're not eating," Ginger said, inching the nachos closer to Sophie. "Are you trying to keep that cute little figure?"

Sophie looked down at her still-flat chest. Willoughby nudged her.

"See?" she said. "I told you they were nice." She rolled her eyes. "There's no way they would ever give Coach Yates attitude."

"Is that what—" Sophie said.

Willoughby gave a little poodle-yelp. "That's like something Julia and them would do."

Victoria froze with a dripping chip halfway to her lips. "Those little princess wannabes?" she said.

There was unanimous disgust around the table.

"No way we're like them," Ginger said.

For the first time, Sophie found herself nodding. Maybe, just maybe ... if these girls saw the Corn Pops for what they were, they might actually be as nice as Willoughby said.

They haven't put me down one time since I've been at the table, she thought. *Corn Pop Julia couldn't get through one nacho without making me feel like I'm a piece of lint —*

"I want to know how you got up the courage to shave your head," Victoria said. She was smiling right into Sophie. "That was so brave."

Squinting suspiciously, Sophie focused hard on Victoria. When one of the Corn Pops was being *that* nice to her, she could smell the fake factor. But Victoria actually looked impressed. It was worth checking out —

"Kitty's my friend," Sophie said. "I didn't want her to be all alone." Now came the final test. "Wouldn't you do the same for Ginger?"

Victoria's eyes widened, as if she were surprised. Then slowly she looked at Ginger, and she bit her glossy lip. "I think I would," she said. And then she gave Ginger a hug.

By the time lunch was over, Sophie had determined that Victoria and Ginger couldn't have committed the sin of backtalking to a teacher. And after all, Coach Yates *had* been grumpier than usual lately. Even Coach Virile had said so.

So the next day at the Round Table meeting, Sophie did her best Goodsy Malone — like defense of Victoria Peyton and Ginger Jenkins before they even came in.

"Sounds like a case of misunderstanding," she told the council. "This can be worked out, see? We don't need to bring in the big guns. Just a sit-down-and-talk. With a neutral party present." She turned to Coach Virile and wished she were wearing a fedora so she could push it back for dramatic effect. "Somebody like Coach here."

Mrs. Clayton looked around the table. "Anyone else?"

"Sure, whatever," said Hannah. She was the eighth-grade girl on the council, a serious brunette with contact lenses that always seemed to bother her. She blinked rapidly at Oliver, the eighth-grade boy. "Sounds like she had it all figured out before we even got here."

Oliver plucked at the rubber band on his braces and nodded.

Miss Imes' eyebrows were aimed at her forehead, but Coach Virile nodded. "I think it's worth a try. I can meet them—"

"How about during lunch tomorrow?" Sophie said.

"It's big of you to arrange Coach Nanini's schedule for him, Sophie." Mrs. Clayton's voice was flat.

"It's okay," Coach said. "I'll set it up with Coach Yates."

Sophie tried not to make her long, relieved breath too obvious. Victoria and Ginger wouldn't miss any practice. Willoughby would be happy.

And I upheld the Corn Flake Code of loyalty, Sophie thought.

It was the bee's knees.

Seven

Not everybody was as happy with Sophie as Willoughby was.

"Don't I know you?" Fiona said when Sophie sat down next to her in fifth-period science. "Didn't you used to eat lunch with us?"

"I had Round Table today," Sophie said. "And yesterday—"

"You were helping Willoughby. I get that." Fiona lowered her voice as the bell rang. "I'm just missing you. And Willoughby. Why's she all about those eighth graders now? What's wrong with *us*?"

Darbie leaned over from the desk on the other side of Sophie. "We've got bigger problems than that," she said. She looked at Fiona. "Did you tell her?"

"Tell me what?"

"Mr. Stires called an emergency Film Club meeting while you and Jimmy were at Round Table," Fiona said. "He and Miss Imes emailed our script to all the parents, and one of them said the kidnapping scene was too 'scary' for kids our age."

"That's our best scene!" Sophie wailed, loud enough for Mr. Stires to look up from taking roll and twitch his mustache.

"Mr. Stires wouldn't tell us who complained," Fiona whispered.

He didn't have to, Sophie thought. She would have bet her video camera it was her father. It made her want to take a bite right out of her science book.

"Let's head to the lab, folks," Mr. Stires said.

But Sophie couldn't keep her mind on test tubes or anything else except how *un*-swell their film was going to be now.

The whole Film Club gathered just outside the door to sixth-period Life Skills before the bell rang. Maggie kept an eye on the clock so they could dive inside the room in time to escape a tardy-detention from Coach Yates. Her mood hadn't gotten any better in the last few days.

"We have to figure something out," Vincent said. "What's everybody doing after school?"

"Bible study," Maggie said.

"What about after that?"

"We don't have school tomorrow," Darbie said. "Let's meet at my house tonight."

Willoughby was already tugging at Sophie's sleeve, and Sophie knew why.

"This is an emergency," Sophie said to her.

"But you said you'd come," Willoughby said. "I asked you first."

"What are you two going on about?" Darbie said.

Fiona folded her arms and looked at Sophie. "Let me guess. You and Willoughby have plans with those eighth graders."

"Sort of," Sophie said.

"That was a yes-or-no question," Vincent said.

Why do you always have to be so mathematical? Sophie wanted to say to him.

"I did promise Willoughby I'd come to her party," she said.

All Corn Flake eyes shifted to Willoughby.

"You're having a party?" Fiona said.

"I hope this doesn't sound rude, Willoughby," Darbie said. "But why didn't you invite us? We're your best friends."

"Why can't they come?" Sophie knew her voice sounded as fake as a Corn Pop smile. "It's your house."

Willoughby grabbed a curl and strangled a finger with it. "I kind of already asked them, but they just want Sophie. I mean, they haven't met the rest of you yet."

"So let me get this straight," Fiona said, hands on hips. "*You're* having a party at *your* house, but somebody else is telling you who can come and who can't."

"Yates Alert," Maggie whispered hoarsely. "We have fifteen seconds."

But nobody moved until Willoughby finally nodded and said, "Sort of."

"That was another yes-or-no question," Vincent said.

This time, Sophie had to agree with him.

Maggie herded them all into the room just as the bell rang. There was a note on Sophie's desk almost before Coach Yates closed the door.

"PLEASE come to my party, Sophie," Willoughby had written. "I NEED you there."

Sophie looked over to see tears threatening to spill out onto Willoughby's cheeks.

"I have to go to Willoughby's party," Sophie wrote to Fiona. "I don't know why. I just do."

At Bible study that afternoon, the fact that Kitty was there, tucked neatly into her wheelchair, was overshadowed by Fiona putting her hand up almost before Dr. Peter could get the words "So, ladies, how was your week?" out of his mouth.

"I guess I'm about to find out," he said, eyes sparkling.

"I just have a question," Fiona said. "What happens if you make a rule and somebody breaks it because there's another rule that is the opposite of that rule?"

Dr. Peter let his eyes cross. It would have been funny if Sophie hadn't known exactly where Fiona was going.

"I'm glad you asked that, actually," Dr. Peter said. "Because it goes back to the story we're studying. Let me ask you something — what did you do Sunday after church?"

They all looked at each other.

"Homework," Gill said.

Harley grunted in agreement.

Maggie was flipping back through her calendar. "We worked on our film," she said.

"It scares me that you have an appointment book, Maggie," Dr. Peter said. "But that's exactly my point. All of you broke the commandment about keeping the Sabbath holy."

"Sorry," Kitty said. And then she gave her nervous Kitty-giggle.

Sophie squirmed a little. "But I thought that's what the story was about. Didn't Jesus change that rule because his disciples were hungry?"

Dr. Peter rubbed his hands together and wrinkled his glasses into place with his nose. "Just as I thought. We need to look at the story a little more closely." He picked up a stack of pastel-colored pads and handed them out, each one matching a beanbag chair color. Kitty giggled and said she'd missed this class *so* much. Sophie just got a squirmy feeling in her stomach. So far this didn't promise to help her with the Corn Flake situation, much less Daddy and the Parent Patrol.

"On this pad," Dr. Peter said, "I want you to write down all the rules you are expected to follow, even the ones you've made for your own group of friends."

"Corn Flake Code," Maggie said.

Gill looked at Harley. "Do we have rules?"

Harley, of course, grunted.

It took the whole hour for everybody to list all their rules, since naturally they had to talk about every one as they went along. By the end of the class, Sophie was no closer to any answers. In fact, the chain around her ankle had gained several links. Dr. Peter said he'd explain it all next week. Fiona was still saying things to Sophie like, "I get it, but I don't get it. Gadzooks!"

Sophie had no word, even in their new slang, to describe how she felt going over to Willoughby's that night.

I want to go, but I don't, she thought in Daddy's truck on the way over. *I'm happy they asked me, and I'm not. I want to help Willoughby, but I don't want to hurt my other Corn Flakes.*

"You look like you're having a scrimmage with yourself over there, Soph," Daddy said. "Want me to referee?"

His eyes were actually sympathetic, but even as Sophie opened her mouth to explain it to him, she could hear Fiona saying, *Somebody said the kidnapping scene was too "scary" for kids our age.*

Daddy doesn't even know anything about kids our age, Sophie thought. So what was the point?

Goodsy Malone shook her head. These old town council members, they didn't know from nothin'. She'd have to handle this on her own, just like always.

She settled back into the seat of the 1928 Pierce-Arrow car and watched through the windshield with trained eyes. Even now there could be members of the Capone organization lurking in the shadows. In fact, didn't she see movement in that yard? Wasn't there someone running straight for the Pierce-Arrow?

"Look out!" she shouted, hand already on her weapon.

The tires squealed, and the vehicle fishtailed to a stop.

Daddy was glaring at her. "What was that all about?"

Sophie blinked through her glasses at the empty road in front of them.

"Don't be screaming like that when I'm driving," Daddy said as he shook his head and jerked the truck back into gear. "I could have had an accident."

His eyes weren't sympathetic anymore.

Daddy waited in the truck until Willoughby let Sophie in the front door. Sophie wondered if Victoria's and Ginger's parents still did that with them.

"I'm glad he's met your dad before," Sophie said, "or he would have come all the way to the door to check him out."

Willoughby gave a poodle-shriek. "I'm glad he didn't! My dad's at work."

Sophie felt the stomach knot forming again. "He's not gonna be here?"

"No, but it's cool," Willoughby said. "He doesn't care if I have friends over."

Sophie gazed at her in awe.

"Okay, squirt, we're out of here." A curly-haired boy of about eighteen followed his deep voice into the room. There was another identical boy right behind him. He messed up Willoughby's hair with his fingers.

"These are my twin brothers," Willoughby said, "Matt and Andy." She wriggled away from the one with his hands in her hair. "And *fortunately*, they're leaving too."

"Make sure you clean up after your party," one of them said.

"By eleven. Dad gets off at midnight," the other one said.

"I know, I know," Willoughby said.

Hands-in-the-Hair waved his cell phone at her as the two of them went out the front door.

"I *know!*" Willoughby said. She rolled her eyes at Sophie. "They're way worse than anybody's parents."

Then why are they leaving? Sophie thought. Her stomach was knotted up tight enough to hold a yacht in place. It was the first time she'd ever been alone in somebody else's house without an adult there. *Not* being in that situation was one of the things she'd written on her rules list that very day in Bible study.

I don't think Jesus would like this, she thought. *Much less Mama and Daddy.*

But before she could mention that to Willoughby, the doorbell rang. Willoughby yelped, and the house was suddenly full of eighth-grade girls.

Sophie recognized some of them from the lunch table the day before, but there were at least ten more besides them. All of them looked like they shopped, had their hair cut and colored, and took modeling classes at the same place. Sophie felt more flat-chested and less Goodsy Malone–confident by the second.

Until Victoria parted the crowd and made a beeline for her.

"Stephi!" she said.

"It's actually Sophie," Sophie said.

"I know, but I like calling you Stephi. You remind me of my cousin Stephanie — you both look adorable in glasses. Come on, I want Ginger to give you a manicure. She's amazing. Have you ever had one?"

"No," Sophie said as she trailed her to Willoughby's family room. *Wait 'til she sees I don't even have any nails.*

But Ginger, who had a full manicure set spread out on the coffee table, didn't even blink when she saw Sophie's gnawed-off absence of fingernails.

"I'm going to put fake nails on you," she said. "They'll be fabulous."

Next to Sophie on the couch, somebody else was getting a pedicure, and on the floor, three girls were pulling DVDs out of their purses. Sophie started to relax. This really wasn't that much different from the Corn Flake sleepovers—

Until a DVD was popped into the player, and a big R appeared on the TV screen.

Sophie tried not to let her eyes pop out. She'd never seen an R-rated movie in her life. That too had been on her rule list.

Victoria swept into the room holding a Diet Dr. Pepper in one hand and positioning the fingers of the other one like she was holding a telephone. "Willoughby!" she called out. "Where's your cell phone?"

Where's yours? Sophie thought as Willoughby tucked her little pink phone into Victoria's hand.

"I get it after you," Ginger said to Victoria. She pressed a shiny squared-off nail onto Sophie's finger and held it up to survey it, frowning. "Too big. You're so petite." She pulled it off. "Parents are so clueless."

"Why are they clueless this time?" said Giving-a-Pedicure.

"I *told* them that Round Table making us have a talk with Coach Nanini wasn't a punishment," Ginger said, "but do they get that? No. They took my cell phone for three days."

"Call Child Protective Services," Getting-a-Pedicure said.

Sophie looked at her quickly to make sure she was kidding.

"Here," Victoria said, tossing the phone to Ginger. "I'll finish Stephi's nails."

"Did you get him?" Ginger said as she poked out a number.

"I had to leave him a text message," Victoria said. "These are darling on you, Stephi." She wiggled her eyebrows up at Ginger. "He'll be here."

He? Sophie thought. *Here?*

"Okay, listen to this." A willowy girl curled up in Willoughby's father's recliner and held up a magazine. "Here's a quiz: 'Are You a Boy Magnet?' "

"Who in here needs to take that quiz?" Victoria said. "We all have boyfriends." She looked at Sophie, who was trying to will herself to disappear under the sofa. "Do you?"

"Uh, no," Sophie said.

"Why not?" said Giving-a-Pedicure. "You're too cute to be single."

"It's because seventh-grade boys are still such babies," Ginger said. She tossed the phone back to Victoria and took over the last of Sophie's press-on manicure. "You need an eighth-grade boy, Sophia."

Sophie didn't even attempt to correct her. She knew nothing would come out but a squeak. An eighth-grade boy? *EWW!*

"We'll get you any guy you want," Ginger said to her. "As long as he isn't already taken."

"What about Scottie Fischer?" Getting-a-Pedicure said.

Ginger studied Sophie. "They would be cute together. Want us to fix you up?"

Yes—to a balloon—and fly me out of here! That definitely sounded better than all of this right now. Sophie almost melted into a relief-puddle when the doorbell rang. Ginger dashed for the door with Getting-a-Pedicure behind her, gauze still stuffed between her toes.

But when Sophie saw half the Great Marsh Middle School boys' basketball team stream into the family room, she ran like a rabbit to the kitchen in search of Willoughby—who was nowhere to be found.

Sophie launched herself at a cooler full of sodas just for something to do while she thought about how she was going to escape. She hadn't put the rule about not hanging out with boys without any adults present on her list. It hadn't even come up in her life yet.

Ginger came in then, draped around a tall boy who looked like he shaved already. Sophie wriggled past them with a Sprite and darted for the stairs to the second floor.

"What's that little seventh grader doing here?" she heard the boy say.

"Shut up. She's valuable," Ginger said.

I'm valuable? Sophie thought. *What — like a bank account or something?*

Suddenly, she didn't feel like a Boy Magnet with a cute little figure and fabulous fake nails. Parking the Sprite on the steps, she headed for Willoughby's room, where she knew there was a house phone. The only thing to do right now was call Fiona and find out what to do. Gadzooks.

"Bunting residence," said the voice on the other end.

Sophie held back a groan. It was Miss Odetta.

"May I speak with Fiona?" she said.

Something beeped in her ear, and for a minute, Sophie thought Miss Odetta had hung up.

"Is this Sophie?" Miss Odetta said, in that voice she used when somebody was about to get a demerit.

"Yes, ma'am," Sophie said. "May I speak with Fiona?"

There was another beep. "What is wrong with this phone?" Miss Odetta said. "This thing does everything but the dishes, and I don't know what any of it means — "

"May I *please* speak to Fiona?" Sophie's voice threatened to squeak out of hearing range.

"She's over at Darbie's house," Miss Odetta said. "Why aren't you there?"

Sophie thanked her and hung up before Miss Odetta could give her a demerit for not being with Fiona.

I deserve one! Sophie thought. *What am I doing here?*

In the distance, another phone rang.

Probably a bunch of high school boys calling on the cell phone to say they're coming over, too, Sophie thought. *I have to get out of here.*

For a crazy moment, she looked at Willoughby's bedroom window. She could always climb out of it and run to Kitty's house, which was only a block away.

But Kitty was probably at Darbie's house too, along with everyone else Sophie felt *safe* with.

The only thing to do now was call home and ask Daddy to come get her. And then she'd have to tell him why—

"Oh, no!" someone screamed from downstairs. Sophie would have recognized that poodle-yelp anywhere. "That was my dad! He got off early!"

Then there was another poodle-cry—a frightened one.

Eight

In a matter of minutes, Willoughby's house was empty of eighth graders, without even a trace of a press-on nail left behind. Willoughby leaned against the front door and whimpered, "Sophie, please—you have to help me clean up before my father gets home."

Sophie was about to say, *I thought he didn't care if you had a party*, but Willoughby burst into tears.

"What do you want me to do?" Sophie said.

"Make it look like nobody was here but you and me. You take the family room. I have to call my brother."

"Okay, but I don't get it—"

"Sophie please—hurry!"

The fear in Willoughby's voice sent Sophie charging into the family room, where she clanked soda cans into a garbage bag and sprayed air freshener over the nail glue smell. She was dumping the trash bag into the outside can when she heard a car pull into the driveway. The thought of jumping the fence and running crossed her mind, but Willoughby stuck her head out the back door and said, "He's here!" It sounded like the poodle was drawing her final breath.

The front door opened as Willoughby motioned for Sophie to sit on one of the snack bar stools while she herself stuck her head in the refrigerator.

"I wish Matt would hurry up with the milk," she said into its depths. "I'm dying for a milk shake."

"Matt went out?" said a deep voice from the doorway.

Sophie flinched, nearly falling off the stool. She'd heard Willoughby's father talk before, but she'd never noticed him growling like a German shepherd. The way he took inventory of the kitchen with his eyes made Sophie wish she had jumped the fence after all, and taken Willoughby with her.

"I just went out to get some milk," said another voice. One of the twins appeared in the doorway with two gallon jugs and a grin—a very shaky grin.

"How long were you gone?" Mr. Wiley snarled at him.

Two hours! Sophie thought.

"Not that long," Matt said. "I knew if I didn't get right back with the stuff, Will was going to go into milk shake withdrawal."

Willoughby pulled her head out of the refrigerator and put out her hands for the milk jugs. "You're a lifesaver," she said to Matt.

Sophie was sure she wasn't talking about milk shakes.

Sophie couldn't even drink the one Willoughby fixed and carried upstairs for her. Her stomach was nothing *but* a knot.

Willoughby flopped down on her bed and covered her face with her hands. "That was close," she said. "Somebody must have been on our phone when he called. Don't they know about call waiting?" She peeked out through her fingers. "It's a good thing he tried me on my cell."

77

Sophie perched uneasily on the edge of a white wicker chair. "What would have happened if he'd caught all those kids here?"

"He would have yelled at Matt and Andy," she said. "They aren't supposed to leave me alone when I have a friend over." Willoughby sat up. "They really wanted to go out, and I really wanted to have this party, so we worked out a plan. I hate that they almost got in trouble. They're cool brothers."

Matt wasn't acting cool just now, Sophie thought. *I think he was scared to death.*

"Aren't you going to drink that?" Willoughby pointed to Sophie's milk shake. Her hand trembled.

"You okay?" Sophie said.

Willoughby plastered on a smile, the same too-cheerful one she'd used with Coach Yates. "I am now. It was worth it, though. Wasn't that a cool party?" She twirled a curl. "I hope Victoria and them had a good time."

Sophie ran a hand over her own short crop of hair. A fake nail hung up in it. "Would they still be worth it if Matt got in trouble?"

"Are you kidding me?" Willoughby's face sobered as she looked at Sophie. "Victoria and Ginger told me they think I have what it takes to be captain of the eighth-grade squad next year. And since they're co-captains this year, they get to be judges when we have tryouts in March. You know what that means?"

"No," Sophie said.

"It means I'm practically guaranteed to make it!"

"But you're the best," Sophie said. "You'd make it anyway."

Willoughby shook her head, sending the curls into a frenzy. "When you get up into *eighth* grade, it gets tougher. It pays to have somebody on your side."

The Corn Flakes are on your side, Sophie wanted to say. But she wasn't sure that would make any difference to Willoughby right now. She had Victoria-worship shining on her face.

"I'm getting my pajamas on," Sophie said.

"Just one thing, Soph," Willoughby said as Sophie reached for her backpack. "Would you please not tell your parents about what happened tonight?"

Sophie pretended to have trouble with the zipper while her mind spun.

This feels like lying. Willoughby's too good at lying.

But what good would it do to tell her parents and get Matt in trouble?

Not to mention herself.

She knew she should have called home the minute she found out Willoughby's dad wasn't home. She also knew that Willoughby was waiting for her answer with fear flickering in her eyes.

She's that afraid for Matt to get yelled at?

There was something else going on, something that made Sophie want to run to Mama and whisper to her about the frightened squeal in Willoughby's voice and the fear-flickers in her eyes.

"It's Corn Flake Code," Willoughby said. "We all promised we'd help each other with our parent stuff."

"You said you didn't have parent stuff," Sophie said.

Willoughby rolled her eyes. "It's not my parent stuff. It's Matt's. When you don't have a mom, you get way close to your brothers. We protect each other."

"From what?" Sophie said.

"Just promise me, Sophie," Willoughby said. She rolled her eyes again, but Sophie knew that this time she was trying to roll away tears.

"Okay," Sophie said. "But I can't come over here when your dad's not home anymore. You *couldn't* protect me from what my parents would say if they knew."

"You have my word." Willoughby flew to the chair and threw her arms around Sophie. "I love you, Corn Flake," she said.

I love you too, Sophie thought later. She sat up in bed, peeling off the phony fingernails while Willoughby slept beside her. *But I don't know if what I just promised was such a good thing.*

Sophie shivered and closed her eyes. Jesus was right there with his kind ones.

Are you disappointed in me? she prayed to him. *I hope not, because I'm really confused, and I really need your help.* She sighed into the pillow. *I really need you to show me what the rules are.*

The Film Club spent most of their long-weekend days together working on their movie. Willoughby missed a lot of rehearsal time because she said she had cheerleading stuff.

Sophie wondered whether she was talking about the seventh-grade squad, or the eighth-grade.

They filmed all the movie except for the kidnapping scene. They were gathered in the sunroom at the back of Kitty's house trying to figure out what to do about what the Parent Patrol had said, when there was a tap on the glass.

"It's Willoughby!" Kitty said.

"I hope she has the pictures for what we're supposed to do with our hair," Fiona said. "She's giving about 50 percent, which is *not* what we all promised."

Kitty ignored her and pushed open the door, letting in a blast of cold late-November air. "Come in before you freeze to death!"

But Willoughby stood in the doorway, shivering and shaking her head. Sophie saw the flicker in her eyes, and she herself started to shake.

"I just need to talk to Sophie," Willoughby said. "In private."

Sophie felt Fiona stiffen beside her.

Throwing her jacket around her shoulders, Sophie slipped outside to join Willoughby. She heard Fiona say in her twenties voice, "What are the rest of us? Chopped liver?"

Willoughby grabbed Sophie's jacket sleeve and dragged her around the side of the house. She was breathing so hard, little puffs of frosty air were coming out of her nose.

"Are you in trouble?" Sophie said. "Did your dad find out—"

"It's not about me," Willoughby said. Her already-big eyes got bigger. "It's Victoria and Ginger."

"Again?" Sophie said. She hoped Willoughby didn't see her sagging with relief.

"They might have to go before the Round Table again."

"Okay," Sophie said. "You know that's not a punishment, even if their parents—"

"You have to say that they were at my house all Wednesday night."

Sophie knew she would have frozen even if the icy wind weren't whipping through her.

"But they weren't," she said.

"They were there part of the time. I really need you to do this, Sophie. Please—"

"Willoughby!"

Even from a block away, the voice was loud and deep and had a growl in it.

"That's my dad—I have to go," Willoughby said.

And she ran as if Al Capone's entire mob were after her.

"I can't lie for them!" Sophie called after her.

But she knew Willoughby didn't hear her as her father growled again. "Willoughby, get home!"

It definitely didn't sound like it was Matt he was mad at.

When Sophie went back into the house, everyone had left the sunroom except Fiona, who was "up to ninety," as Darbie would say.

"What's going on?" Fiona said.

Sophie swallowed hard. The tangle of rules seemed to be caught in her throat. "Willoughby wants me to do something I can't do, and I didn't get to tell her I couldn't do it because her father yelled at her."

"I thought she had Superfather," Fiona said. "What is going *on*?"

"I'll tell you after I talk to Willoughby."

Fiona's gray eyes went into slits. "Why do I have to wait? I'm your best friend."

"Because I don't know which rule I'm supposed to be following!" Sophie said.

Fiona looked closely at her. "You're about to freak out."

"And how," Sophie said. One thing she *did* know, though: the reason she was now so valuable to the eighth graders.

She wanted to email Willoughby as soon as she got home, but Lacie was on the computer, moaning about the huge history paper she was "never going to finish."

Sophie tried calling the Wiley house, but when one of the twins answered the phone, he told her Willoughby couldn't come to the phone and hung up before Sophie could ask him when she could. She imagined his lips trembling the way they had Wednesday night.

Please help me with all these rules, she begged Jesus when she went to bed. *I need to know what to do!*

One rule was very clear: she couldn't lie for Victoria and Ginger. It was one thing to keep a secret for Willoughby, and another to tell a big old whopper for girls she didn't even know—girls who said things like, "She's valuable," even if they also said Sophie was cute and a boy magnet.

As she thought about that during first period, she watched Colton Messik saunter to the pencil sharpener and do a fake burp in Anne-Stuart's ear as he passed.

EWW.

"Sophie," said a trumpet-voice at her elbow.

Sophie looked up at Mrs. Clayton.

"Round Table during lunch today. We have some repeaters."

Sophie felt her stomach harden.

It was still in a mass of knots when she and Jimmy got to the council room and joined Hannah and Oliver and Coach Virile, Mrs. Clayton, Miss Imes, and Coach Yates. Sophie didn't see how Coach Yates' face could be any more pinched-in. She was starting to look like a Pharisee.

"It's those cheerleaders again," Hannah whispered to Sophie and Jimmy while the teachers talked to each other in under-the-breath voices. She blinked about two hundred times. "No offense, Sophie, but I didn't think a little chat with Coach Nanini was going to change them."

"Let's come to order," Mrs. Clayton said. "I want us to talk before we bring our offenders in." Her eyebrows pointed. "I think you'll all remember Victoria Peyton and Ginger Jenkins, who were before us last week for a confrontation they had with Coach Yates. Any further problems, Coach?"

Coach Yates shook her head. "They've basically been avoiding me."

"At least they have *some* brains," Oliver muttered.

"They're coming before us again today," Mrs. Clayton went on, "about a different matter. It seems that they were seen out after curfew on Wednesday night, which means Ms. Barnes, the eighth-grade squad coach, has suspended them from the cheerleading squad for two weeks."

"The end of life as they know it," Hannah said.

Mrs. Clayton shot her a bullet-look. "Let's try to keep our personal feelings out of this."

Oliver strummed the rubber band on his braces. "Who saw them out after curfew?"

"What difference does that make?" Hannah said.

"Could be somebody that wants to frame them. That would make it more interesting."

"That would be fascinating," Mrs. Clayton said dryly, "except that it was a reliable source, and no one has come forward to provide them with an alibi."

"There was one attempt," Miss Imes put in. "But that was an unsigned note."

Unsigned by Willoughby, Sophie thought. That definitely wasn't Corn Flake Code, and it made Sophie homesick for the old Willoughby of before-Victoria-and-Ginger days.

Jimmy raised his hand. "So if they've already gotten a punishment, why are they coming here?"

"Because we're about helping kids become better than they are," Coach Virile said. "And after working with these girls just one time, I could see they needed some guidance." His big face softened. "It's not too late."

"Ms. Barnes wants them to have some Round Table rehab before she lets them back on the squad," Mrs. Clayton said. "So let's bring them in and make our recommendation."

Ginger and Victoria both smiled at Sophie when they came in and took their seats as if they were about to be offered the title of cheerleading cocaptains for the rest of their lives.

Sophie considered asking for a restroom pass. But that wasn't something Goodsy Malone would do.

Goodsy narrowed her eyes at the both of them. There were kids who needed help, see, and then there were lyin' little flapper

*girls who didn't care about nothin' or nobody. They used people up
and then tossed 'em aside like—like yesterday's garbage, see—*

Willoughby wasn't yesterday's garbage.

And neither was she.

"Ladies, you know why you're here," Mrs. Clayton said.

"I assume it's to tell us we're not suspended," Victoria said.

Sophie watched Miss Imes' eyebrows shoot up, while Coach
Nanini's unibrow lowered almost to his nose.

"Wherever did you get that idea?" Mrs. Clayton said.

Victoria's eyes flicked to Sophie. Ginger's had never left
Sophie's face.

Sophie adjusted her glasses and looked back at them. She
saw her answer dawn on them and freeze their faces.

"We are here to offer you some help," Coach Nanini said.
"Council?"

Sophie raised her hand. "I recommend that we give you
Campus Commission after school," she said. "It'll really teach
you a lot. You know"—Sophie drilled her eyes right into
Victoria—"like not to use people."

The teachers all looked puzzled. Ginger and Victoria didn't.

Sophie barely got to her locker after they adjourned before
Willoughby was there. Her face was a furious red, and her big
eyes looked ready to lunge from her face, right at Sophie.

"You said you'd help!" she said. The poodle voice was out
of control.

"No, I didn't," Sophie said.

"Yes, you did. You stood right here in this very spot and
said we all had to be loyal to each other, no matter what!"
Willoughby stomped her foot. "If what you just did to me is
what you mean by loyal, then I don't want to be a Corn Flake
anymore!"

Then she turned with a squeal of her sneakers and was gone.

Nine

By sixth period that day, it was final. Willoughby had officially dropped out of Film Club.

"How much revising will you have to do on your film, then?" Miss Imes said when Sophie and Fiona gave her the news after school. "You only have two weeks left."

Sophie hadn't even thought about that. She was too busy trying to swallow Willoughby's other decision—that she was no longer a Corn Flake either.

Anybody can play a flapper girl in a movie, Sophie told Jesus on the way home on the bus. *But nobody else can be Willoughby in my life.*

Who else would yelp like a poodle at Sophie's funniness?

Who else could do a cheer every time Sophie got above a C on a math test?

Or twirl a curl around her finger when she got nervous? Or throw her arms around Sophie just because?

Sophie wished just this once Jesus would answer in actual words—just appear in the seat next to her on the bus and tell her how to get Willoughby back.

She closed her eyes and imagined him looking kindly, sadly at her. It occurred to her that Willoughby needed to be imagining him right now too. Because unless doing what he wanted her to do became more important than what Victoria and Ginger wanted her to do, things were going to stay just the way they were. Somehow that thought added more weight to that chain around her ankle.

Going home didn't help at all. Daddy was there, white-faced with the news that Mama was going to have to stay in bed until Baby Girl LaCroix was born.

"Four *months*?" Lacie said.

"Don't worry, Lace," Daddy said. "You won't have to cook *every* night. There's always McDonald's."

"Can Mama get up to go to the bathroom?" Zeke said.

"Yeah, Z-Boy, she can do that," Daddy told him.

"Is something the matter with the baby?" Sophie said.

Daddy made a not-too-successful attempt at a smile. "No, she's just an eager little rookie. She wants to come out and play now, and she's not ready."

"Does Mama get to take a bath?" Zeke said.

"Yeah, Z."

"So what's the game plan?" Lacie said. "Obviously we're all going to have to help if we don't want the whole place to fall apart."

"We need a chart like Mama made for Kitty's sisters when she was in the hospital," Sophie said.

"Can she still read with me?" Zeke said.

Daddy patted Z's head, eyes on the girls. "Thank you for having that attitude, Lace, Soph." Sophie thought his eyes looked wet. "You two are on the top shelf looking down."

"It's family, Dad," Lacie said. "We all have to take a hit for the team." To Sophie, Lacie's eyes looked wise as she pushed up her sweat-jacket sleeves and said, "Okay, how does tuna salad sound for dinner?"

While Zeke put in his vote for raisins in the salad, Sophie kept watching Lacie — pulling cans out of the pantry, making an out-of-my-way bun out of her ponytail and sticking a pencil through it, giving Zeke the raisins and a measuring cup so he could help.

Why did I ever think Victoria and Ginger seemed older than Lacie? she thought. *Lacie could be, like, their mom right now.*

There must be a difference, she decided, between acting grown up and really being grown up.

"I can chop the celery," she said.

But being a grown-up was harder than it looked. Dinner had to be fixed, cleaned up, and thought up for the next night. Zeke had to be bathed, chased, and read to. Laundry had to be washed and dried and folded, not to mention collected from every corner of Zeke's room to begin with.

It meant coming home right after school and taking over for the ladies from the church who took turns keeping Mama fed and occupied all day so she wouldn't "go bonkers," as she put it.

It also meant missing Film Club just when Sophie really needed to be there. By Tuesday night, only the second day of their no-Mama routine, Sophie not only felt like she had a chain around her ankle, she was convinced it was attached to a wall.

Some of that was because of Daddy. Even though he was super-busy with Mama and Zeke when he was home, he still had a corner of his brain reserved for running Sophie's life.

"How are the grades, Soph?" he asked when she came down to the study to type her English homework. "You're not involved in too many activities, are you, Baby Girl?" he asked when she was still up at 9:30, writing up her science lab. And when she went downstairs to pick up her laundry, he said, "How are you holding up? Can you handle all this?"

Sophie sagged against the dryer, laundry basket on her hip. It was tempting to tell him she felt like she was dragging a ball and chain, especially when his eyes actually got soft and he took the basket from her.

"I know it's tough," he said. "You and Lacie are being champs about it. Mama and I appreciate it, but you have to let me know if it gets to be too much."

Sophie wanted to leap up for a hang-around-the-neck-legs-dangling Daddy hug—just to feel carefree again for a minute.

But then Daddy said, "After all, you're still a little girl." He passed through the laundry room door with her basket of folded clothes. "By the way, how's that twenties gangster film coming together?"

Sophie got in front of him and pulled the basket out of his hands.

"Fine," she said. She headed for the stairs so she wouldn't add, *No thanks to you.*

"I can take that up for you," he called after her.

"I've got it," she said.

Glasses off and face down in her pink pillow a few minutes later, her thoughts screamed.

Let me get this straight—I have to run the whole house with Lacie and practically give up Film Club so I can raise my baby brother—but I'm still a little girl who can't handle a kidnapping scene where nobody even gets hurt.

I don't get it. I don't get it!

She tried to imagine Jesus, but she wasn't sure just now that she wanted him telling her what to do either. She pawed fitfully at her Bible, but she couldn't remember where the story was that they'd been studying with Dr. Peter.

Dr. Peter.

Sophie felt a spring of hope that bounced her up, but she plopped back down again. Forget Bible study. She had to watch Zeke tomorrow.

And watch life as she knew it disappear.

There was a tap on the door, which Sophie answered with a pillow-muffled grunt.

"Mama wants you to come in and say good night," Daddy said.

Sophie climbed off the bed and hoped she could work up a smile before she got to her parents' room.

Mama held out her arms to Sophie when she arrived and ran her hand down the back of Sophie's head.

"I miss our time together, Dream Girl," she said. "But I know you're busy helping."

"It's okay," Sophie lied.

Mama pushed her back so she could look at her. "Are you sure?"

What am I supposed to say? Sophie thought. She didn't know whether she was expected to be a grown-up or a little girl right now.

Mama was still searching her face with her tired Sophie-brown eyes. "Anything you want to talk about?" she said.

Sophie just shook her head. There was another long look and a pause.

"I'm right here," Mama said. She gave a wispy smile. "More than I want to be. You can still talk to me."

Can I? Sophie thought. She could feel her throat getting thick.

"Just promise me something," Mama said. "Promise that if you can't talk to me or Daddy, you'll at least talk to Dr. Peter."

"I won't even get to see Dr. Peter," Sophie blurted out. "I can't go to Bible study because I have to watch Zeke."

She wanted to chomp her tongue off as Mama's mouth dropped at the corners.

"But it's okay," Sophie said. Her voice squeaked. "It's fine."

"Time for bed, Baby Girl," Daddy said from the doorway.

Sophie escaped to her bedroom, where she cried herself to sleep, because she didn't know what the rules were anymore.

As Sophie boarded the bus the next morning, she spotted Victoria and Ginger, minus their cell phones, sitting in sullen silence on the eighth-grade side. Their eyes looked right through her as if she weren't even there.

It's tough being a law enforcement officer, Goodsy Malone thought as she took her usual watchful position by the window. Not everybody is going to like you, especially those thugs that can't obey the law.

But she didn't have time to think about that right now. She had an invalid girl in a wheelchair to rescue from the lousy Capone men that had nabbed her right out of her house. So far, they hadn't hurt her. At least that was what Goodsy could gather from listening in on the phone calls they let her make to her rich father, mob family leader Shawn O'Banyon. Goodsy had also gathered that the sick girl—Bitsy O'Banyon—was with at least two women. She'd heard their voices in the background during phone calls.

It pays to have a trained ear, is what I say, thought Goodsy. Even now she could detect words she knew she wasn't supposed to hear—

"I don't see why we should keep hanging out with her now," one voice said. "She can't have parties. We can't use her cell phone—"

"And she doesn't have any control over that Stephi girl at all," the other one said. "So what's the point?"

Sophie pressed herself closer to the window. Goodsy didn't have time for eavesdropping. She had mobsters to deal with.

Which she did all day. Goodsy hid behind a literature book during a stakeout—and Sophie nearly blew a quiz on the short story she was supposed to read.

Goodsy put on a disguise so she could spy on Capone—and Sophie got docked points for wearing sunglasses in the gym.

Goodsy checked the addition and subtraction on Al Capone's records, ate lunch in Capone's favorite Italian restaurant, and experimented with bomb-making so she wouldn't be caught by surprise when Capone's men tossed their next one.

By sixth-period Life Skills, Fiona was hoarse from coughing Sophie back on track. Fiona hadn't had to use her comeback-to-the-real-world signal in a long time.

"Are you even here at all today?" she wrote to Sophie in a note while Coach Yates was showing a film.

I don't know, Sophie thought.

Because no matter how deeply she escaped into Goodsy Malone's world, her own world was still the same chained-up, knotted-together mess when she returned to it.

Willoughby still wasn't speaking to the Corn Flakes, or even looking at them.

Their film still wasn't done, and there was no time for Sophie to work on it.

Mama was still in bed so Baby Girl LaCroix wouldn't make a too-early entrance into the world.

Daddy was still treating her like a little girl, unless he needed her to be Zeke's mom or run the dishwasher.

The rules that had once made her life so easy to live were all over in a corner of her mind, arguing with each other.

And the people who used to be there to untie the knots were now out of reach, especially Dr. Peter.

"It's Boppa's turn to drive us to Bible study today," Fiona said when she and Sophie and Maggie and Darbie were at their lockers after school. "I hope he doesn't play that elevator music the whole way."

"It's better than Aunt Emily's 'oldies,'" Darbie said. "I'd like to hear some 'newies' once in a while, but she thinks it's all evil or something—"

"I'm not going," Sophie said.

"No way," Maggie said.

"Yes, way. I have to watch Zeke."

"Bushwa!" Fiona said. She linked her arm through Sophie's as the four of them headed for the front of the school.

"Who else is going to do it?" Sophie said.

"Boppa," Maggie said.

"What?"

"Boppa," Maggie said again. Sophie followed her pointing finger to the Expedition parked at the curb. Boppa was behind the wheel, and Zeke was in the second seat, yakking away.

"All aboard," Boppa said through the rolled-down window. "First stop, church. Next stop, Bunting's Day Care."

"You're keeping Zeke?" Sophie said.

"So you can go to Bible study," Boppa said. He wiggled his caterpillar eyebrows. "Matter of fact, I have him for the rest of the week."

"Coolio!" Zeke crowed.

"He might not be so happy after he spends an afternoon with Miss Odetta," Fiona muttered to Sophie as they climbed into the third seat. She squeezed Sophie's hand. "But I am."

Ten

Sophie didn't have time to wonder how it had all come about, because the minute she walked into the Bible study room, Dr. Peter gave them red carnations to pin on, and fake cigars and black felt fedora hats. Sophie squealed as she dipped hers over one eye.

"This is swell!" she said.

"What's the deal?" Gill said. She put the fedora on top of her ball cap.

"The deal is, we're doing this Bible study twenties-style, see?" Dr. Peter said. He parked a phony cigar between his molars and talked out the other side of his mouth. "You dolls sit down and shut yer yaps. I'm the boss here, see, and you dames do what I say or else."

Kitty giggled and stuck the carnation behind her ear.

"So yer a tough guy, huh?" Sophie said in her best Goodsy Malone voice.

"Yeah."

"Says you." Sophie chewed on the cigar and gave him a Goodsy glare.

"Yeah, says me. Yer all a buncha lousy disciples, dirty rats in my book, 'cause ya been nabbed for stuffin' yer cake holes with grain on a Sunday." Dr. Peter glowered at all of them from under the brim of his hat. "And the Boss don't like that. It's against the rules, see?"

Kitty giggled again.

"Is he for real?" Maggie said to Darbie.

"That bulge in his jacket ain't his wallet," Darbie said. "He's packin' heat."

"So, what now?" Fiona said.

"What do you have to say for yourselves?" Dr. Peter said.

Sophie smothered a grin. "Get outta town," she said. "That ain't what the law means. I got a buncha hungry dolls here, see? What am I supposed to do, let 'em starve?"

"Who are you, their mommy?" Dr. Peter said. He stuck his hand inside his jacket. Fiona gave a shrill flapper-girl scream and rolled onto the floor, dragging Darbie with her.

"Huh?" Maggie said.

"Don't get your knickers in a knot, girls," Sophie said. "He's all talk. He ain't gonna shoot us over a coupla lousy grains a wheat."

"It's the principle of the thing!" Dr. Peter said.

"We can't eat your lousy principle," Sophie said. "See, that's the difference between you and me, Mr. Stinky Cigar."

"Oh yeah? How's that?"

"You'd let your own grandmother go hungry over a lousy rule 'cause you ain't got no heart. Me — us — we got heart. When somebody needs somethin', we do it for 'em; don't matter what day it is."

Dr. Peter's hand went farther into his jacket.

"I'm telling you, he's got a rod in there," Fiona said.

"He'll pump us fulla bullets!" Darbie cried.

"They're kidding," Maggie said to Kitty.

"So lemme ask you this," Dr. Peter said, narrowing his twinkly eyes. "You just gonna forget about Sunday altogether? Treat it like any other lousy day?"

"Says you!" Sophie said. "It's the Sabbath, and we're keepin' it holy. If we gotta do a little work to help somebody, that's still holy, see?"

"Yeah?" Dr. Peter said.

"Well, yeah," Sophie said. "I mean—" Her Goodsy voice faded into a Sophie squeak. "I get it."

Dr. Peter nodded. "Y'know," he said, "I like a smart doll like you."

Then he pulled his "weapon" out of his pocket and sprayed them all with Silly String.

Later, while they were pulling it out of their hair and eating Baby Ruth bars (Dr. Peter said they were invented in the twenties), Sophie was still thinking about the story.

"So the only time you can break a rule is when it would really help somebody to break it," she said. "Right?"

"Tell me some more," Dr. Peter said.

Sophie picked her words carefully. "Like if we had a rule with our friends that we would always help each other when we were in trouble—but one friend wanted somebody to lie to help her, only that really wouldn't help her—we should break the rule."

"Right," Dr. Peter said. "Only you wouldn't really be breaking it, because love and compassion and truth are never against the law."

Sophie could almost see that soaking into everyone's brains.

"Another important part of that," Dr. Peter said, "is that the original rule, to be loyal and help each other, still stands. Just like we should always try not to work on Sunday, unless we have to so we can feed somebody who's hungry in some way."

Sophie nodded. It felt like one small knot was starting to come undone.

"You were talking about Willoughby, weren't you?" Fiona said when they were all—except Kitty—in the car with Boppa and Zeke.

"Yeah," Sophie said. "And I think I know what to do to get her back in the Corn Flakes."

"Then tell," Darbie said. "I've been wretched all day missing her."

"And how," Fiona said.

Sophie tried to sit taller. "Even though she thinks we broke the rule, we still have to help her."

"How are we going to help her see that those eighth graders are bad for her?" Fiona said. "She's, like, obsessed."

"We do what Dr. Peter said. We feed her." Sophie shrugged. "You know, like take her a party."

"Right now?" Maggie said.

Fiona snorted. "Like that's going to happen."

There was a cough from the driver's seat. "Why not?" Boppa said. "There's never a better time for a party than right now." He picked up his cell phone and punched a number.

"What's he doing?" Maggie whispered.

Fiona rolled her eyes. "You got me."

Sophie listened, wide-eyed, as Boppa talked to her mother. When they got to Sophie's, Mama was on the couch, ready to act as Take-Willoughby-a-Party coordinator.

She sent Boppa and Zeke to the store for sodas and chips, while Sophie and Maggie foraged in the kitchen for other snacks, with Lacie pulling stuff off the shelves for them so they wouldn't mess up her pantry. Mama sent Fiona and Darbie to Daddy's computer to print up signs that read "We love you, Willoughby" and "We want you back!" At the last minute, before the girls piled back into the Expedition, Sophie grabbed a box of Corn Flakes from the pantry.

When Boppa pulled into Willoughby's driveway, he turned to the girls and said, "You take as long as you want, ladies. I'll wait out here."

"I have to admit that was swell of Boppa," Fiona said as they hauled their party-in-bags up to the front door.

Sophie glanced back at the car where Boppa was watching them in a pool of light from the streetlamp. Later, she wanted to tell him he was no longer on the evil Parent Patrol—he or Mama.

"Yo, Willoughby!" Fiona yelled as she hammered the door-bell. "Open up!"

Sophie heard footsteps on the other side, and then a pause. For a moment she was afraid Willoughby wasn't going to open the door. But then she did, and Darbie and Maggie waved the signs. Willoughby burst into tears.

"Does that mean she wants us to go away?" Maggie said.

"No!" Willoughby cried. "It means I love you!" She pulled them in, still wailing and laughing, and hugged each one of them until Sophie was sure there would be broken ribs.

"I'm sorry—" Willoughby said.

But Fiona stuffed a potato chip in her mouth. "We know," she said. "Now hush up and let's party."

"I brought you a present," Sophie said. She held up the cereal box.

"Am I still a Corn Flake?" Willoughby said as she hugged it against her.

"Is Al Capone Italian?" Darbie said.

Willoughby sobered. "I don't know—is he?"

"You have missed way too many rehearsals," Fiona said.

Willoughby let out a poodle-shriek, which brought an ear-to-ear smile to Sophie's face. It also brought Willoughby's father down the stairs.

"What's going on, Willoughby?" he said. Sophie could tell the growl wasn't far away.

"The girls came to see me—"

"When you're grounded?" Mr. Wiley's voice rose to dog-fight level. "What are you thinking—you can't have friends in here when you're grounded. What's the matter with you?"

"I'm sorry," Willoughby said.

"Sorry doesn't cut it."

"But I—"

It was as if Willoughby's father had forgotten there were four other girls standing there, staring at their toes, rigid as poles. Sophie's stomach was tying itself into a noose when Fiona poked her to say something.

"We should go," Sophie said. Her voice came out small.

Maggie got the door open, and they all shot out of it.

"Bye, y'all," Willoughby said in a quivery voice.

"Get to your room!" her father said.

The door slammed, shutting away the sight of Willoughby, hugging her Corn Flakes box and cringing. The girls skittered down the steps, but not before Sophie heard a thud and a cry like a wounded poodle.

One look at the other Corn Flakes, and she knew they had heard it too. They stood frozen at the bottom of the steps, until Maggie said, "Let's get out of here."

"Right," Darbie said. "I don't want to hear any more."

But Sophie couldn't move. "What about Willoughby?" she said.

Fiona grabbed Sophie's wrist and pulled her along. "I don't think she gets to party tonight, Soph."

"But what are we going to do?"

Darbie stopped and huddled the girls in with her arms. "I don't think we can do anything. I mean, he's her father."

"He shouldn't hit her," Maggie said.

Fiona's eyes bulged. "You want to go tell *him* that?"

"I didn't know he was a mean dad, did you?" Darbie said.

Sophie could hardly swallow, and the words "I should have known" barely came out.

"Should we tell someone?" Darbie said.

"I thought we said we'd help with parent stuff, not get each other in *more* trouble," Fiona said.

Sophie shook her head. "Dr. Peter said you have to break the rule if it helps somebody, and if we don't—"

"Just stop." Darbie put her hand up. "Maybe we're about to make a holy show out of something that's nothing. We do that sometimes." She pulled the girls in closer. "Why don't we ask Willoughby what happened before we tell any adults?"

"Brilliant," Fiona said. She was nodding harder than she needed to, Sophie thought. "Tomorrow, third period, we ask her."

Sophie looked back at the door. "I know what I heard," she said.

"We're just double-checking, Soph," Fiona said.

Because we don't want to believe it's true, Sophie thought as they hurried toward the Expedition.

"Not a word about this to Boppa yet," Fiona whispered.

Sophie actually didn't say anything at all on the way home or after she got there. She wasn't sure she could speak anyway, not with the knots that were now taking over her throat too. All she could do was close her eyes and imagine the kind eyes and beg Jesus to show her just which rule to follow.

"You do the talking, Soph," Fiona said the next day as she and Darbie hurried along with Sophie to the PE locker room at the beginning of third period to meet Maggie and Willoughby.

"You always say the right things," Darbie said.

All Sophie could think of to say right now was, *Jesus—please help!*

Because it wasn't just about a Film Club project anymore, or parents who wouldn't let them do adult things. It wasn't even about eighth-grade cheerleaders using a seventh-grade girl to get them out of trouble.

Now it was about Willoughby being with a father who growled like a dog—and maybe even hit her—hard enough to make her cry out.

Willoughby wasn't in the locker room when they arrived, and Maggie said Willoughby hadn't waited for her after second period.

"She'll run in here late again," Darbie said. "All in flitters."

"Get ready," Fiona said. "Sophie can ask her while we're changing her clothes."

Willoughby did burst in with only forty-five seconds left until roll call. "The team is ready," Fiona told her.

But as Maggie and Darbie stripped off Willoughby's backpack and jacket, and Sophie and Fiona went after her ankle boots, Willoughby pulled away.

"Y'all go ahead," she said, flashing them the plastic smile. "I don't want to make you late."

"Corn Flakes don't let any of their own be late, see?" Fiona said, flapper-girl style.

"Shut yer yap and let me have that shirt," Darbie said.

She slid Willoughby's sleeve off her arm. Sophie had to put her hand over her mouth to keep from gasping out loud. Bruises blued Willoughby's skin from shoulder to elbow. From the way Fiona was frozen over the other arm, Sophie was sure she saw the same thing there.

"I can really do this myself," Willoughby said. She turned her back to them and fumbled with her locker combination.

Fiona motioned everyone away with her head and gave Sophie a hard look.

"So," Sophie said in a voice that was over-the-top cheerful, "did you get punished because we came over yesterday? We didn't mean to get you in trouble."

"Not by *my* dad," Willoughby said. Her poodle-shriek came out thin and shrill. "He acts like he's all grouchy and mean sometimes, but he doesn't ever punish us." She twirled around, arms now covered. "He's a cool dad."

"He grounded you," Maggie said.

"For like ten minutes," Willoughby said. "And he apologized after you left."

"You girls that anxious to get detention?" Coach Yates yelled from the end of the locker row.

Willoughby jumped, and Sophie saw the fear-flecks in her eyes. She was the first one out of the locker room, still wearing the phony smile.

"She was lying," Maggie said as the rest of the Corn Flakes hurried out behind her.

"Uh, you think?" Fiona said.

Darbie edged close to Sophie in the roll-call line. "Did you see those bruises?" Sophie felt her shiver. "I'm never going to complain about Aunt Emily and Uncle Patrick again."

"Wiley!" Coach Yates yelled.

Nobody answered.

Coach Yates looked up from her attendance sheet, and for a second, her eyes looked worried. "She was just here. Where is she?"

"Should I answer for her?" Fiona whispered.

Sophie shook her head. It was time to break the rule — the one that said they would handle all their parent problems themselves.

This one, she knew, was way too big, even for the Corn Flakes.

Eleven

At lunch, sandwiches and chips and even Maggie's mother's homemade *sopapillas* went uneaten as the Corn Flakes talked in hushed voices. Willoughby wasn't with them, and Maggie said she hadn't shown up for fourth-period math either.

"So none of us have seen her since we dressed out for gym," Fiona said. "It's like she evaporated."

Darbie's eyebrows came together under her red bangs. "For all we know, she's still running around in her PE clothes."

"If she's cutting classes, she's gonna be in so much trouble with her dad." Maggie's words sounded even heavier than usual. They seemed to press everyone deeper into worry.

"We have to tell a grown-up," Sophie said. "We know her dad's hurting her—we heard—we saw the bruises—and you remember that other time when we were helping her change and she said she fell over the coffee table? I bet—"

"She didn't say he hit her, though," Fiona said.

They all stared at her.

Fiona rolled her eyes. "Okay, so she didn't have to. But what if we tell, and they put her in some foster home?"

There was a stunned silence, the kind of scary quiet that usually sent Sophie straight to Goodsy Malone's world. But somehow she knew even Goodsy didn't have an answer. And she didn't even have to close her eyes to see who did.

"I say we stick with our Code," Fiona said. "Or we're just going to make things worse."

"I say we stick with the Code too," Sophie said. "Only the Code says we always help when somebody's in trouble. The Jesus kind of help. Not lying and hiding stuff."

Fiona sat back and folded her arms. "If we're just going to call the police or something, no way."

"No," Sophie said. "First we tell Willoughby what we're going to do, and then we tell a grown-up we can trust."

"Like Dr. Peter," Darbie said.

Sophie wanted to hug her.

"How are we going to tell Willoughby if we can't even find her?" Maggie said as she dumped her untouched lunch into the garbage can.

"We keep looking until we do," Sophie said. She stuck out her pinky finger.

"Corn Flake promise," Darbie said.

Maggie hooked on.

Finally, Fiona did too. "I hate this," she said. "I wish our biggest problem was still how to make a kidnapping scene so every parent in America won't yell."

"And how," Sophie said. "I wish we could all just be kids."

She felt strangely old all afternoon as she took every possible chance to find Willoughby. She even got a restroom pass from grouchy Coach Yates so she could search the stalls. When she came back, disappointed, Coach Yates met her at the door.

"How long does it take to use the restroom, LaCroix?" she said.

Sophie groped for a comeback, but she only felt herself crumpling.

"Sorry," she said, "I was looking for Willoughby." Coach Yates' eyes sprang open, enough for Sophie to add, "Do you know where she is?"

"No, I don't know where she is. If you kids can't get yourselves to class, what am I supposed to do about it?"

I don't know, Sophie thought. *Care, maybe?*

Coach Yates pressed her lips together until they turned white. "I apologize, LaCroix," she said. "I'm just concerned about—a student. It's been bugging me for two weeks. You're a good kid—I shouldn't take it out on you."

Sophie hoped her mouth wasn't hanging completely open.

"Go on back inside," Coach said. "And let me know if you hear from Wiley, okay? She's a good kid too."

Her dad doesn't think so!

Sophie put her hand up to her mouth to make sure she hadn't said it out loud, but her lips were closed.

We have to find Willoughby soon, she thought, *or I really am going to tell somebody.*

By the next morning, it truly seemed, as Fiona said, Willoughby had evaporated. She hadn't answered Sophie's emails—or anyone else's, it turned out—and there had been no answer on her house phone or her cell phone. Sophie had avoided both Mama and Daddy, and she had imagined Jesus until she fell asleep, partly so she *wouldn't* imagine what might be happening to Willoughby at her house.

Nobody—Corn Flakes or Lucky Charms—had any news about her first period—nobody except Mrs. Clayton. She called Sophie out into the hall right after the bell rang.

"Willoughby Wiley is coming before the Round Table today at lunch," she said.

"Willoughby?" Sophie said. "She's here?"

"In Mr. Bentley's office, I assume." Mrs. Clayton's bullet eyes weren't firing. "She cut four of her classes yesterday. The librarian found her hiding out in the reference section."

Sophie didn't know whether to shout, "Yes!" or just plain cry. Willoughby was really in trouble now. And when her dad found out—

"Usually they would just give a student in-school suspension for that," Mrs. Clayton said. "But Mr. Bentley feels there's something else going on, and I agree. He would rather see the Round Table work with her. Maybe Coach Nanini."

Sophie did say "Yes!" then.

But Mrs. Clayton had more. "There's a problem, though," she said. "With you."

"Me?"

"Willoughby informed me during our preliminary meeting before school this morning that maybe you shouldn't be on the council today because you 'fixed' the outcome for two of her friends, and you might do the same for her. She doesn't want that."

Sophie could only stare at her.

"I'm not assuming that what she says is true," Mrs. Clayton said. "In fact, I'm inclined to believe it isn't. But the fact is that you and Willoughby are very close, and I'm not sure you could be completely objective. She does have a point there."

Sophie's mind was spinning like a bicycle wheel, but she managed to poke a stick in the spokes long enough to say, "But nobody knows Willoughby better than I do! I could really help her!"

Mrs. Clayton shook her head of cemented hair. "She may need your help in other ways, but I think you ought to sit this one out, Sophie."

How am I supposed to see justice done? thought Goodsy Malone as she scraped her chair up to her desk, *when I can't even be in the courtroom?* She slumped in her seat. *I gotta talk to her, see? I gotta tell her we need to rat on her old man, but it's for her own good.*

Goodsy pulled the rod from her shoulder holster and let it thud to the top of the desk. *Why try to fight violence on the streets if people's homes weren't even safe for them?*

Someone across the room coughed. Goodsy looked up—

Fiona nodded toward Sophie's desktop. Her hairbrush was lying where she'd dropped it, and everyone else had their faces in their lit books. Sophie pulled hers out, but all she could see on the pages was Willoughby with fear-flecks in her eyes.

Why did she tell Mrs. Clayton about me helping Victoria and Ginger? she thought. *It's like she doesn't want me there.*

But why?

Sophie asked herself that question all through PE and math class. It was the only thing she could talk about at lunch.

"I don't get it either," Fiona said. "She knows you're the fairest person in life."

"She's making a bags of it," Darbie said. "Poor thing."

"Here comes Jimmy," Maggie said. She shook her head soberly. "It didn't go so well."

Jimmy did look as if he'd rather be delivering a baby than the news he obviously had for them.

"Just tell me fast," Sophie said. "I can't stand it any longer."

Jimmy shoved his hands into his pockets. "She's not getting ISS, so nothing will go on her record. We gave her Campus Commission."

"After school?" Fiona said.

Jimmy nodded.

"Her dad's gonna be mad," Maggie said. "Way mad."

"Mad?" Darbie said. "He'll be furious."

"It's not like it's detention," Jimmy said.

"Her father won't get that," Sophie said.

"Yeah, but—" Jimmy hunched his shoulders as if Sophie might smack him. "You would have voted the same way if you'd been there."

Sophie had to nod. And then something shifted in her mind.

"That's why Willoughby didn't want me there," she said. "She knew I would vote that way because it's fair. It's what I did for those eighth graders the second time."

"She did look kinda surprised when Hannah suggested it and Oliver agreed with her." Jimmy shrugged. "I guess she thought they wouldn't."

Sophie shot up from the table. "So where is she now?"

"Going to class, I guess."

"We're there," Fiona said.

For the second day in a row, the Corn Flakes tossed their uneaten lunches into the trash. Sophie led them at a dead run to Miss Imes' classroom, but even ten seconds before the bell rang, when Darbie, Fiona, and Sophie had to get to science, there was still no Willoughby.

"Maybe Mrs. Clayton kept her after the meeting," Miss Imes said. "Surely she wouldn't cut class again after we just went easy on her."

"Willoughby doesn't see it that way," Fiona said as they tore for the science room.

"Neither does her father," Darbie said.

Sophie didn't say anything. She was too busy asking herself why they hadn't told an adult about Willoughby's father already. She had an old thought, one she hadn't had in several weeks.

I wish I could talk to Mama and Daddy about it right now.

Two days ago it would have seemed like a ridiculous idea. But today, it almost didn't matter that Daddy still thought she was a little girl. Right now she felt like one—a little girl with too many adult things in her head.

"You okay, Sophie?"

Sophie looked up to see Mr. Stires standing beside her desk. The rest of the class was gathered in small groups.

"I'm sorry," Sophie said. "I'll go be in Fiona's group."

"I told her to go on without you." Mr. Stires sat in the desk beside hers. His always-cheerful face looked confused, as if he didn't know how to be anything but happy.

"I heard about Willoughby," he said. "I don't understand it. Do you?"

"Sort of," Sophie said.

"You want to tell me?"

Sophie caught her breath. Mr. Stires probably never would have appeared on a list of adults she would talk to about a problem. But here he was, right at the moment when she needed a grown-up.

"I don't know why Willoughby cut her classes yesterday," Sophie said. "All I know is that she's afraid of her father. He's kind of—mean to her. Actually—really mean."

There. It was out. Mr. Stires wasn't Daddy or Dr. Peter, but at least—

"It makes sense now." Mr. Stires rubbed his fingers across his toothbrush mustache. "When Mr. Wiley called me and said your kidnapping scene was far too dark for seventh graders, he was angry. Too angry for the situation—"

Mr. Stires stopped suddenly, as if he'd said too much. It was enough for Sophie—enough to make her feel even smaller than she already was.

I just automatically thought it was Daddy, she thought. *I should have known.* Daddy wasn't Mr. Wiley, not even close.

"Do you think I could have a pass to the office?" Sophie said. "I want to call my dad."

Daddy answered his office phone on the first ring. Before Sophie could even get out "Hi, Daddy" all the way, he said, "What's wrong, Baby Girl? You okay?"

Sophie started to cry. She couldn't stop the whole time she was telling Daddy about Willoughby and her father, and what might happen now.

Daddy listened without interrupting. When she was through, there was such a long pause Sophie thought they had been disconnected.

"Daddy?" she said.

"Yeah, Baby Girl," he said. "I'm here. I'm just thinking." He pushed out some air. "Okay, here's what we'll do. You go on back to class and do your best to get through the rest of the day. I'll take care of this."

Sophie didn't even ask him what he was going to do. What *she* had to do was done, and she was suddenly very tired.

This is backwards from the way we were gonna do it, she thought as she took the hall back to the science room. *But I still need to tell Willoughby.*

Mrs. Clayton had to be finished with her by now, and Willoughby would be in Life Skills sixth period.

There was barely time before the end of science to join Fiona, Darbie, Vincent, and Jimmy in their group and fill them in on her phone call to Daddy. Even Fiona looked relieved. The boys were white-faced.

"So," Fiona said, "now we find Willoughby."

"We'll run interference for you," Vincent said. He and Jimmy cleared a people-free path in the hall so Sophie could be the first one at Coach Yates' door when kids started filing in.

But when Maggie arrived, she shook her head.

"She wasn't in math," she said.

"Are you talking about Willoughby?"

Sophie whirled around to face Cassie Corn Pop. She pushed her dislike out of the way and said, "Yes, I'm talking about Willoughby. Do you know something?" *Something that might actually be true?* Sophie wanted to add. "Just—do you know where she is?"

"I know where she isn't," Cassie said. By now Julia was at her side, looking curious. Cassie was apparently ready to take her moment in Julia's spotlight. It was all Sophie could do not to grab her and shake her.

"*Where?*" Sophie said instead. She didn't care that her voice was squeaking out of control.

Cassie glanced at Julia as if to make sure she was paying attention before she brought her face close to Sophie's and said, "She's not hiding out here at school anymore. I just saw her running across the parking lot." Julia gasped, and Cassie's eyes took on a shine. "Girl," she said, "she's out of here."

Twelve

✳ ⬠ ✺

"id I just hear what I think I heard?" Fiona said.

Sophie turned from watching Julia and Cassie disappear into the classroom, Cassie still basking in Julia's impressed gaze. "Did you think you heard that Willoughby just left school?" she said.

"Yeah."

"Then you did."

"Well, let's go find her then," Darbie said. "Why are we foostering about?"

"We definitely have to get to her before somebody from the school does." Fiona glanced at her watch. "How far do you think she'll get in forty-five minutes?"

"No," Sophie said.

"No what?" Fiona said.

"No, we can't just look for her ourselves. We have to tell an adult that she left school."

Fiona grabbed Sophie's arm and hauled her into the classroom. "You'll get her in more trouble, and it won't be just Campus Commission this time," she said through her teeth.

"And her father—" Darbie said.

But Sophie pulled away. "She's going to be in a worse kind of trouble if somebody doesn't stop her right this minute. We have to tell somebody who can do that."

With Fiona and Darbie still protesting behind her, Sophie went to Coach Yates, who had her whistle to her lips, ready to blow the class into silence. One look at Sophie's face, and she had Sophie out in the hall.

The story came out easier than it had with Daddy, as Sophie raced to the part where Willoughby was seen running from the schoolyard. For a few seconds, Coach Yates closed her eyes.

"I'm not surprised," she said. "I've been trying to get Willoughby to tell me this for weeks."

Sophie wondered if Willoughby was the student Coach Yates had said she was concerned about, the one who was making her grumpy. She could almost see Willoughby flashing a too-cheerful smile the day Coach Yates took her aside. There was no way Willoughby was telling anybody, even her best friends.

"All right," Coach Yates said. "I'll get word to the office. You did the right thing, LaCroix. I said you were a good kid."

"You said Willoughby was a good kid too," Sophie said.

"She is." Coach Yates opened the door for Sophie. "That's why we have to get her some help."

Sophie tried to explain that to Maggie and Fiona and Darbie.

"Dr. Peter told us really helping is never against the rules," she said, "even the rules we make up ourselves. Jesus would do this."

"We're not Jesus," Fiona said stubbornly.

Darbie shook her head, scattering her bangs. "Jesus would go look for her."

"So why can't we look too?"

They stared at Maggie.

"Mags is right," Sophie said. "We can still look for her. We just shouldn't be the *only* ones."

Fiona's face unclouded slightly. "Where do we start?"

They mapped out a plan. As soon as the last bell rang, Sophie sprinted straight to the eighth-grade locker area. If anybody looked at her like she was an intruder, she didn't notice. She had eyes only for Ginger and Victoria. She'd heard them say they wouldn't hang out with Willoughby anymore, but she had to try everything.

The moment they appeared, Sophie was on them.

"Did you talk to Willoughby today?" she said.

The two girls looked at each other and had one of those unspoken best-friends conversations with their eyes. Sophie was surprised to see that they didn't seem to exactly agree.

"No," Victoria said. "Look, Stephi—we haven't talked to her in, like, a week, okay?" She gave her blonde-over-blonde hair a toss and swept away, and what seemed like half the boys in the eighth grade followed her.

Ginger didn't. She spoke low and fast.

"Tell anybody I told you this, and I'll ruin your dating life forever," she said. "I talked to Willoughby. She was hysterical when she got Campus Commission for skipping, and I felt responsible because we showed her where to hide out when she wanted to cut class." She raked a hand through her elfin-hair. "I guess we forgot to tell her how not to get caught. Anyway, she told me today she was going to some neighbor's just to get her head straight. I told her to pack a couple of changes of clothes. Getting *her* head straight was going to take some time."

"Ginger!" Victoria called from the lockers. Before Sophie could ask another question, Ginger was gone.

I don't care about my "dating life" anyway, Sophie thought as she rushed off to tell her Corn Flakes. *EWWW!*

"Willoughby's neighborhood is Kitty's neighborhood," Fiona said when Sophie told them.

"You don't think she would try to hide out at Kitty's?" Darbie said.

"No," Fiona said. "But if we go there, we might see her."

Fiona called Boppa for a ride. Darbie went in search of the Lucky Charms, and Maggie phoned Kitty to tell her they were coming. Sophie prayed, and by the time they piled into the Expedition, she had a brilliant idea to share.

"Don't you want to wait 'til we get there to tell us?" Fiona said, shifting her eyes significantly toward Boppa.

"No," Sophie said, "'cause Boppa can help."

Although Fiona looked ready to pull out Sophie's nose hairs when they arrived at Kitty's, Boppa was checked out on the plan, complete with Kitty's phone number programmed into his cell phone.

"I'll call the minute I see her," he said, and he pulled off in the Expedition to patrol the streets for Willoughby.

The Charms set up for the kidnapping scene in Kitty's front yard while the Flakes explained to Kitty why they were having a film rehearsal at the very moment that Willoughby was missing.

"She's not going to let us find *her*," Fiona said. "So we have to let her find *us*."

Sophie gave a satisfied sigh. Fiona was finally getting it.

Vincent yelled that he was ready with the camera, and everyone got into position. Kitty had the phone in her lap in the wheelchair.

"Action!" Vincent called out.

Al Capone/Jimmy and his right-hand man, Thug Nathan, barely had time to sneak up behind poor little sick Bitsy

O'Banyon when the phone rang. Sophie leaped out of the bushes and leaned in as Kitty held the receiver away from her ear.

"She's headed down Valmoore Drive," Boppa said. "She hasn't seen me yet. I'm keeping my distance. She's right around the corner from you."

"Now!" Sophie said between her teeth.

Vincent abandoned the camera. He, Jimmy, and Nathan tore off like a herd of giraffes. Maggie and Darbie helped Kitty out of the wheelchair so she could go inside with the phone. She'd watch for her cue with her mom through the window. Sophie saw Kitty clinging to her before they closed the drapes almost all the way.

Sophie's job was to pray again: *Please let this work. We're really trying to play by your rules now.*

"Here they come!" Fiona said from her stakeout by the mailbox. She ran back to the Corn Flakes just as the Lucky Charms rounded the corner. Jimmy had Willoughby over his shoulder, screaming like a whole litter of poodle puppies. Nathan was carrying a suitcase.

Does she believe everything those eighth graders tell her? Sophie thought.

"Can you get this dame to shut up?" Jimmy/Al Capone said as he deposited Willoughby in front of Darbie and Fiona, the flapper girls. Sophie/Goodsy and Maggie/Loyal Sidekick Malloy stood apart and waited for their cue.

"Shut your cake hole and nobody'll get hurt," Fiona/Flapper Fran said to Willoughby.

"What are you doing?" Willoughby said. Her eyes were frantic as she looked over her shoulder and back at them, and then over her shoulder again.

"Making you look like somethin', for one thing," said Darbie/Soozy Floozy. "Get that jacket off her. Where's the fur coat?"

Fiona produced the oversize fake-fur coat Maggie's mom had made.

Make the change fast, Sophie thought. *It's cold out here.*

Willoughby was already shivering before Fiona and Darbie pulled her jean jacket off. When Nathan let out a long whistle at the sight of her black and blue arms, she began to shake like a wet dog.

"Let me go!" she screamed. "I don't want to rehearse. I have to go!"

Somehow they got the fur coat on her, but not before Sophie saw there were new bruises that hadn't been there the day before.

Hurry up, you guys, she wanted to call to the Capone gang. *Get her in the chair.*

"We can't let you go, see?" Jimmy/Capone said. "Because we gotta kidnap you."

"I don't have time!" Willoughby cried.

"Nobody has 'time' to be kidnapped, sister," Fiona/Flapper Fran said. She nodded toward the chair. Willoughby followed with her eyes and screamed louder, "No! Let go of me!"

Jimmy/Capone and Thug Nathan looked like they wanted to let her go, especially when Willoughby began to kick. But Vincent helped them get her into Kitty's wheelchair. Fiona and Darbie were ready with Kitty's mother's clothesline.

"Not too tight," Jimmy said in his own voice as they wrapped the line around Willoughby and the chair. "Her arms—"

"My arms are *fine*!" Willoughby screamed. "Now would you just get me out of this thing—I can't rehearse today!"

Sophie took her cue, only she didn't go to Willoughby as Goodsy Malone. It was Sophie herself who knelt down in front of the wheelchair and took both of Willoughby's hands. Willoughby tried, but she couldn't pull away.

"We're not rehearsing," Sophie said. "This is real life."

"Your life," Fiona put in.

"Please, Sophie," Willoughby said. Her words were choking out in sobs. "You don't understand—I have to get away!"

"We do understand," Sophie said.

"We know about your dad," Darbie said.

Willoughby froze. "What do you know? There's nothing to know—" her voice broke. "He's a good dad."

"Even a good dad makes mistakes sometimes."

Sophie had never been so happy to hear her father's voice. When she saw Dr. Peter walking up with him, she knew it was more than Kitty and her mom making that phone call at the right time. This was a Jesus answer.

"Why don't you all come inside for hot chocolate?" Mrs. Munford called from the porch. "You'll catch your death of pneumonia out there."

Nobody rolled their eyes. In fact, all the kids ran to her like lost-and-found four-year-olds. Except Sophie, who was wrapped around Daddy's leg.

"Let's talk, Willoughby," Dr. Peter said when he had untied her.

Willoughby looked at Sophie, tears glistening on her cheeks as if they were freezing. "Why did you tell on my dad?" she said.

"Because she's your friend," Dr. Peter said before Sophie could get her mouth open. She made a note in her head to hug him for that later. "She knew you were hurting, and she wanted you to get help. That's a holy thing."

"But my dad's gonna get in trouble!"

Who cares? Sophie wanted to shout at her. *He's mean to you. He SHOULD get in trouble! Why—*

Daddy tightened his grip on Sophie's shoulder. And then Sophie knew, and she empathized like no other. Mr. Wiley was Willoughby's dad, no matter what. If Sophie hadn't had her own dad holding her up at this very moment, she wasn't sure she could even stand.

"Your dad's a single parent," Dr. Peter said to Willoughby. "That's a big, scary job, and sometimes the stress gets to him, I'm sure. But there's help for that, Willoughby, not trouble. You want things to be better with him?"

"They used to be!" Willoughby said. "He used to be a cool dad. Sometimes he still is—" She threw up her hands as if all the confusing thoughts were in them, and she couldn't hold them any longer. Then she sank against Dr. Peter's chest.

"It's okay, little friend," Dr. Peter said. "We'll get that cool dad back again."

Boppa took the rest of the kids to their houses. Sophie noticed that when they pulled away in the Expedition, Fiona was in the front seat talking away to him.

But in the truck with Daddy, Sophie had so many things she wanted to say, none of them would come out. When they pulled into the driveway at home, Daddy kept the engine running and the heater blasting.

"I'm proud of you, Baby Girl," he said. Then he shook his head. "You're not a baby girl anymore, though, that's obvious. You're growing up right before my eyes."

It did come out then. "I'm not grown yet," Sophie said. "I thought I was, but I wasn't—not like Lacie or you or Mama—or even Goodsy Malone—I tried to be, but I'm so confused about what 'grown-up' even is—and sometimes I don't know which rules to follow—but I'm really trying to figure it out, Daddy—really."

119

Daddy's mouth was twitching, but in the light from the lamp in the yard, Sophie could see a wet shine in his eyes.

"You know what a real grown-up is, Soph?" he said.

Sophie shook her head.

"A grown-up is a person who knows what she can't handle and turns it over to somebody who can—but she also knows what she knows and she doesn't let anybody else take that away from her." He reached a big hand over and squeezed her tiny shoulder. "I want you to teach our new baby girl that when she gets old enough."

"For real?" Sophie said.

"Who could she want more for a friend than you?" Sophie could see him swallowing. "*I* sure want you for my friend."

"Your friend?" Sophie said.

"I'm still your dad, Soph. I have to steer you right when you start flying off to places I don't think you're ready to go yet." His face went soft. "But I also hope you can trust me as a friend when you've got trouble."

It was Sophie's turn to swallow. "But sometimes you don't get it, Daddy," she said.

"No, I don't," Daddy said. "And I'm going to work on that. I think it's time I let you fly just a little bit—" He put up his hand. "Not too far—just a little."

Sophie felt her stomach start to untie, but still—

"What does that mean?" she said.

"That means I bought myself a new laptop and a new desktop computer today."

"Huh?" Sophie said. *Talk about flying off into weird places—*

"And *that* means my old laptop is in Lacie's room at this moment as we speak, and my old desktop is on your desk."

"Says you!" Sophie cried.

"Yeah, says me." Daddy locked his fingers and stretched out his arms. "Incredible father that I am." He grinned. "Now, there are going to be rules for the Internet—"

Sophie nodded happily. Rules were fine. In fact, rules were the cat's pajamas.

She closed her eyes, and there were the kind eyes. And the best rules were right there in them.

Glossary

bee's knees (beez kneez) the way someone from the 1920s said "that's really cool"

bushwa (boosh-wah) complete nonsense

cat's pajamas (cats puh-JAM-uhs) when something's really impressive; you could also say it's the "cat's meow"

chemotherapy (key-mo-THER-a-pee) really strong chemicals that are used as a treatment for cancer

eejit (eeg-it) the way someone from Ireland might say "idiot"

empathize (EM-puh-thize) feeling for someone and putting yourself in their place, because you went through the same thing in the past

flappers (FLA-purs) girls from the 1920s who cut their hair short and wore really cool hats and short skirts (at least short for that time!); parents and other adults were shocked because they didn't act like "proper young ladies"

Flitters (FLI-turs) a feeling you get when you're really excited, like when your body gets all shaky because you're waiting for something to happen

foostering about (foo-stur-ing a-bout) an Irish way of saying "stop wasting time"

gadzooks (ghad-zooks) an exclamation of surprise, especially when something is a little different from what you expected

giving cheek (ghiv-ing cheek) talking back to someone, or acting a little snotty

leukemia (loo-KEY-me-uh) a type of cancer; it attacks your healthy blood cells, especially in your bone marrow, so that you become very sick

make a bags of (mayk a bags of) do a poor job at, or screw things up

nontraditional (non-trah-dish-un-al) something that doesn't follow the way you normally do things

pussyfoot around (pussy-foot uh-rownd) carefully avoiding something; talking about everything but the real issue when someone brings it up

rod (rhod) a slang term for a gun

says you (sez you) a statement of disbelief; telling someone that just because they said it doesn't make it true

scintillating (SIN-tuh-late-ing) something that is really fun, interesting, and even exciting

sumptuous (SUMP-shoe-us) really impressive and over the top

sympathize (sim-pah-thize) feeling sad and concerned for someone when bad things happen

telly (tel-lee) a shortened word for television

up to ninety (up too nine-tea) so incredibly angry, your blood is almost ready to boil, and you're ready to explode on someone

wretched (ret-chid) really upset and concerned about something or someone

Sophie Loves Jimmy

One

Cynthia Cyber, Internet Investigator, leaned toward the computer screen, eyes nearly popping from her head. Could it be that a kid would actually be enough of a bully to print something like THAT for all the middle-school world to see? Impossible—and yet, there it was, a sentence that was already showing its ugly self on computers in bedrooms all over Poquoson, Virginia, and maybe even beyond. It was a sentence that could ravage the social life of its seventh-grade victim before she even checked her email.

"I cannot allow it!" Cynthia Cyber, Internet Investigator, cried. She lunged for the keyboard, fingers already flying—

"It's a seven-passenger van, Little Bit," said a voice from the driver's seat. "You don't have to sit in Jimmy's lap."

Sophie LaCroix jolted back from Sophie-world at several megahertz per second—or something like that. She found herself staring right into Jimmy Wythe's swimming-pool-blue eyes. She had no choice. She really was in his lap.

A round, red spot had formed at the top of each of Jimmy's cheekbones. Sophie was sure her entire *face* was that color.

"Do you want to sit on this side?" Jimmy said as Sophie scrambled her tiny-for-a-twelve-year-old body back into her own seat. "We could trade."

"I don't think that's what she had in mind." Hannah turned around from the van's middle seat in front of them, blinking her eyes against her contact lenses practically at the speed of sound. She was Sophie's inspiration to keep wearing glasses. "Personally, I think seventh grade's a little young to be dating. I know I'm only a year older, but—"

Mrs. Clayton didn't turn around in the front seat, but her trumpet voice blared its way back to them just fine. "There is actually a world of difference between seventh graders and eighth graders."

Yeah, Sophie thought, fanning her still-red face with a folder. *Eighth graders think it's all about the boy-girl thing. I am SO not dating Jimmy Wythe. Or anybody else! EWWW.* She scooted a couple of inches farther away from Jimmy.

It wasn't that Jimmy wasn't a whole lot more decent than most of the boys at Great Marsh Middle School. He was one of the three guys who made films with Sophie and her friends. They didn't make disgusting noises with their armpits and burp the alphabet in the cafeteria—like some other boys she knew. But *date* him—or anybody else?

I do not BELIEVE so!

"So, are you guys going out or what?" Hannah said.

"Not that it's any of your business." Oliver, the eighth grader next to her, gave one of the rubber bands on his braces a snap with his finger. Why, Sophie wondered, did boys have to *do* stuff like that?

"Oh, come on, dish, Little Bit," Coach Nanini said from behind the wheel. He grinned at Sophie in the rearview mirror in that way that always made Sophie think of a big happy gorilla with no hair. She liked to think of him as Coach Virile.

She had to grin back at him.

"We're not going out," Jimmy said. The red spots still punctuated his cheekbones. "We're just, like, friends."

Mrs. Clayton did turn around this time, although her helmet of too-blonde hair didn't move at all. "That's very noble of you, Jimmy, to get Sophie out of the hot seat like that. You're a gentleman."

"Ooh, Mrs. C," Coach Virile said, still grinning. "Don't you know that's the kiss of death for the adolescent male?"

"It's okay," Jimmy said. He pulled his big-from-doing-gymnastics shoulders all the way up to his now-very-red ears. "It's what my dad's teaching me to be."

"Bravo," Mrs. Clayton said. "I'd like to bring him in and have him train the entire male population of the school."

Coach Virile's voice went up even higher than it usually did, which was pretty squeaky for a guy whose beefy arms stuck out from both sides of the driver's seat. "I thought I was doing that, Mrs. C."

"I wish you'd step it up a little," she said.

Sophie glanced sideways at Jimmy, who was currently ducking his head of short-cropped, sun-blond hair. *I guess he is kind of a gentleman,* Sophie thought. She had never heard him imitate her high-pitched voice like those Fruit Loop boys did, or seen him knock some girl's pencil off her desk just to be obnoxious. And somehow he managed to be pretty nice and still cool at the same time. The Corn Pops definitely thought so. The we-have-everything girls were always chasing after him.

"So if you're not going out," Hannah said, "why were you in his lap?"

She was turned all the way around now, arms resting on the back of her seat as if she were going to spend the rest of the trip from Richmond exploring the topic. Oliver groaned.

"Inquiring minds want to know," Hannah said.

NOSY minds, you mean, Sophie thought. But she sighed and said, "I wasn't really sitting in his lap. Well, I was, only that wasn't my plan. I didn't even know I was doing it, because I was being—well, somebody else—and Jimmy's window was a computer screen—all our stuff's piled up and blocking my window so I couldn't use it—anyway, it all started with the conference. I really got into it."

Coach Virile laughed, spattering the windshield. "We can always count on you to be honest, Little Bit."

"Let me get this straight," said Oliver. "You were pretending to be, like, some imaginary person?"

"More like a character for our next film."

Jimmy, still blotchy, nodded. "For Film Club. Sophie always comes up with the main character."

"I play around with it some before I tell the whole group," Sophie said. "I try not to get too carried away with it in school." She didn't add that if she got in trouble for daydreaming, her father would take away her movie camera.

"Ya think?" Hannah said. She put on her serious face. "A little advice: don't tell that to a whole lot of people at Great Marsh. You'd be committing social suicide."

"Especially don't let it get out on the Internet," Oliver said. "Everybody'll think you're weird."

"I *am* weird," Sophie said. "Well, unique. Who isn't?" That was the motto of Sophie and her friends, the Corn Flakes: Keep the power God gives you to be yourself.

"I may be weird," Hannah said, "but I do *not* go around acting out imaginary characters, okay?"

You wouldn't be very good at it, Sophie thought. She ran an elfin hand through her short wedge of honey-colored hair and squinted her brown eyes through her glasses.

"What?" Hannah said.

130

"Well," Sophie said slowly, "you might not be unique in that way, but you are somehow. Everybody is."

Hannah's eyebrows twitched. "I try not to let that get out. I'd like to get through middle school without being the punch line of everybody's jokes, thank you very much."

"Speaking of bullying . . ." Coach Virile cleared his throat.

"Yes," Mrs. Clayton said. "What did you glean from the conference?"

"Can I 'glean' if I don't know what it means?" Oliver said.

"It means what did we learn," Sophie said. It came in handy to have a best-best friend who almost knew the whole dictionary. Fiona, she knew, would be proud.

Hannah gave Oliver a poke. "So what did you glean, genius?"

Oliver held up his folder, which had the shield of the Commonwealth of Virginia on it, and the words "Governor's Conference on Cyber Bullying." He flipped it open and read, "'Seventeen million children in America use the Internet. Twenty to thirty percent of them report being victims of bullying through email, instant messaging, chat rooms, websites, online diaries, and cell phone text messages.'"

Sophie hadn't remembered any of that. She'd been way wrapped up in the stories actual kids told, right from the stage, about how people had written heinous things about them on the Internet (*heinous* was one of Fiona's best words, meaning worse than awful) and everybody believed them. One victim changed schools. Another one refused to even go to school. And there was actually a boy who fought back with his own website and got suspended for the rest of the year while the original bullies were never caught.

Cynthia Cyber was outraged. This could not be allowed to go on! Fortunately she had taken on the job of Internet Investigator, ready to do battle to clean up cyberspace —

"Are you doing that imaginary character thing right now?" Hannah said.

Sophie froze and looked at her hand, which was poised in the air, fingers curled around a not-there computer mouse.

"Yeah, she's doing it," Jimmy said. He gave Sophie a shy smile. She noticed his teeth were as straight as slats in a fence.

"You can't tell me you two aren't going out," Hannah said.

"All right, Round Table," Mrs. Clayton said. "Let's stay focused."

Yeah, can we please? Sophie thought. Sometimes she wondered if Hannah and Oliver even took Round Table seriously. *She* definitely did. After all, the four of them, plus Mrs. Clayton and Coach Virile and a few other teachers, were the group that was trying to stop bullying at Great Marsh Middle School by teaching kids how to treat each other and helping bullies be better people instead of just punishing them. To Sophie, it was an awesome responsibility, which was why she had spent the whole day at the conference in Richmond figuring out how the Round Table could help stop an even worse kind of bullying—the stuff that happened on people's computers.

"How about you, Jimbo?" Coach Virile said.

"I know what *Jimbo* was thinking about," Hannah muttered.

"Uh—that cyber bullying is simple," Jimmy said. "Like, all you have to know is how to log on to the Internet, and do email and get in chat rooms, and download stuff."

"Which is why it's spreading like a wildfire," Mrs. Clayton said. She shot the two back seats a bullet-eyed look. "And since there's no adult supervision on the Internet, it's up to you kids to stop it."

"Not just you four," Coach Virile said. "But you're the leaders."

Oliver snapped both sets of rubber bands. Sophie rolled her eyes at Jimmy, who rolled his back.

"I don't see how we're gonna stop it," Oliver said. "It's all under the adult radar, like you said, so people hardly ever get caught. Not like when they do regular bullying at school."

"We adults definitely have to do our part," Mrs. Clayton said. "I have absolutely no online life. I'm going to have to get hip to this Internet thing."

Oliver snorted, and Hannah covered her whole face with her hands. As Sophie turned to grin at Jimmy, she saw in the rearview mirror that even Coach Virile's eyes were twinkling.

"I'm so glad you're all amused," Mrs. Clayton said.

"What about you, Little Bit?" Coach Nanini said. "What did you learn?"

That Cynthia Cyber is going to kick buns as an Internet investigator, Sophie thought. But she gave Hannah a being-careful look and instead said, "It seems like the first thing to do is keep trying to get kids to stop treating each other like enemies so cyber bullying won't happen in the first place."

"Good luck," Hannah said.

"We *are* having good luck with that, though," Coach Virile said. "For just about every student who's come before Round Table, we've been able to get some change going."

"Except that one fat kid," Oliver said.

Mrs. Clayton shot him another bullet look.

"Sorry. That poor overweight kid that ripped off Sophie's—"

"Eddie Wornom," Coach said.

At the sound of that name, Sophie shivered. Stealing wasn't the only thing Eddie had done to her since she met him back in sixth grade. Even working with Coach Virile on Campus Commission hadn't changed Eddie, except to make him worse. He was away at military school now, and that was fine with Sophie.

"It would take a miracle to rehabilitate Eddie," Jimmy whispered to Sophie.

"Yeah," Sophie said. "That would be right up there with the loaves and fish."

Jimmy laughed from someplace way down in his throat. "If Eddie had been at the loaves and fish, there still wouldn't have been enough food to go around."

"You know it."

They settled into a comfortable silence. It occurred to Sophie that she had started out that morning wishing her Corn Flakes were with her—Willoughby and Maggie and Darbie and Kitty and especially Fiona. She had missed them some during the day, like when she went to the restroom and there was nobody to giggle with. Hannah wasn't a giggler.

But most of the time she and Jimmy had talked—more than they did when the other Lucky Charms, Vincent and Nathan, were around.

But for Pete's sake, Sophie thought now, *why does Hannah think we're going out? Like Mama and Daddy would let me, even if I wanted to.*

Besides, Sophie could never figure out where seventh-grade couples "went" when they were "going out." Yikes. They were *twelve*.

"All right, Round Table," Mrs. Clayton said. "You have an assignment."

"Is it a lot?" Hannah said. "I'm going to have a ton of home-work from missing the whole day today."

"You'll manage," Mrs. Clayton said. "Before we meet next Monday, I want each of you to come up with some ideas for putting the things we learned at the conference to work in our own anti-bullying campaign."

Sophie smiled what she knew was her wispy smile. She was already coming up with a film they would show to the whole school, starring Cynthia Cyber—

"What time is it?" Hannah said as they pulled into the school driveway.

"Three-thirty," Coach Nanini said. "You can still catch the late bus."

"There's a line out there for it already." Hannah sighed loudly. "I hate it when it's so crowded. It smells the whole bus up when everybody's been playing sports."

"Well, excuse them for perspiring," Oliver said.

Once again, Sophie and Jimmy rolled their eyes at each other. *It was almost as much fun rolling them with him as it was rolling them with the Flakes*, Sophie thought.

"I think somebody's trying to get your attention, Little Bit," Coach Virile said, pointing through the windshield.

Sophie grinned. It was hard to miss Willoughby, who was waving both of her red-and-white-and-blue pom-poms and yelling, "SO-phee!" in her biggest cheerleader voice.

"How does all that sound come out of that little person?" Coach said.

Although Willoughby wasn't quite as small as Sophie, she was still petite, and looked even more so under her mop of darkish, wavy hair that was even now springing out of its clips as she bounced up and down shouting at Sophie.

Sophie called good-bye to everybody in the van even as she wriggled her way through the line to Willoughby. When Sophie reached her, Willoughby grabbed her by the sleeve and dragged her away from the stream of kids waiting for the late bus.

"You aren't going to *believe* this," Willoughby said instead of "hello." Her very round hazel eyes were bright with excitement. "We've been dying to tell you all day, and I told the rest of the Flakes I'd tell you since I was the only one staying after school and we figured you'd be back to catch the late bus——"

"What *is* it?" Sophie said. Sometimes Willoughby's thoughts went as wild as her hair.

"You will never guess who's coming back to school."

"Who?"

Willoughby sucked in a huge breath. "Eddie Wornom," she said.

"No WAY!" Sophie shook her head. "He's at military school."

"Not anymore. At least that's what B.J. and Cassie were saying in fifth period."

Sophie let out a relieved sigh. "You know you can't trust a Corn Pop. They're just trying to scare you."

Willoughby's eyes were as big as Frisbees. "You think?"

"I *know*. What do the Pops do better than anything else?"

"Put on lip gloss?"

"Besides that."

Willoughby nodded slowly. "Spread rumors."

"Exactly." Sophie gave Willoughby a quick hug around the neck. "We have to just ignore stuff like that. They said that at the conference, which I wanna tell you all about, only I've gotta go."

"IM me tonight," Willoughby said.

"You coming or what?" the bus driver yelled.

Sophie scrambled up the steps and hurled herself into an empty seat just as the door sighed shut and the bus lurched around the curve in the driveway. Sophie lurched with it, rocking into the person next to her.

She looked up into the eyes of Eddie Wornom.

Two

Sophie pulled back and stared. She'd *thought* it was Eddie. It was Eddie's sandy-blond-with-bangs hair and matching almost-invisible eyebrows. But this guy's hair was way shorter than Eddie's. And the cheeks weren't Eddie's pudgy ones, and the mouth wasn't curled up and poised for some lame remark like, "Hey, Soapy. When's the breast fairy gonna come visit you?"

This kid was taller than Eddie. She could tell that even though he was sitting down. He was also thinner. And he didn't look like he was capable of burping the alphabet. Sophie could see his now-sticking-out Adam's apple move up and down.

"Hi, Sophie."

Sophie jerked back like a startled rabbit. How was Eddie Wornom's voice coming out of this kid's mouth? This kid who didn't say it like he wanted to hurl at the same time?

"Do I know you?" Sophie said.

"Uh, yeah," he said.

It *was* Eddie. What was he doing on the bus when he hadn't even started back to classes yet? *He's probably just here to torment me*, Sophie thought. She clutched the edge of the seat and waited for what was sure to come. Something from the you-sure-didn't-get-any-brains-while-I-was-gone department.

Eddie swallowed again. It looked like it hurt. "Everybody says I look really different," he said.

Sophie could only stare. And think of all the other times she'd been this close to Eddie Wornom. Every one of those times, she'd felt like she was either going to throw up or pass out from terror.

The bus lurched again, this time at its first stop. As a clump of kids gathered at the door, Sophie popped up and tore down the aisle toward the back, looking for a familiar face. After all, it was only a matter of time before Eddie went Fruit Loop on her, she was sure of that.

When she spotted two of the Wheaties, she dived into their seat and hissed, "Scoot over! Please!"

The Wheaties were a group of soccer-playing and every-other-kind-of-ball-playing girls the Corn Flakes got along with. They were very un-Corn Pop and very cool.

"What's up?" said Gill, the bigger of the two. A couple of straggly strands of her lanky red hair trailed out from under the blue toboggan cap she wore pulled down to her eyebrows. Beside her, by the window, her friend Harley grunted, which was all she usually did, since Gill did most of the talking. Harley just smiled a lot under the brim of her Redskins ball cap, until her cheeks came up to her eyes and squinted them closed.

"I got stuck sitting next to Eddie Wornom!" Sophie whispered.

Harley grunted again.

"I thought he was gone," Gill said.

"I guess he's back." Sophie looked furtively up the aisle to the seat she'd just vacated. "For once, B.J. and them weren't lying."

Both Gill and Harley grunted this time. The Corn Flakes had never told the Wheaties that they called the popular girls

Corn Pops, but they knew the Wheaties didn't like the Pops any more than they did.

"It's in our Code not to put them down just because they do it to us," the Corn Flakes had told the Wheaties more than once. But it wasn't easy for any of them.

"Where is he?" Gill said.

"Second row back on the other side," Sophie said.

Gill rose up out of the seat just far enough to keep from getting yelled at by the bus driver and shook her head. "That kid isn't fat enough to be Eddie Wornom."

"I guess he lost weight," Sophie said. "What's he doing now? I can't see."

Gill craned her neck. "He's got Tod Ravelli sitting with him. Colton Messik's behind them. The Three Stooges."

The three Fruit Loops, Sophie thought, groaning inside. "What are they doing?"

"Tod's all up in Eddie's dental work, tellin' him something. Colton's clapping like an ape."

"What about Eddie?"

"He's not saying anything—for once."

Harley grunted. She too was up on her knees, watching.

"What?" Sophie said.

Gill looked at Harley, and they both nodded. "We think Eddie's smiling too big," Gill said. "It's like he's straining his mouth or something."

"Just wait ten seconds," Sophie said miserably. "He'll start yelling swear words."

"That's all he knows," Gill said.

A block later, the first two seats erupted with snorts and too-loud laughs that clearly said *we're ripping somebody apart up here*. Sophie could almost see herself being shoved into a trash can, or worse.

When the bus stopped at the corner of Odd Road where Sophie lived, she scooted hurriedly past the Fruit Loops without even glancing at them. She definitely didn't look up from the sidewalk as the bus pulled away. She was sure she would have seen Eddie hanging out, waggling his tongue.

There was only one thing to do, and that was to get online *immediately* and find out what the rest of the Flakes knew. Fiona, Darbie, and Sophie were in different classes than Maggie and Willoughby for some periods, so Fiona and Darbie might have heard different things. Julia and Anne-Stuart were the Pops in their section, and although they didn't talk as loud as B.J. and Cassie, they were the ones who decided what rumors were spread and how.

But Sophie headed for the family room to check on Mama first. She was enthroned on the couch, hands folded over her pregnant tummy, dozing in front of the TV with the sound muted. Sophie watched her for a minute.

Everybody always said Mama and Sophie looked alike with their wispy smiles and round brown eyes and pixie-like bodies. But lately Mama didn't even look like herself, much less like Sophie. Everything about her was puffy — not just her tummy. And her usually bouncy, highlighted-to-cover-gray curls were pulled up into an untidy bun on the top of her head so it didn't get ratty from lying down all the time.

The doctor had told Mama she had to remain completely off her feet if Baby Girl LaCroix was going to stay put until it was time for her to be born in March. Being inside the house made Mama milky-pale, and not being involved in absolutely everything Sophie and her older sister, Lacie, and her little brother, Zeke, did kept the wispy smile from appearing as often as it used to.

Since this was only December, Mama still had a lot more time to spend, as she put it, being a beached whale. As Sophie watched the air puff out between Mama's lips in sleep, she felt a wave of I-need-to-do-more-to-cheer-her-up.

Right after I check my email I'm going to bring her a snack, Sophie thought. *Peanut butter and celery, with honey for dipping—*

She was about to turn and tiptoe out when Mama's eyes fluttered open and she gave Sophie a swollen smile.

"Hey, Dream Girl," she said. "How was the conference? I want to hear everything." She struggled to sit up. "Not that I would understand any of it. You know I'm computer challenged."

"That's okay." Sophie dropped her backpack on the floor and hurried to adjust Mama's pillows. "You do a lot of other stuff really well."

"Not these days," Mama said. She fluttered a hand toward the covered basket beside the couch. "And if I even look at a pair of knitting needles again, I'll probably poke somebody with them."

Sophie nodded. The basket was overflowing with sweaters and booties and blankets for Baby Girl LaCroix that Mama had knit and knit until two nights ago when she said she was sick of the sight of yarn and wanted to put the whole pile down the garbage disposal. Daddy had rescued it and carried Mama upstairs to bed.

Sophie sniffed the air, but she didn't smell supper. "Where's Lacie?"

"She has the night off from cooking," Mama said. "Daddy's bringing home Chinese."

"Yes!" Sophie said. Not only did she love egg rolls, and moo goo gai pan because it was fun to say, but this meant she didn't have to help in the kitchen, and there would be more time to find out stuff from the Flakes. She edged toward the door.

"Why don't you go do your thing?" Mama said. "You can tell all of us about the conference over chow mein. I'll send Zeke up when Daddy gets here."

Sophie was glad Zeke was with Fiona's grandfather Boppa. A lot of the time, *she* had to watch him after school, which meant endless hours playing Spider-Man.

"Love you," Sophie said as she backed toward the stairs.

"Love you more," Mama said and closed her eyes again.

Sophie flew to her room and turned on her computer. It had been Daddy's at one time, and when he had given it to her, he'd built a special desk for it so she could have more privacy in their busy house. It had been kind of a reward for taking more responsibility helping with Mama. It didn't exactly go with the flowy chiffon curtains Mama had hung around Sophie's bed or the princess lamp on the table that had given light to so many of Sophie's daydreams, but that didn't matter. Right now Cynthia Cyber, Internet Investigator, had work to do—

I have to stay focused on the real world right now, Sophie told herself as she clicked on the Internet icon. And Eddie Wornom was about as real as this world got.

Sure enough, there was a group email from Fiona—WORDGIRL—to all the Flakes. The subject was EDDIE WORNOM ALERT!!!!

IT'S OFFICIAL, CORN FLAKES: EDDIE WORNOM IS COMING BACK TO GREAT MARSH MIDDLE SCHOOL. HEARD JULIA AND ANNE-STUART TALKING ABOUT IT 5TH. ASKED COACH YATES ABOUT IT 6TH. SHE SAID HE WAS IN THE OFFICE ALL AFTERNOON AND THE SCHOOL'S GIVING HIM ANOTHER CHANCE. WE HAVE TO BE VIGILANT. IT COULD GET UGLY.

Sophie was just reaching for the dictionary to look up *vigilant* when an instant message popped up. It was from IRISH. Because Darbie was from Northern Ireland, she used IRISH for just about everything.

IRISH: I won't believe that blackguard is back.

Sophie could almost hear Darbie saying that in her lilty Irish voice. She always pronounced blackguard, another word for absurd little creep, like blaggard.

DREAMGRL: He IS back!!!! I saw him on the late bus.
IRISH: Evil!

Before Sophie could answer, another IM popped up, this time from Kitty. Nobody IM'd and emailed more than Kitty. Because of her leukemia and the chemotherapy that made her sick, she was being homeschooled. The Internet kept her from feeling like she was missing absolutely everything.

MEOW: Hi, Sophie.
DREAMGRL: Hi, Kitty. Did you hear about Eddie?
MEOW: Yes! for once I'm glad I'm not at school!
DREAMGRL: LOL!!!

It had taken Sophie a while to learn that LOL meant "laugh out loud." Now that she could spend more time online, she was getting the language down.

DREAMGRL: I SAW him
MEOW: Eddie?
DREAMGRL: Yes. On the late bus
MEOW: Was he mean?

143

Sophie grabbed a hunk of her hair and toyed with its blunt-cut ends. She had to decide what to say next so she didn't break Corn Flake Code. It was hard when you were talking about the most heinous boy on the planet.

```
MEOW: Did he cuss on the bus?
DREAMGRL: No
MEOW: Belch?
DREAMGRL: Nope
MEOW: Was he even awake? LOL
DREAMGRL: LOL!!!
```

Sophie paused. It would be okay to just state a fact, right?

```
DREAMGRL: He isn't as fat as he used to be.
MEOW: POS
```

Sophie definitely knew that code. POS meant "parent over shoulder." When you saw that, you really had to be careful about what you wrote. Sophie was glad she didn't have that problem anymore, like she did when she'd had to use the computer down in Daddy's study. There was always POS going on back then.

Cynthia Cyber squinted through her glasses at the screen. She was instantly alert when she saw POS. That could mean bullying was happening that a kid didn't want a mom or dad to know about. She cupped her hand on her mouse, finger ready to click on anything heinous that might flash before her—

The bell sound announced another instant message. It was from Go4Gold. It took Sophie a second to realize that was Jimmy.

```
Go4Gold: Sophie?
DREAMGRL: Hi, Jimmy.
```

```
Go4Gold: I have an idea for what Mrs C told us
to do.
DREAMGRL: For Round Table?
GO4Gold: Ya. Wanna meet before school tomorrow?
DREAMGRL: Where?
GO4Gold: Library. 7:30?
DREAMGRL: I'm there.
```

"SO-phee! SUP-per!"

Something banged against the door, as if someone had thrown a bag of potatoes at it. Sophie knew it was Zeke, probably trying to launch himself up onto the doorframe so he could climb down like Spider-Man. Meanwhile, bells were dinging on the computer.

```
IRISH: You still there?
MEOW: Where did you go?
Go4Gold: See ya tomorrow
DREAMGRL: Gotta go eat
```

Sophie clicked offline and gave an impatient sigh. When Sophie slid onto her cushion at the big square coffee table in the family room, Daddy was tapping chopsticks against her plate. Never a good sign.

"We're not interfering with your busy schedule, are we, Soph?" he said.

There was just enough of a gleam in his dark blue eyes to tell Sophie she wasn't in the penalty box yet. That was what Daddy called it when they were in real trouble. He talked about everything like it was a sports event.

"Sorry. I just had to log off," Sophie said.

"Could you stay off for about seven seconds after supper?" Lacie said. "I have to look something up for my history paper."

Daddy looked from Lacie, with her dark hair and her intense eyes, back to Sophie. "You two aren't going to start fighting over Net time, are you?" he said.

"We're not fighting," Lacie said. She gave Sophie a work-with-me-here smile and nodded so definitely toward Mama her ponytail jerked.

Sophie got it. These days Lacie always made sure they didn't do anything to upset Mama. Sophie knew her mother would never actually poke somebody with a knitting needle, but being pregnant did seem to make a person very emotional.

"We're just working out the schedule," Lacie said to Daddy.

"Take all the time you need," Sophie said, smiling hard. "Just let me know when you're off."

Daddy bunched his eyebrows at Sophie again. "So you can get on to do homework, I assume."

Sophie stifled a sigh. Every time she thought she and Daddy were going to get along forever, he did something new to make her want to take her moo goo gai pan and eat it in the closet.

"So!" Mama said. She dunked an egg roll into the sweet-and-sour sauce with one hand while she pushed the fortune cookies out of Zeke's reach with the other. "Tell us about the cyber-bullying conference, Sophie."

"Spider bullying?" Zeke said with a chow mein noodle hanging out of his mouth.

Lacie gave him a lesson in *cyber* versus *spider* while Sophie told Mama and Daddy about the conference. When she was through, both their brows were puckered like she had the flu and they were deciding whether to call the doctor. Sophie held her breath.

"That's a real eye-opener," Daddy said. He ran a big hand over his hair, which went in several different directions just the way Zeke's did. "But it makes sense. You kids are the constantly connected generation. You always have to be IMing or emailing or chatting—"

"Or talking on a cell phone." Lacie smiled so sweetly Sophie was surprised sugar didn't collect on her lips. It didn't work on Daddy.

"Forget it, Lace," he said. "No cell phone."

"That's it," Lacie said, still grinning. "My life is over."

Sophie had to admit that if anybody deserved a cell phone, it was Lacie. She made straight A's and was freshman class president at the high school and played every sport, *and* she did a lot of the cooking and took turns with Sophie watching Zeke now that Mama had to stay down. She was also in the church youth group, where she had learned not to be a complete snot about all of that, especially to Sophie. Sophie thanked Jesus for that every day.

"Sounds like I'd better get more in the loop on this cyber stuff," Daddy said.

Sophie wondered if that was the same as getting hip. And then she squirmed. She wasn't sure she wanted her father in her loop. But he was watching her as if he could see into her brain.

"I brought home a bunch of stuff for parents," she forced herself to say. "It's in my folder."

Daddy smothered the top of Sophie's head with his hand. "Way to be a team player, Soph," he said. "Any other kid would've destroyed anything that would let parents invade their world."

Sophie wriggled out from under his hand. "Nobody I talk to online is bullying," she said. She didn't add that she was *very* glad not to have POS going on. "Since I'm so wonderful, could you give me a ride to school tomorrow at seven-fifteen?"

"Why—do you have a date?"

"Rusty!" Mama said.

Daddy held up his palm. "Kidding. Just kidding."

On IM, Cynthia Cyber thought, that would be KJK.

Sophie wisped a secret smile. If Jimmy was thinking what she was thinking, Cynthia was about to become a star.

Three

Sophie worked at staying out of Cynthia-world the next morning as her footsteps echoed in the still-empty halls on the way to the school library. Round Table was serious stuff, and she wanted to be sharp. There would be time enough for Cynthia Cyber when she and Jimmy started planning their movie. Cynthia would, of course, be perfect as the main character, and Fiona could be her personal assistant—

Jimmy was waiting for her at one of the tables, looking just-showered with his blond hair still in wet spikes. He looked sort of soft, like Zeke did right after he woke up, and before he started squalling that he wouldn't eat a pancake unless it was shaped like a superhero.

"Hi," Sophie said.

Jimmy jumped up and pulled out a chair for her, and then glanced around like he was making sure nobody had seen him. Sophie didn't blame him. The Fruit Loops could work with that for days. *Especially with Eddie back*, she thought.

She sat down and raised her eyebrows at Jimmy.

"So, my idea," he said. His voice was morning-husky. "I think Round Table should do a website. Y'know, like, on cyber bullying."

"Oh ..." Sophie said. She could practically see Cynthia snapping her face from the computer monitor to stare.

The two red spots reappeared at the tops of Jimmy's cheeks. "You hate it."

"I don't hate it," Sophie said slowly. "I just thought—"

She stopped. Jimmy looked like someone was about to kick him in his very-straight teeth.

"It's just that I don't know how to do a website," she said.

Jimmy sprang into a smile. "Oh—well, me neither. Somebody else—like Mrs. Britt—would have to design it. We'd just give her ideas."

"Mrs. Britt? The computer lady?"

"Yeah. Vincent says she's, like, this genius."

Sophie nodded. Vincent would know. He spent as much time exploring websites as the Flakes did emailing each other. Vincent sometimes had a dazed look, like he'd gotten lost in there somewhere.

Still, it wasn't a movie.

"I have some ideas," Jimmy said. "And since you're creative, you could probably come up with some too." He shrugged like he couldn't think of anything else to say.

Sophie was squirmy. "I don't visit websites that much. Y'know, Fiona usually does the research for our films, she and Darbie and Vincent—"

"Maybe we could still use your character you were thinking up yesterday."

Sophie pushed her glasses up with her finger. "You mean, like, Cynthia Cyber could be on a website?"

"Sure. Who is she?"

"Internet Investigator."

"Sweet."

It was suddenly Christmas morning on Jimmy's face, so Sophie tried not to sag in her seat. Making a website wouldn't be the same as being Cynthia Cyber in a movie—

Springing up from her desk chair, she raised both hands in the air. *Victory—she had tracked the cyber bullies straight to their email address.*

"You okay?" Jimmy said.

"Yeah," Sophie lied.

Jimmy reached for his backpack, fumbled with it, and dumped half the contents onto the table. A granola bar slid into Sophie's lap.

"I brought that for you anyway," Jimmy said. There were two more red spots on each cheek. He practically buried his head in the backpack and emerged with a piece of paper and a pencil. "I'll write stuff down," he said.

Sophie had to giggle. "You can be Maggie." Maggie always kept records in the Treasure Book of everything for Corn Flakes Productions and Film Club. "You don't *look* like Maggie," she said. "I mean, like, she's a girl and you're a boy—"

"I'm glad you see that," Jimmy said.

Sophie stuffed her hand over her mouth so she wouldn't guffaw the librarian out of her office.

"Okay," Jimmy said. "We could have, like, a quiz that people could take to see if they're bullying or being bullied."

Sophie tugged at a short strand of hair. "So—what would Cynthia Cyber do?"

"She could tell how to score it."

"Oh," Sophie said. "So there would just be a picture of her or something?"

"No," Jimmy said. "She could talk and move her head and stuff."

"Like a little mini-movie?"

Jimmy bobbed his head so hard, Sophie found herself nodding too.

"Okay," she said. "I guess you could write that down."

"I could write down that if somebody scores in the cyber-bully range, Cynthia Cyber gets, like, huge and covers the whole screen and her nostrils go all big—"

"And she gets laser eyes," Sophie said.

Okay, so maybe this wouldn't be so bad.

The warning bell rang, and Jimmy scowled at it.

"Man, we were just getting started."

"You started on something without us?" said a familiar voice behind them.

Sophie turned and smiled at Fiona, who had Nathan and Vincent and the other Corn Flakes behind her. Fiona didn't exactly smile back. She craned her neck toward the paper on the table. Sophie wondered if that could be called FOS, "friend over shoulder."

"What's up, dude?" Vincent said, his voice cracking.

He punched Jimmy on the arm. It was such a boy-thing, one of the many reasons Sophie was glad she was a girl. Willoughby came up behind her and hugged her neck.

"Are you planning a movie without us?" Maggie shook her head, splashing her dark silky bob against her cheeks. "I don't think you can do that." Maggie's voice was solid and square like the rest of her. If you wanted to know what the rules were, you only had to ask Maggie.

"It's not a film." Fiona's shiny gray eyes swept across Jimmy's notes. "It's a website."

"We don't do websites," Maggie said.

Fiona gave a sniff and tossed aside the wayward strand of straight, deep brown hair that fell over one eye. "It doesn't look like *we* are doing it."

Nathan punched Jimmy on the other arm. Then his face turned red beneath his mop of curly hair. That was mostly how he communicated.

"What's the deal, man?" Vincent said.

Jimmy looked at Sophie, who looked up at the group. "We have to do a project for Round Table," she said.

Darbie perched her slender long-legged self on the edge of the table and tapped the paper. Sophie couldn't see her face because her reddish hair fell forward, but she had a feeling Darbie wasn't smiling, either.

"It's a website?" Darbie said.

"On cyber bullying," Sophie said.

Fiona folded her arms. "No offense," she said, "but neither one of you knows anything about designing a website."

"I know," Sophie said, "so we're going to get Mrs. Britt to help us—"

"Mrs. Britt? What about us?" Fiona's big eyes got bigger. "Hello—Vincent's king of the computer geeks. I have a program that shows you how to make websites—I was gonna surprise you with one for the Corn—for us."

"I didn't even know you liked websites, Sophie," Darbie said.

Even her pronouncing it "Soophie" the way she always did didn't make her sound any friendlier at the moment, as far as Sophie was concerned. She looked at each of them, with their arms folded and their eyes all slit-like. Willoughby was wrapping a curl around her finger so tight it was turning blue.

"She *doesn't* care about websites," Maggie said. "Neither do I. I don't even have a computer at home."

It doesn't have anything to do with you! Sophie thought.

But she didn't say it. After all, she never did anything that didn't have *something* to do with them.

Sophie looked at Fiona, whose magic gray eyes were obviously waiting for something. Sophie just wasn't sure what.

153

Thankfully the second warning bell rang. Sophie dived for her backpack, banging her forehead on the table.

"You okay?" Jimmy said.

"Uh-huh," Sophie said.

"Here." Jimmy held out her backpack. Sophie took it, smiled, and ran.

There was no time to talk to Darbie and Fiona during their first-and-second-period language arts/social studies block. But the minute the bell rang and they were headed for third-period PE, Darbie was all over Sophie in the hall.

"You okay, Sophie?" she said in a voice that sounded suspiciously like Jimmy's. Her dark eyes were dancing. "Let me get that backpack for you." She flexed her arm muscles.

Sophie rolled her eyes at her and glanced nervously at Fiona. Her eyes were *not* dancing, and that prickled up the back of Sophie's neck. "Oh, thank you, darling," Sophie said to Darbie, in a voice she hoped sounded like a romance novel.

Willoughby hurried up to them, dragging Maggie behind her. Even her hair was in exclamation points.

"I know you can't have a boyfriend, Sophie," she said. "But Jimmy really *likes* you!"

"Not only *can't* I have a boyfriend," Sophie said, "I don't *want* a boyfriend."

"That's a good thing," somebody said, "because you'll never *get* one."

Sophie didn't have to turn around to know it was Julia Cummings, queen of the Corn Pops. Julia sailed past, thick auburn hair swishing across her shoulders. She didn't look at Sophie, either, but Anne-Stuart, Julia's second-in-command, cast Sophie a watery-eyed look and sniffed. Sophie had never seen skinny, everything-pale Anne-Stuart when she didn't need a tissue.

"You know that isn't true, Sophie," Willoughby said when the Pops were gone. "You could *so* have Jimmy for a boyfriend if you wanted one."

"I *don't* want one!" Sophie cried.

Darbie's eyes sparked mischief.

"But the Corn Pops don't know that, do they?" she said.

Four

Willoughby's eyes grew to dinner-plate size. "You mean we're going to make them think Jimmy and Sophie are going out?"

"That would be lying." Maggie looked at Sophie. "Wouldn't it?"

They *all*, even Fiona, looked at Sophie, who grinned at the image in her mind of the Corn Pops with their mouths hanging open like chimpanzees because they believed their favorite target had a boyfriend.

"We would just be playing," Sophie said finally.

"And if they can't figure that out," Darbie said, "that's their problem."

They stopped outside the girls' locker-room door.

"Is everybody in?" Darbie said.

"I'm not gonna do it," Maggie said. "But I won't give it away."

Willoughby gave one of her shrieks that always sounded to Sophie like a poodle yelping. "I probably won't be able to stop laughing."

Fiona arched an eyebrow at her. "So what else is new?"

"B.J. and Cassie are behind us," Darbie whispered.

Fiona put her lips close to Sophie's ear. "You don't really like Jimmy, do you? I mean, boyfriend-girlfriend?"

"No!" Sophie said. *"Ewww!"*

Fiona knotted up her pink rosebud of a mouth. "It really would be excellent to freak out the Corn Pops—it wouldn't be mean."

"Hurry up!" Darbie whispered.

Fiona's eyes took on their magic shine. "Come on, Soph, dish," she said in a too-loud voice. They pushed through the door and headed for their locker row. "Did Jimmy ask you out or not?"

Sophie's prickles disappeared. "I'll never tell," she said. Her voice squeaked, which it always did when she was about to give way to giggles. Willoughby already had.

"He's a fine bit of stuff, Sophie," Darbie said.

"What's that mean?" Maggie said.

"It means he's a hottie," Fiona said as she twirled the dial on her lock. "Right, Soph?"

"Total hottie," Sophie said.

Several lockers down, Julia laughed and fluffed her hair out of the neck of the GMMS T-shirt she'd just pulled over her head.

"Like she even knows what a hottie is," Cassie said in a coarse whisper. She rolled her close-together eyes.

Fiona winked at Sophie over the top of her open locker door. "Come on, Soph. Tell us how you feel about him."

"We're your best friends," Willoughby said, and then buried her face in her wadded-up sweater.

Sophie gave an elaborate sigh. "All right, if you must know ..."

All of the Flakes, including Maggie, leaned toward her. Sophie sneaked a glance at the Pops. Their bodies were tilted in her direction too.

"Well?" Fiona said.

"Sophie, we're desperate to know," Darbie said.

Sophie closed her eyes and tried to remember something she'd heard on the soap opera Mama watched when she was really bored. If they were going to drive the Corn Pops nuts, she had to be convincing.

"I think ..." she said.

Corn Flake heads nodded.

"No, I don't think—I *know*—it's real this time." Sophie put her hand on her chest. "I'm in love."

Willoughby gave the poodle shriek. The bell rang for roll check. The Pops pushed past them, faces looking ready to burst like water balloons.

When they were gone, the Corn Flakes jumped up into one big high five.

"We got them," Sophie cried.

Fiona smacked her palm twice. "We got them *good!*"

They were still laughing when they reached the gym and staggered into their roll-check line. The Corn Pops, in the next line over, stared at Sophie, lower lips hanging, just the way Sophie had imagined. And then Julia moved hers.

"Hey, Sophie," she said.

Sophie was a little surprised. That was the second time today Julia had said something to her. Ever since the Pops had been kicked off the cheerleading squad for being mean, they barely spoke to the Flakes. They knew if they bullied the Corn Flakes at all, they would be suspended forever.

"I just want to say something," Julia said.

Sophie shrugged. "So say it."

Behind her, Darbie whispered, "Look out. She's wretched because Jimmy likes you and not her."

"And you can't go running to the Tattletale Table." Julia flung her hair over her shoulder with her head. "Because I'm just expressing my opinion."

"It's a free country," B.J. put in. She narrowed her eyes below her buttery-blonde bangs so hard that her pudgy cheeks drew upward.

Julia gave the hair another fling. "I just don't think it's fair that you and Jimmy Wythe are the only seventh graders that got to go to that conference. Tod is class *president*, and *I'm* vice president. We're, like, the *real* leaders of the class."

"Coach Yates alert," Cassie said between clenched teeth.

Behind Julia, Anne-Stuart snapped a cell phone closed and stuffed it in the pocket of her hoodie. Julia handed hers off to Cassie, who stuck it in the elastic of her track pants.

"It seems like you're trying to take everything away from us," Julia said.

Sophie would have felt sorry for her if Julia's eyes hadn't clearly said what her mouth didn't: *You just aren't cool enough, Sophie LaCroix.*

So Sophie shrugged again. "I'm not trying to take anything away from you. Honest. You don't have anything I want."

While Julia was still blinking at her, Sophie knelt down and retied her shoe. Within a heartbeat, Fiona was squatted next to her.

"That was spectacular," she whispered.

"It was just the truth," Sophie whispered back. "I don't want to be her. I just want to be me."

Coach Yates gave a blast on her whistle, and Sophie and Fiona bolted up.

"All right, people," Coach Yates yelled. She yelled everything, but Sophie had discovered that in spite of how mean she looked with her graying ponytail pulled too tight and that evil whistle always at the ready, Coach cared about the kids. She just did it at full volume. Sophie didn't think she deserved her nickname, Coach Hates.

"We're starting a gymnastics unit today!" she hollered. "You'll be in groups of five with one student aide—"

Before the Corn Flakes could even grab onto each other, she added, "Coach Nanini and I have assigned the groups."

"You mean we'll have boys in our group?" Maggie whispered. Sophie thought her Cuban-brown face looked a little pale.

"Group One!" Coach Yates yelled. "Darbie O'Grady. Anne-Stuart Riggins. Sophie LaCroix. Nathan Coffey. And Edward Wornom."

No! Sophie *wanted to yell back at her. How could the coaches do this to her?* They both know Eddie blames me for every scrap of trouble he ever got into! They both know he'll be heinous to me!

Arguing with Coach Yates only got a person after-school detention. Maybe she could talk to Coach Virile.

But Coach Virile was walking toward Group One's mat with his arm around Eddie's shoulders, their heads close as he talked. It didn't look like Coach was warning Eddie. It looked more like he was pumping him up for the Olympics.

Darbie tucked her arm through Sophie's. "This is going to be murder," she said. "I hope the coaches keep their eyes on him."

There aren't enough eyes in this whole school to stop Eddie Wornom, Sophie thought.

Coach Yates was still calling out groups when Darbie and Sophie got to their station. Right in the middle of the Group Six announcement, somebody let out a squeal that echoed through the gym like screeching tires.

It was Julia, literally doing cartwheels toward the Group Six mat, where Jimmy was waiting. Sophie could see the red spots already oozing onto his cheeks.

"I don't think that's because Jimmy's a gymnastics champion," Darbie said.

Willoughby tapped Sophie's shoulder as she ran past her. "Me and Maggie and Fiona are in Group Six too. We'll protect Jimmy for you."

"Student aides are going to teach you the forward roll," Coach Yates yelled, and then gave an extra-long toot on the whistle.

"Who's going to protect us?" Darbie whispered as they hurried toward their mat.

"We just have to keep our power to be ourselves," Sophie said.

Darbie snapped a ponytail holder around her hair and muttered, "Somehow I don't think that's going to be enough."

Sophie tried not to agree with her, even in her mind. *No, she told herself, we can do this. We have to start with Step One in anti-bullying: ignore him.*

A solid-looking eighth-grade girl named Pepper—who had a curved-in waist and thighs bigger than Sophie's hips—demonstrated the forward roll for them and told everybody to try it.

Eddie volunteered to go first.

"Get ready for some eejit thing," Darbie whispered.

Sophie nodded. Eddie did everything the idiot way.

Eddie knelt at the end of the mat, tucked his head under just the way Pepper had told them, and rolled over twice. When he stood up, his gym shorts were down around his hips, revealing a pair of plaid boxers underneath.

"Nobody needs to see that," Darbie whispered.

"Woo-hoo, Eddie!" Anne-Stuart said with the customary sniff.

Eddie hitched up the shorts and said to Pepper, "Sorry. These are from before I lost weight. I'll get new ones."

"You did lose weight," Anne-Stuart purred. She sounded to Sophie like a cat with a sinus problem. "You look good, Eddie."

Eddie shrugged one shoulder and sat down. Sophie and Darbie stared at each other.

He must've learned to be sneakier in military school, Sophie thought. She shivered. This was worse than Eddie just picking her up and trying to stuff her into the garbage. At least back then she had known what she was dealing with.

The Flakes discussed it at lunch.

"Like I said in my email," Fiona told them, "we're going to have to be more vigilant than ever."

"Does vigilant mean 'careful'?" Maggie said.

"It means don't take your eyes off him if he's within a mile of you."

Maggie frowned. "I can't see a whole mile."

"That's why we have to work together," Fiona said. "Report all suspicious Eddie activities to each other, and if we find out something outside of school, we have to email each other."

"I don't have a computer, remember?" Maggie said.

Willoughby slung an arm around her. "That really stinks," she said.

"I feel like I don't know what's going on sometimes."

"I hate that for you," Fiona said.

Darbie put her mini-can of Pringles in front of Maggie. "Don't worry, Mags. We won't let you miss anything."

"Mags can't possibly keep up if she's not online," Fiona told Sophie when they were walking to fifth-period science. "Nobody can. I think I can fix that, though."

Cynthia Cyber nodded at her generous assistant, Dot Com. She was as rich as any of the cyber bullies, but she used her money only for good. If she could get their loyal but computerless staff member online somehow, what strides they could make together in cleaning up the Internet for good. After all, Maga Byte knew all the rules and wasn't afraid to point out when they weren't being followed—

Sophie found herself staring into her science book. Cynthia Cyber was so cool. Maybe there was a way she could fit Dot Com and Maga Byte into the website too.

But that thought was interrupted by Mr. Stires raising his voice. Mr. Stires, their round-faced, bald-headed teacher, was always so cheerful even his toothbrush mustache looked happy. He never spoke above a chuckle.

But right now he was barking. "Why are you using cell phones in my class?"

By the time he stopped in front of Julia and Anne-Stuart, his face was as red as Nathan's. And that was red.

"They're probably text-messaging," Vincent said.

"We are not," Julia said with a roll of her eyes.

Anne-Stuart, of course, sniffed.

"What's text-messaging?" Maggie whispered, but Fiona shook her head.

"May I see, please?" Mr. Stires said.

Anne-Stuart thrust her phone toward him. Julia smiled up, both hands busy with hers under the desktop. Mr. Stires stared at Anne-Stuart's display window amid the somebody's-in-trouble silence in the room.

"This looks like a website," Mr. Stires said.

"It is," Anne-Stuart said. "We were web browsing for our science homework." She delivered a stony stare to Vincent. "And we found one on E. coli."

"Isn't it interesting?" Julia said to Mr. Stires.

"I'm more fascinated by the fact that you can web-browse with your cell phone." Mr. Stires chuckled. "I've read about them, but I haven't seen one yet."

"Look at it all you want," Anne-Stuart said.

Fiona scribbled something on a piece or paper and snapped it onto Sophie's desk.

I'm appalled by what they get away with, it said.

Me too, Sophie wrote back.

Vincent looked openly over their shoulders. "If you had cell phones, you could text-message that to each other. You know that's what they were doing."

Sophie leaned across the aisle toward Jimmy. "We have to put stuff about text-messaging on our website."

"No doubt," he said.

Sophie caught Fiona looking from one of them to the other. Her eyes went flatter and flatter, until they were no more than suspicious dashes. Fiona scribbled on the note paper and thrust it onto Sophie's desk.

I thought you said you didn't LIKE him, like him, it said.

As Sophie crumpled up the note, she wished for the first time ever that she had a cell phone. She could almost see the text message: I DON'T WANT JIMMY FOR A BOYFRIEND!!!!!!!

But watching Fiona slant her gaze over at Jimmy, Sophie wasn't sure even that would do it.

Five

Sophie decided it was a really good thing it was Wednesday and they had Bible study after school. Not only was way-cool Dr. Peter Topping their teacher, but he used to be Sophie's therapist. That meant he could help the Flakes deal with just about any problem by using the Jesus stories.

As the Flakes rode to the church in Fiona's family's big Expedition, with Boppa driving, Sophie tried to decide *which* of her problems to ask Dr. Peter about.

There was Eddie Wornom's coming back to school, acting like he was any normal person, when Sophie knew better. It was like waiting for a snake to strike.

Just as bad in a different way, there was the thing of doing a website instead of a movie. It was turning out to be sort of fun, but not like it would be to *become* Cynthia Cyber and banish a bully from the Internet with fire in her eyes. Or lasers—

But the issue that niggled at her the most was Fiona.

I really want to talk about THAT one at Bible study, Sophie thought. *But how am I going to do it with her sitting right there?*

When they first arrived there was no time to talk about anything, not with so much going on.

Willoughby surprised them by showing up. She hadn't been to Bible study since she'd made cheerleader in September.

"Ms. Hess is only having cheerleading practice twice a week now," she said. "And my dad said he really wanted me to come back to this."

She gave Dr. Peter a shiny smile. Sophie knew Dr. P. was working with Willoughby and her dad on some family stuff, which, as far as Sophie was concerned, meant everything was going to be just fine.

Kitty was there too. Since the Flakes didn't get to see her every day, there was a lot of hugging that had to be done. Dr. Peter made sure frail Kitty with her chemotherapy-puffed face was settled in the pink beanbag chair before all of that started. She got to come to Bible study only if she was feeling not-too-awful, and Dr. Peter liked to keep her that way.

He is the best, the best, the best, Sophie thought as she watched him wrinkle his nose to scoot his glasses up and twinkle his blue eyes at the hugging.

When Gill and Harley arrived, he high-fived both of them and plunked Harley's Redskins cap on top of his short, gelled-stiff curls to see how Sophie thought he looked in it.

He always knows what to do for every person, she thought. That decided it. She would talk to him about Fiona after class.

As soon as they all were in their every-one-a-different-color beanbags, Fiona's hand shot up. Sophie froze. Fiona was *not* going to bring up Jimmy, was she?

"Shoot, Fiona," Dr. Peter said. He rubbed his hands together like somebody was about to give him a big, juicy cheeseburger.

"I have several issues, actually." Fiona looked at Sophie. "But let's start with this one: Eddie Wornom is back." Fiona held up her palms. "Need I say more?"

Sophie let out all her air.

"Up to his old tricks, is he?" Dr. Peter said.

"That's the problem," Darbie said. "He's acting the perfect gentleman." She nodded at the girls, who all nodded with her.

"He's definitely up to something," Fiona said.

"Being a gentleman." Dr. Peter's eyes looked like they were going to twinkle right through his glasses. "That's pretty low."

"It's just an act," Maggie said.

Dr. Peter raised his eyebrows. "And we know this because—"

"Because he isn't capable of being anything but heinous," Fiona said. "He's proved it, like, a million times."

Willoughby gave half a poodle yelp. Kitty whimpered. Harley grunted.

"Looks like we're all in agreement on that," Dr. Peter said. "And I think I have just the story to help us sort this out."

Sophie snatched up the Bible from the floor next to her seat, the one with the purple cover to match her beanbag. She loved this part, where Dr. Peter asked them to imagine they were somebody in the story while he read it out loud.

"Matthew chapter 18," he said. "We'll start at verse 23."

"Who do we have to be?" Maggie said.

"Not somebody evil, I hope," Sophie said. "I don't like it when we have to be the Pharisees."

"Those blackguards," Darbie said.

Dr. Peter grinned. "I wish you girls wouldn't hold back on expressing how you feel. No Pharisees this time. I want you to imagine that you are the forgiven servant."

Sophie closed her eyes and immediately pictured herself in a butler's uniform like she'd seen in a movie once, with a black bow tie and tails on her jacket. She knew they didn't wear those in Bible times, but Dr. Peter always said to go with the visual that made the story clear. Servants in Sophie's world were butlers with towels over their arms, always bowing and saying, "As you wish, madam."

Dr. Peter cleared his throat and read. "'The kingdom of heaven is like a king who wanted to settle accounts with his servants.'"

"You mean, like bank accounts?" Gill said.

"More like loan accounts," Dr. Peter said. "The master's servants often borrowed money from him, and it was time for them to pay him back."

"Okay. Go on," Gill said.

"'As he began the settlement,'" Dr. Peter read, "'a man who owed him ten thousand talents was brought to him.'"

"How much is that?" Maggie said.

A lot, Sophie thought. *Can we get on with the story?*

"Between fifteen and twenty million dollars," Dr. Peter said.

Gill whistled.

"'Since he was not able to pay—'"

"You think?" Willoughby did the poodle thing. "Where's a servant going to get millions of dollars?"

"Exactly," Dr. Peter said. "Shall we go further?"

Please! Sophie thought. It was hard to keep Jenkins the Butler in view with all these interruptions.

"'Since he was not able to pay, the master ordered that he and his wife and his children and all that he had be sold to repay the debt.'"

Jenkins/Sophie fell frozen to the floor. Sell his family—his babies? He buried his face in his hands. He would rather die than be separated from them.

"'The servant'—that's you, ladies—'fell on his knees before him. "Be patient with me," he begged, "and I will pay back everything."'"

Then Jenkins/Sophie flattened himself on the rug before the master, barely daring to breathe unless the master told him to. After all, his whole life was in this powerful man's hands—and not just HIS life.

"'The servant's master took pity on him,'" Dr. Peter read on, "'canceled the debt and let him go.'"

Jenkins/Sophie could hardly believe what he'd heard. He stayed facedown, gasping for air and breathing in rug fibers. Choking and shaking, he pulled himself back up to his knees and clasped his hands over the front of his starched white shirt, now stained with tears. "Thank you, sir," he cried. "Thank you—thank you—thank you."

"'But when that servant went out, he found one of his fellow servants who owed him a hundred denarii.'"

Maggie said, "How much—"

"Just a few dollars," Dr. Peter said. "About a day's wages for a servant. 'He'—well, you, the servant—'grabbed him and began to choke him. "Pay back what you owe me!" he demanded. His fellow servant fell to his knees and begged him, "Be patient with me, and I will pay you back." But he refused. Instead, he went off and had the man thrown into prison until he could pay the debt.'"

Sophie's eyes flew open. "I don't want to imagine myself doing that!" she said. "That's heinous!"

"You aren't the only one who thinks so," Dr. Peter said. "Let's read on."

"I hope this guy's lips get ripped off or something," Gill muttered.

"'When the other servants saw what had happened, they were greatly distressed and went and told their master everything that had happened.'"

"That's what I'm talkin' about," Willoughby said.

" 'Then the master called the servant in.' " Dr. Peter paused.

Jenkins/Sophie felt his stomach tighten. Had the master changed his mind? Or was he going to congratulate him for sticking to the rules about people owing you money? Straightening his bow tie, Jenkins/Sophie marched up to the master and said, "How can I help you, sir?"

" 'You wicked servant!' " Dr Peter's voice gave Sophie—and Jenkins—a jolt.

Jenkins/Sophie lowered his head and stared at the very rug where only a few hours ago he had felt so relieved, so free.

" 'I canceled all that debt of yours because you begged me to. Shouldn't you have had mercy on your fellow servant just as I had on you?' In anger his master turned him over to the jailers.' "

Jenkins/Sophie felt a shock go through him. He couldn't even move his lips to beg. Besides, he knew it would do no good.

"He got what he deserved," Maggie said.

"Did he go to prison for the rest of his life?" Kitty said. Her voice was quivery. She got into the Bible stories almost as much as Sophie did.

"He would be a slave for six years, he and his family," Dr. Peter said. "Not fun."

"So this story means don't borrow money and get in debt," Fiona said. "Like, with credit cards and stuff."

"What if we substitute the word sin for the word debt?" Dr. Peter said. "How does that work in verse 32?"

Sophie followed it on the Bible page with her finger.

" 'I canceled all that [sin] of yours because you begged me to,' " Darbie read out loud. " 'Shouldn't you have had mercy on your fellow servant just as I had on you?' "

"Now," Dr. Peter said, rubbing his hands together again, "if we put 'God' in place of 'he,' the master, what does the story mean?"

Sophie read it to herself. *"You wicked servant,"* [God] said. *"I canceled all that [sin] of yours because you begged me to. Shouldn't you have had mercy on your fellow servant just as I, [God], had on you?"*

Something pinged in her head.

"You get it, don't you, Sophie-Lophie-Loodle?" Dr. Peter said.

"God forgives us for our sins," Sophie said, "so we should forgive other people for theirs."

"A round of applause for Loodle!"

"I totally get that," Fiona said when they were finished clapping. "What I don't get is what that has to do with Eddie Wornom. No offense or anything."

"None taken." Dr. Peter leaned forward in his beanbag, forearms dangling over his knees. "Looks like we need to watch our Eddie and see how it fits."

"Just once, Dr. Peter," Darbie said, "couldn't you just tell us the answer?"

"No, but I'll help you figure it out."

They all groaned.

"What did the master do to the servant in the end?"

"Threw him in the slammer," Gill said.

"Right, to pay off his debts. So, he wasn't forgiven his debt anymore. What does that say about God's forgiveness?"

Sophie raised her hand. "That we don't get it unless we forgive other people the way he does."

Dr. Peter looked at the rest of the group. "Is she good, or is she good?"

"She's the best," Kitty said.

"Now let me ask you this." Dr. Peter scooted forward some more. "Do you think the servant could ever have paid his master back if the master hadn't forgiven him?"

"Twenty million dollars? On a servant's salary?" Fiona snorted. "No way."

Sophie was sure Fiona was the only one in the room who would know about servants' salaries. The Buntings had a nanny and a cook and a gardener at their house.

"So if we're talking about sins and God, you have to figure only God can dig us out of some of the sin-holes we get ourselves into," Dr. Peter said. "So what two things do we have to do that we've learned from the servant?"

There was a thinking silence.

"He went to the master and begged him," Darbie said.

"Okay—so Number One, we go to God and ask him to forgive us for our sins. And then, Number Two—"

"We gotta forgive other people." Maggie was writing it down in a notebook.

Fiona raised her hand. "What I don't get is why the servant was so evil to the guy that owed him. You'd have thought he would be so happy he'd be in a generous mood." She grinned. "I always ask my dad for stuff when he's just landed a big client or something."

"He was evil," Dr. Peter said, "because he didn't learn anything from being forgiven. The master gave him forgiveness, but he didn't really receive it. Really understanding that you've been forgiven changes something in you."

"Oh," Gill said.

Dr. Peter smacked the sides of his beanbag. "Okay, that's a lot to think about. Let me give you your assignment and then we'll eat."

"Ready," Maggie said, pen poised over the notebook.

"Every day between now and next Wednesday, I want you to confess your sins to God in your quiet time. Think of the things you did or didn't do that probably disappointed

God. Be really specific. Lay them all out for him, and ask him to cancel those things out in his mind as if they never happened, because you can never make up for all that stuff. See if it doesn't make you feel like you're starting over with a clean record after you do it."

"I get it!" Willoughby said with a mini-yelp. "Like the beginning of every report-card period—you don't have any tardies or anything."

"Only you can do this as many times a day as you want." Dr. Peter twinkled a smile.

"Did you say there was food?" Gill said.

"How 'bout hot chocolate and Christmas cookies?" he said. "I want to get you in the right mood."

The door opened and Kitty's mom, Mrs. Munford, backed in and pivoted around with a tray of steaming mugs with snowmen on them. Darbie's aunt Emily followed with two plates heaped with red-and-green-sprinkled cookies. Sophie felt a pang of missing Mama. She would have so been here with her double-fudge brownies if she could.

"So what are we getting in the right mood for?" Fiona said when they were all circled around the cookie piles, mugs in hand.

"For a project I hope you'll do," Dr. Peter said. "It's mostly for you filmmakers, but Gill and Harley, you can be involved if you want."

The Wheaties exchanged glances and shook their heads. "We're not actors," Gill said.

"You want us to make a movie?" Sophie rose to her knees. "That would be—"

"Fabulous!" Fiona said.

"You haven't even heard what it is yet," Dr. Peter said. "I'm thinking we need a movie for the little kids at church on the true meaning of Christmas. Something they can really get. I know it's short notice, with Christmas just three weeks away."

"Leave it to us, Dr. P," Darbie said. "Sophie will dream up characters, and we'll work out a script—"

"I already have the script." Dr. Peter reached behind his beanbag and pulled up a folder.

"We don't do it that way," Maggie said.

"But we could." Sophie gave Dr. Peter an extra-big smile in case his feelings were hurt. "What's it about?"

"You know 'Twas the Night Before Christmas'?" he said. "It's like that, but it's about Jesus instead of Santa. It could probably use some doctoring up."

"Sounds ... fascinating," Sophie said. Fiona was already midway through a not-so-tactful eye roll.

"The only problem is that it requires some male types."

"We have boys," Sophie said. "I mean, not boyfriends—you know, just boys we do movies with."

"You know Jimmy will help." Darbie nudged Sophie with her elbow. Willoughby collapsed against Maggie. Dr. Peter looked bewildered.

"Okay, then, so I take it you're up for it?" he said.

"We'll make it amazing," Fiona said. "With or without boys."

Darbie nodded. "We're in."

Sophie was too jazzed to even speak. Yes! A chance for Cynthia to make a film after all. Surely there would be a spot for her—

Dr. Peter passed out enough scripts for each of them and the Lucky Charms, in case they agreed to help. But when they climbed into the Expedition with Boppa and read the script, Sophie wasn't so sure they would.

Six

I n the first place, there was obviously no room in the script for Cynthia Cyber. But that wasn't the only problem.

"Is it just me," Fiona said, "or is this the corniest thing you've ever read?"

"It's absolutely cheesy," Darbie said.

Maggie looked up soberly. "You and Fiona write way better than this, Sophie."

"No doubt," Fiona said.

"We can't hurt Dr. Peter's feelings, though," Sophie said.

"Let's just change some of the lines so they don't sound like Miss Odetta would say them." Fiona leaned forward and rubbed the back of Boppa's bald head. "No offense, Boppa."

Miss Odetta used to be Fiona and her brother and sister's nanny. Now she was married to Boppa, and she was so old-fashioned, she gave Fiona demerits when she didn't act like a lady.

"I take it you don't want it to sound completely proper," Boppa said.

Boppa's caterpillar eyebrows filled the rearview mirror, but Sophie knew his eyes were smiling.

"There's sounding proper and then there's sounding like a grammar book," Fiona said. "Those little kids will be climbing up the walls after the first five minutes."

Darbie suddenly let out a giggle, which didn't happen often. "One thing works," she said. "There's a married couple in it. Sophie and Jimmy can play them."

"What?" Sophie grabbed the script from Darbie.

"Should I write that down?" Maggie said.

Sophie's voice squeaked up into the only-dogs-can-hear range. "We don't even know if the Lucky Charms will do this with us yet."

"Do we really need them?" Fiona said. "We used to play the boy roles all the time before."

"No offense, Fiona," Darbie said. "But I think we're too old for that now. Besides"—her eyes sparkled—"Sophie and Jimmy would be—"

"Okay, okay." Fiona swatted her hands like she was beating down a bee swarm. "We'll ask them."

"We should have a meeting," Maggie said. She still had her pen ready.

"My house?" Darbie said.

"No," Fiona said. "We'll meet on the Internet tonight at seven. Go to our website. You'll see a private chat room I just set up for us. Well, my dad did. Anyway, I'll call Vincent, and he can call Nathan. Darb, you let Kitty and Willoughby know."

Darbie smiled slyly at Sophie. "You call Jimmy, Soph," she said.

"No!"

"I can't meet in a chat room," Maggie said. Her voice was as matter-of-fact as always, but Sophie could see a left-out look in her eyes.

"Aw, Mags, we forgot again," Darbie said.

"Come home with me now, Mags," Fiona said. "Boppa can call your mom. Besides, I want us to talk to my dad about something."

"You actually have a chat room for us?" Darbie said.

Fiona nodded. "I can be very useful when it comes to websites." She slit her eyes at Sophie. They had completely lost their magic. "I *know* I'm better at it than Jimmy Wythe," she added.

Sophie felt stung. Fiona was suddenly looking a lot like a Corn Pop, and it made her shiver.

I didn't get to talk to Dr. Peter about it, either, she thought.

But it looked like she'd better. And soon.

The Flakes and the Charms all gathered in the chat room that night. It was Sophie's first time chatting, but once she figured out it was just like IMing, only with a bunch of people, she caught on right away.

It was a good thing it didn't matter who said what because it was hard to keep the screen names straight. Besides Darbie's IRISH and Fiona's WORDGRL and Kitty's MEOW and Jimmy's Go4Gold, there was Willoughby as CHEER and Nathan as SWASH. That was short for Swashbuckler, since he was all into swordplay. Vincent was COMPTRGEEK. He was the only person Sophie knew who was proud to be a geek. *That's taking the power to be yourself to a whole new level,* she thought.

By eight o'clock, plans for Dr. Peter's Christmas movie were a done deal. The parts were doled out, with Jimmy and Sophie as the husband and wife by popular vote. Except for Fiona, who pointed out that Vincent should be the husband since he actually looked older than Jimmy. Vincent almost freaked out right on the screen. He liked to stay behind the camera. After that, Sophie could feel Fiona pouting out there in cyberspace.

It wasn't MY idea, Fiona, Sophie wanted to type in.

But at least it wasn't some creepy Fruit Loop. She thought it might not be *too* evil with Jimmy. Fiona shooting eye darts at her was a worse image.

The rehearsal schedule fell into place, and Maggie was ready to research pictures of costumes for her mom, Senora LaQuita, to make. That led to some discussion.

COMPTRGEEK: How's Mag going to do that when she doesn't have a computer?
WORDGRL: She does now.
CHEER: You bought her one?
MEOW: I knew you were rich Fiona but WOW!!!!!!!!!!!!
WORDGRL: My dad gave her one of our old ones. Boppa's setting it up at her house tomorrow.
IRISH: Boppa?
WORDGRL: I found out he knows all about computers. Who knew?
DREAMGRL: He got hip.
SWASH: Huh?
MEOW: POS Gotta go!!!!!!!!!!
CHEER: BYE everybuddy.

Sophie smiled at her screen. The Internet was like having everyone there with her any time she wanted. And now even Maggie got to do it.

Fiona's being pretty rude to me right now, Sophie thought, *but she really is good inside.*

Sophie just wished she would be "good" about the Round Table website. And Jimmy.

I'm gonna write her an email, Sophie thought.

She had just clicked out of the chat room when the happy little bell told her she had an IM.

ANGELEYES: Hi Sofee

Who's that? Sophie thought. She knew from the conference not to respond to people she didn't know.

ANGELEYES: It's me Anne-Stuart.

Sophie stared. Anne-Stuart was IMing her? And her screen name was Angel Eyes? Oh, brother.

She must be up to something, Sophie thought. Carefully Sophie typed and then clicked Send.

DREAMGRL: Hi
ANGELEYES: I'm sorry Julia said you couldn't
get a boyfriend. That was kinda mean. Don't
tell her I said that, k?

Before Sophie could even think how to answer, the bell dinged again.

ANGELEYES: Well, bye
DREAMGRL: Bye. Thanks

Something pinged, like the IM bell going off in her mind.
She did apologize. I'm supposed to forgive her.
Which reminded her—
Sophie crawled through the chiffon curtains and onto her bed, where she closed her eyes. Dr. Peter had said to confess every day.

It wasn't hard for Sophie to talk to Jesus. Dr. Peter had taught her to imagine him and tell him everything. She never imagined him answering because that would be like writing his lines for him. But she could always "see" his kind eyes, and there was always an answer sometime, somewhere, if she watched for it.

Jesus, she thought to him, *it's a good thing you have time for everybody because I'm going to confess all my sins to you, and that could take a while.*

She started off with the first sin she could remember, which was when she was four and she didn't come when Mama called her for lunch because she was busy pretending she was Sleeping Beauty, and she was right in the middle of the sleeping part.

By the time she got through with the sins of year four, Sophie decided she'd better stick with just the ones from that day.

So, Jesus, she prayed, *I'm really sorry I didn't help Lacie clean up the kitchen this morning because I went to school early.*

And I think it hurt Fiona's feelings when I was working with Jimmy on the website and didn't invite her. Only I didn't do that on purpose. I didn't know she would care—only I should have known because she always gets funky if she thinks I might get a different best friend. Like I would be best friends with a boy! But I'm sorry I forgot that about her.

Sophie scrunched her eyes shut tighter. So far, none of her sins seemed so bad. She was going to have to look harder.

I think I'm sorry that we played that trick on the Pops. I just wanted them to feel lame the way they're always making us feel. Only that's against our Code, and since you, like, wrote the Code for us, I guess I'm in trouble with you. Will you please forgive me?

But Jesus, don't you have to admit we really got them good?

Sophie sank back against the pillows with a sigh. This was harder than she'd expected it to be.

Wow, she thought. *It must take some people the whole night to confess.*

Some people, like Eddie Wornom.

Sophie scrunched her eyes again. She was pretty sure she better get forgiveness for that thought.

When Sophie got on the bus the next morning and sat behind the Wheaties, they both turned around and stared at her.

"What?" Sophie wiped at her nose. "Do I have a booger hanging out or something?"

"No," Gill said. "We just don't get why you'd want a boyfriend. Boys are lame."

"I don't want one," Sophie said.

"That's not what I heard. I heard you and Jimmy Gymnast were going out."

"Heard from who?" Sophie said.

Gill twisted her mouth. "See, that's the thing. I don't exactly know."

"How could you not know who told you?" Sophie put up her hand. "Forget it. Just so you know, Jimmy Wythe and I are not going out."

"We didn't think you'd do something stupid like that," Gill said. "That's why we asked you."

But no one else Sophie saw that day bothered to ask. All she heard from the time she stepped off the bus were things like—

"So you and that gymnastics dude are going out."

"Congratulations, Sophie. He's cute."

Half those people Sophie didn't even know. By the time she got to third period, she'd received five notes from girls who had never noticed she was alive before, not to mention a slew of comments from faceless voices in the hall saying everything from "Poor Jimmy" to "Y'all make the cutest couple!"

Almost the only person who didn't say anything to her was Jimmy himself. He spent all of first-and-second-period block behind his literature book with about six red blotches on each cheek.

181

So when someone behind her in the gym locker hall said, "Why am I the last person to know Little Bit loves Jimbo?" she would have decked him if he hadn't been Coach Virile.

He grinned down at her, and Sophie gave him her most dramatic sigh.

"Is there anybody in this whole school who isn't talking about it?" Sophie said.

"Nope. It's the main topic of conversation."

Sophie put her hands on her hips. "Can I make an announcement on the intercom that Jimmy and I are not going out? Can't a girl and a boy just be friends?"

"Around here? Evidently not," Coach Virile said. "So it's only a rumor, huh?"

"Yes!"

He bent over and put his hands on his knees so he was closer to Sophie's level. "I'm actually glad to hear that because I think middle school is way too early for"—he made quotation marks with his fingers—"'relationships.' There will be plenty of time for boyfriends when you're older, Little Bit."

"That's what I keep saying, but nobody believes me!"

"It'll die down, just as soon as they find something else to gossip about." Coach Virile gave her another grin. "Doesn't anybody talk about football anymore?"

I HOPE it dies down, Sophie thought as she pushed her way through the girls' locker room. *And the sooner the better.*

But that didn't look promising when she arrived at her locker. Two girls were standing in front of it, and they practically pounced on her.

"So *you're* Sophie," one of them said.

The other one smacked the girl on the arm. "I told you it was her."

"Wow," said Girl #1 to Sophie. "I thought you'd be cuter."

"No offense," said Girl #2.

"I need to open my locker," Sophie said.

"Oh, sorry," said Girl #1. She grabbed Girl #2's hand and they went off whispering.

Sophie turned to the Flakes, who were already half dressed.

"What's going on?" she said.

"Simple." Maggie jerked her head toward B.J. and Cassie, who were hissing to Julia and Anne-Stuart.

"They talked about you guys going out all first and second periods," Willoughby said.

"But it isn't true!" Sophie said.

Darbie took Sophie's discarded clothes and shoved them into her locker for her. "We made them think it was, remember?"

"Only they've embellished it," Fiona said.

"Does that mean they exaggerated?" Maggie said.

"More like they decorated what we said with lies." Fiona's voice tightened. "Or are they?"

"Some eejit told me you'd been dating in secret since last year," Darbie said. "And we know that's a lie."

Willoughby looked wide-eyed at Sophie. "It *is* a lie, right?"

"Hel-*lo*!" Sophie looked at Fiona, who didn't look back.

"Sorry," Willoughby said.

Sophie plunked herself down on the bench to put on her shoes. "I hope Jimmy doesn't think I'm telling everybody all this stuff."

"Maybe you should ask him," Maggie said.

"You want me to ask him for you?" Willoughby said.

"I can do it," Sophie said.

"Let Willoughby do it," Fiona said.

But sending somebody else sounded to Sophie too much like something one of the Pops would do if she actually liked a guy. They always made everything so complicated with boys.

Still, Sophie's mouth went dry as she headed for Jimmy in the gym. But before she could get to him, he came to her. His red spots had been reduced to two, and he was smiling.

"Pretty funny, huh?" he said. "All the stuff they're saying about us."

"Funny?" Sophie looked at him closely. "You aren't mad about it, are you? Because I didn't start it—"

"What's to get mad about? I'm laughing all over the place."

"Oh," Sophie said. He was right, of course. Du-uh—that's what you did with bullies.

He bent his blond head toward her and lowered his voice. "Did you know we were getting married?"

"What?"

"Planning the wedding and everything. I mean, come on—who's gonna believe that?"

He had the most perfect are-these-people-lame-or-what expression on his face, Sophie spit out a laugh. Jimmy grinned and pretended to wipe her saliva off his shirt.

"All right, lovebirds, break it up!" Coach Yates yelled.

"See you at the wedding," Jimmy whispered to Sophie.

"Do we have to invite *her*?" Sophie whispered back.

Seven

Jimmy's words nudged at Sophie like mischievous elves. So when Pepper asked her if she wanted her to try to get Jimmy switched with Nathan so they could be in the same gymnastics group, Sophie just laughed out loud. Now, if Pepper had asked her to switch *Eddie* with Jimmy, that would have been a different matter.

Eddie *did* do his forward rolls and his tripods and his headstands like Pepper told him to. But Sophie wasn't fooled. After all, he was still hanging with Tod and Colton outside classes. And she'd seen Eddie come out of Coach Virile's office about five times.

He isn't fooling Coach Virile, either, Sophie thought. She launched into her forward roll—and couldn't stop rolling. When she did, she was in the middle of the gym.

Before she could even get up, Eddie was there, sticking his hand down to her.

"Want help?" he said.

Somewhere in the direction of Group Four, Sophie heard Colton clapping like an ape.

"I'm *fine*." Sophie scrambled up by herself. *How stupid do you think I am?* she wanted to ask. Yeah, she still needed to watch Eddie—along with the thousand other things she had to do.

She and Jimmy met Thursday and Friday mornings before school to write their website proposal for Round Table. Both days Fiona shot her so many pointy looks during first period, Sophie felt like she needed Band-Aids.

I know she gets all possessive, Sophie thought, *but for Pete's sake, I'm spending all the rest of my time with her!*

Thursday and Friday at lunch and after school, and all day Saturday, the Flakes and Charms worked on their Dr. Peter Christmas movie. Most of that time they were rewriting the script. The whole thing. There didn't seem to be a line in the original that didn't make everyone's eyes roll. A couple of times Sophie thought Fiona's might disappear up into her head.

"It is the wee hours of the morning, sir," Fiona read in a fake-deep voice Saturday afternoon. "What business have you with us?" She looked at the group with her mouth open. "Nobody talks like that."

"It's set in the Victorian era," Vincent said.

"I bet they didn't talk like that then, either," Fiona said stubbornly.

"So what do you want it to say?" Maggie tapped her gel pen on the open Treasure Book.

Jimmy let an easy smile spread across his face. "How 'bout 'Yo, dude, what's up? It's three o'clock in the morning.'"

"Yeah," Sophie said. "'What you want?'"

Jimmy laughed. "'It better be good because when somebody wakes me up, man, it can get ugly.'"

"You know it," Sophie said, giggling.

"Do I write that down?" Maggie said.

"Yeah, that's good!" Nathan said.

Fiona knotted her lips. "I don't know, Jimmy. It's pretty lame."

Jimmy blinked. Sophie glared at Fiona.

"It isn't lame, it's a gas," Darbie said.

"It won't go with Victorian costumes then," Fiona said.

Sophie was immediately serious. "Don't change the costumes!" She'd already fallen in love with the gown Senora LaQuita was making for her. It even had a corset underneath that made her stand up very straight.

"You know what would be mega-funny?" Vincent said. His big, loose grin took up half his face. "If we did everything Victorian, even, like, with those proper voices, but we used modern language, like you guys just did."

"That would be class!" Darbie said.

"It isn't supposed to be funny." Maggie tapped harder with the gel pen.

"Why not?" Vincent said. "The kids'll laugh, but they'll still get the point."

"Yeah! Kind of like a Disney movie," Willoughby said, "where it's all slapstick, and then you have a serious part where you end up crying."

"Yeah," Jimmy said. He tilted his head at Sophie. "You're not saying anything."

Eyes half closed, Sophie nodded slowly.

"Uh-oh, she's dreaming," Fiona said. "I know that look."

"But is she dreaming the same thing we're dreaming?" Vincent said.

Sophie blinked at him. "That depends."

"On what?" Darbie said.

"On whether I can be called Louisa Linkhart and act *way* proper."

"Oh, yeah, we can't use Cynthia Cyber, huh," Jimmy said.

Fiona's face went stiff. "Who's Cynthia Cyber?"

"Internet Investigator," Jimmy said. "She's for the website."

Fiona rolled her eyes *and* her head. "Come *on*, Jimmy," she said. "You can't have some Internet chick in a Victorian movie. That *is* lame."

Jimmy turned even redder than Nathan.

"He knows that," Sophie said through clenched teeth. "He just said that."

"Okay!" Vincent said. "I vote we let Sophie be this Louey Linkey chick and act as proper as she wants. That'll make it really funny when she says, like—"

"'You get your tail out of here unless you have a death wish,'" Sophie/Louisa said. She made every letter distinct.

"I love that!" Willoughby cried.

Everyone joined in with their individual versions of Willoughby's poodle yelp. That was, everyone except Fiona, who slit her eyes like a full-fledged Corn Pop.

It got worse on the way to Fiona's after rehearsal. Sophie was going to spend the night, but all Fiona did on the ride was concentrate on her cuticles.

This is gonna get ugly, Sophie thought.

They were barely in Fiona's room when Fiona dropped her backpack on the floor and, hands on hips, ripped out with, "How come you didn't tell *me* about Cynthia Cyber?"

Sophie sank down on the bed and counted the leopard spots on the pillowcase trim before she answered. It was better to think things through, she knew, when it came to a word-fight with Fiona.

"I didn't tell you because you're not working on the website," Sophie said finally.

"Still," Fiona said. She sat heavily next to Sophie. "You're asking Round Table if we can all help, right?"

Sophie hadn't actually considered that, but she nodded. She could feel Fiona's eye darts going right through her.

"Sure," she said. "I mean, if it's okay with Jimmy."

"Is he the boss of you now?" Fiona said.

Sophie grabbed the pillow and smacked her with it.

Fiona grabbed it and smashed it down beside her. "Don't change the subject," she said.

"What subject?" Sophie said.

"And don't try to stall me, either. I want to know if you have to check everything out with Jimmy now. It sure seems like it."

Fiona's eyes narrowed as she punched her fist down into the pillow. Sophie felt like it was her stomach that had taken the hit.

"No," Sophie said. "But we're both doing the website. It wouldn't be right for me to just say we're gonna do something when he has half the say." She gnawed at her lip. "I can't be rude to him like you're being."

"I'm just being honest." Fiona glared at the pillow. "And I wasn't just talking about the website."

"Then *what*?"

"I'm hungry." Fiona headed for the door like she was starving. But Sophie knew she wasn't.

It's a hard enough job Internet investigating, Cynthia Cyber thought as she followed Dot Com to the kitchen. Why does she have to make it even MORE complicated?

Fiona didn't have much to say the rest of the weekend. Sophie chewed on that until Monday. Finishing the website proposal with Jimmy that day helped. When they took it to Round Table at lunch, Hannah didn't give them twenty-five reasons why it wouldn't work. Oliver only snapped his rubber bands once, and that was when Sophie mentioned involving people outside of Round Table.

"I think it should just be the people who went to the conference," he said.

"Feeling exclusive, are you, Oliver?" Miss Imes said, her eyebrows pointing up as sharply as her voice.

"No," Oliver said. "But if this is such a big deal and people could get really wrecked by the whole cyber-bullying thing, it should be done by the people that know what it's all about."

Miss Imes nodded her head of crisp, almost-white hair. "Excellent reason. I underestimated you."

The rest of the group gave Oliver polite applause, while Sophie chewed at her bottom lip again. Fiona wasn't going to like this. At all.

Fiona *didn't* like it. Even after Sophie explained to her at least twelve times that it was a Round Table decision, Fiona still drilled her eyes into Sophie. "They're the ones who are losing out, then," she said.

She opened her mouth as if she were going to say more, and then she snapped it shut.

"*What?*" Sophie said. "If you're thinking Jimmy's my new best friend or something, we have *so* been through this before — first Maggie, then Darbie."

Fiona rolled her eyes. "That was back when I was imma-ture," she said. "Just forget it, okay? And tell those Round Table people I could help you build an awesome website."

Then she knotted her mouth, and Sophie knew the con-versation was over. *Besides*, Sophie thought, *the Round Table website is already amazing.*

They had Jimmy's quiz, and sample situations of cyber bul-lying where web visitors could click on what they thought were the best solutions. When her picture popped up, Cynthia Cyber would then tell them if they were right or wrong. The drawing that Mrs. Britt chose to represent Cynthia Cyber wasn't exactly how Sophie imagined her, but at least she was there.

Sophie tried to get Dot Com and Maga Byte in there too, but she and Jimmy decided that would make it too confusing. They already had so much information to include to help kids who were being bullied. They settled on a list of basics with little graphics of computers to click on for more information.

1. WHEN YOU'RE CYBER-BULLIED FOR THE FIRST TIME, DON'T RESPOND. THAT WILL ONLY MAKE THE SITUATON WORSE. MOST BULLIES GO AWAY IF YOU IGNORE THEM.

2. IF YOU'RE BULLIED AGAIN, PRINT OUT THE BULLYING MATERIAL AND SAVE IT IN CASE YOU NEED EVIDENCE. BLOCK ALL EMAILS FROM THE SENDER. THE HELP MENU ON YOUR EMAIL PROGRAM WILL SHOW YOU HOW.

3. IF THE BULLYNG KEEPS UP AND YOU FIND OUT WHO'S DOING IT, TELL YOUR PARENTS OR ANOTHER ADULT. ASK THEM TO CALL THE BULLY'S PARENTS.

4. IF THAT DOESN'T WORK, REPORT THE HARASS-MENT TO SCHOOL OFFICIALS AND SEND YOUR EVIDENCE TO THE BULLY'S INTERNET SERVICE PROVIDER.

5. IF A CYBER BULLY THREATENS YOU WITH PHYSICAL HARM, TELL YOUR PARENTS AND ASK THEM TO CALL THE POLICE. *CYBER STALKING IS A CRIME!*

On another webpage they had everything about how to prevent Internet bullying. They included things like "netiquette"—online manners. And how to have a strong code of personal behavior so you don't bully, even though no one may ever catch you.

One of the best parts of the website, Sophie thought, was the "Acceptable Use Policy" that everyone in the school would have to sign before they could use school computers. That seemed so wonderfully official to Sophie, and she and Jimmy always referred to it as the AUP. They didn't come up with the idea themselves—a lot of schools were doing it—but Cynthia Cyber heartily approved.

Working on the website could have occupied all of Sophie's time, if she hadn't also been working on the movie and helping at home, plus chatting, emailing, and IMing on the computer. Her Internet time got cut back, though, when Lacie complained that she could never get online to do her homework. Daddy limited Sophie to an hour a day. It was like losing a finger or something.

And then there was school. It was getting hard to keep up, but Sophie knew she had to maintain at least a B in everything to keep her camera. Actually, school wouldn't have been so bad if she hadn't ended up with Anne-Stuart every time a teacher assigned a group activity. *What happened to us making our own groups?* Sophie wondered more than once. Anne-Stuart was never openly snotty to her—especially not in Language Arts/Social Studies block where they had both Mrs. Clayton and Ms. Hess patrolling the classroom. But the too-nice approach she was using made Sophie feel like she needed Pepto-Bismol. Sophie thought she must be getting tips from that snake Eddie Wornom.

"Doesn't it bother you that Julia is always in groups with Jimmy?" Anne-Stuart said to Sophie one day in Miss Imes' class when their group was figuring out story problems.

Sophie glanced at the group in the corner. Julia had her desk touching Jimmy's and appeared to be writing something on his paper. When she saw Sophie looking, she smiled a plastic smile and waved.

"She's totally flirting with your guy," Anne-Stuart said.

It did no good to protest for the ninety-fifth time that Jimmy wasn't her "guy."

Another day, Anne-Stuart showed up first period with an elastic bandage wrapped around her right wrist, saying she'd hurt it in PE the day before. She asked Sophie, in a cotton-candy voice, if she would email the group's notes to her that night since she couldn't write. The bandage disappeared by third period, and, come to think of it, Sophie didn't remember seeing Anne-Stuart hurt it in the first place.

But I'll email her the notes anyway. That's what a Corn Flake does, Sophie told herself. Thankfully, there weren't that many notes.

There was definitely a lot going on, but Sophie remembered to confess everything to Jesus at night before she went to sleep.

I'm sorry I keep thinking the Corn Pops are the most heinous people in the galaxy. Even if they are, I shouldn't be thinking that. I just wish they'd stop with the Jimmy thing already. HE'S NOT MY BOYFRIEND.

I gotta confess that I'm getting sick of Fiona pouting about the website. But I guess I would feel kinda hurt if it was me.

I hate it that I wanted to flush Zeke down the toilet today when he used my curtains for a Spider-Man web and tried to swing from the window to the bed. I hope Daddy can fix my curtain rod this weekend.

She always fell asleep before she got through the whole list. She liked getting a fresh start every day, but the teasing about Jimmy started the minute she set foot in the school. When she wished she could shove them all into the nearest garbage can, she knew there would be plenty more to confess that night.

But none of that teasing could compare to what happened Sunday.

Eight

When Sophie sat down to check her email after church, there were five messages. Three were from Fiona, which she was almost afraid to read. One was from Jimmy. The fifth one had an address she'd never seen before.

She hesitated with the cursor pointed at the Read icon. The website said not to open mail from unknown senders—but maybe this was just somebody who had never emailed her, like one of the Wheaties.

I'll just look at it, and if it's trash I'll delete it, she decided.

Sofee, the email said. *Check out this cool website.*

Sophie clicked on the website address. The minute she saw it, she turned to ice.

Who's getting together at GMMS? it said. And before the visitor could even wonder, there was the answer, complete with a photograph of Jimmy and Sophie huddled up like they were peeking out an imaginary window together.

"That was when we were practicing for the movie during lunch Friday!" she said out loud. "It was right out in the courtyard! Who took that?"

Sophie's hand was so cold she could barely scroll down the page.

There was a "quote" from Sophie's own screen name.

DREAMGRL: I've been after him for a long time.
Now he's mine.

Then came a cut-out photograph of Sophie's head. When Sophie clicked on the icon, there was a recording in her own voice saying, "I'm in love." Her photographed mouth moved like a robot's.

Below that was a picture of Jimmy with his mouth open and a written quote: "I wanted Julia, but she's going out with Colton now. Lucky guy. Sophie's okay, but—"

For More, Click Here, the instructions read. Sophie did, and heard Jimmy's voice saying, *"She's got some serious mental problems."*

It ended with—

To Follow Jimmy/Sophie, Check This Website Daily. To End, Click Here.

Sophie did and was rewarded with a loud kissing sound.

Even after the images disappeared from the screen, Sophie sat staring at it. *It's not true!* she thought over and over. *It's all made up!*

And then it pinged in her head. She'd just been cyber-bullied. *Okay—okay*, she thought. *What am I supposed to do?*

She smacked her forehead with the heel of her hand. *Du-uh. I WROTE the rules!*

No more going to that website. That was Step One. But she was still shivering. She decided to skip a couple of steps and tell Daddy.

It was DOS—"daughter over shoulder"—as Daddy perused *Who's Getting Together* on his computer in the study, making disgusted noises in his throat.

"Isn't Jimmy that kid you're doing the website with?" he said.

"Yes."

"You two aren't—"

"Daddy!"

"I'm just asking. They've got a picture of you both here."

"We were practicing for our movie!"

"And the recording of your voice?"

"I don't know how they got that. We were just messing around in the locker room, playing a joke."

"That's your screen name, isn't it? Dream Girl?"

"But I never wrote that! I don't even think it!"

Daddy put his hand on top of Sophie's head and gently pushed her down to sit beside him. "Okay, Baby Girl, I'm on your side. I'm just showing you how easy it is for people to get images and sound bites and 'prove' anything they want to." He grunted. "These kids should be working for the tabloids."

"What are those?"

"Those newspapers in the grocery store checkout line with the stuff about space aliens and Elvis coming back."

"That's so totally what this is!" Sophie said. "Only how did they get all this stuff? How did somebody get my email address?"

And did Jimmy really say I had some serious mental problems? she added to herself. She was suddenly having a hard time swallowing.

"All right, here's the game plan," Daddy said. "I'm going to move your and Lacie's computers into the family room."

"Why?" Sophie said.

"Why? You gave me the rules—right there in that stuff for parents from the conference. It said to not let your child use a computer in a private place like the bedroom." Daddy grinned at her as he ruffled up her hair. "That will teach you to be such a good kid, huh?" His blue eyes got softer. "Look, I know you feel like you're being punished for what somebody else is doing, but I just think I need to keep a closer eye on what goes on with your computer use. I promise I won't POS you too much."

Sophie's eyes bulged. "I shouldn't have given you that stuff," she said.

Daddy laughed. After he moved the computers into the family room, Lacie glared at Sophie for the rest of the day.

Sophie could barely drag herself into the school on Monday. If *she* had seen the website, the rest of GMMS had probably seen it too.

But nobody mentioned it before school or during the first block. Not even Fiona.

Maybe they really have moved on to the next thing to gossip about, Sophie thought. *Just like Coach Virile said.*

Cynthia Cyber sighed. At last the young people were starting to understand: if cyber bullying got them no attention, they would soon stop. She rubbed her hands together and went for the mouse again. There was still much work to be done—

"There is a rule at this school about cell phones in class." Mrs. Clayton's voice trumpeted across the room.

Sophie turned around to see Tod blinking innocently. He looked like a character from Dr. Seuss, the way everything on his face came to a point at the end of his nose, but he wasn't fooling Sophie. There was a cell phone someplace on his person.

"It's a good rule too, Mrs. C.," he said. "How would anybody get any work done if people were sending out pictures to everybody's cell phones?"

Julia smacked him on the back of the head with her binder. Anne-Stuart went into a coughing fit.

"Is that what's going on?" Mrs. Clayton was now on him like an angry goose. Ms. Hess was closing in from behind.

"I don't know." Tod shrugged. "I don't have a cell phone."

"Frisk him, Mrs. C!" said Colton as he grinned at Tod. "Make sure he isn't lyin'."

"Shut *up*!" Tod said.

"*Everyone* be quiet!" Mrs. Clayton's trumpet voice hit a new high. Even Ms. Hess jumped.

"Now," Mrs. Clayton said, "this is your warning: leave your cell phones in your lockers when you come to this class. Any that I find in this room will be confiscated and you can retrieve them from Mr. Bentley."

Mr. Bentley was the principal. You didn't want to have to go to his office.

"What was that whole thing about the cell phones?" Darbie said when the Corn Flakes were on their way to PE.

"Did it happen in your class too?" Maggie said. "Everybody was looking at their phones and laughing." She squared her shoulders. "They're not supposed to have them in class."

Sophie looked at Willoughby, who lagged behind them. "You have a cell phone," she said. "Do you know?"

Willoughby wouldn't look at her.

"You do know," Fiona said. "Come on, dish."

"I don't want to," Willoughby said.

"Why not?" Darbie said.

Willoughby wound a curl around her finger. "Because it's about Sophie."

They all stopped. Sophie felt herself go cold again.

"Was it a text message?" Fiona poked Willoughby. "What did it say about Sophie?"

"It wasn't a text message." Willoughby sounded like every word was painful to say. "It was a picture."

"You can't get pictures on a cell phone," Maggie said flatly.

"You can if it's a camera phone," Fiona said. "Was it of Sophie?"

Willoughby gave a miserable nod. "She was putting on her shorts in the locker room." Her eyes popped at Sophie. "You couldn't really see your underwear or anything."

"I admit that's pretty rude," Fiona said. "But it's not like *that* bad."

"There were words with it, though." Willoughby looked like she was going to throw up. "It said, 'Hey, Jimmy, look who has the ugliest body at GMMS.'"

She threw her arms around Sophie, but Sophie peeled her off. Although her lips were frozen, she managed to say, "We have to tell. It says so on our website."

"Let's see it, Will," Darbie said.

But Willoughby shook her head. There were tears shining in her eyes. "I erased it. I didn't want Sophie to see it."

Sophie sagged. "Then we don't have any evidence."

"And you *know* nobody else around here is going to turn them in," Darbie said. "The blaggards."

Maggie jerked her head toward the locker room. "We're gonna be late."

But as the rest of the Corn Flakes hurried inside, Fiona tugged Sophie to a stop.

"I know the Pops are being mean, Soph," she said. Her eyes looked motherly. "But they wouldn't even be doing it if it didn't look like you and Jimmy were practically engaged."

"It doesn't look like that!"

Fiona wiggled Sophie's sleeve. "Evidently it does to them. I'm just saying, think about it."

It was impossible to think about anything else from then on. Sophie could barely change into her PE clothes for fear there were hidden cameras everywhere. The other Corn Flakes kept close watch on the Pops while she wriggled into her shorts. They were on backward, but she left them that way.

During class she went through the gymnastics moves like an icicle. Anne-Stuart did hers perfectly, which made Sophie wish she had faked a heart attack and gone to the nurse instead. Eddie acted like he was zipped inside a sleeping bag — that was how much attention he paid to anybody. Sophie didn't even try to guess what was going on with him.

In fact, by the time she got to fourth period, Sophie was in such a frozen state she stared for a good two minutes at the paper Miss Imes put on her desk before she realized it was a test. A test she'd forgotten to study for. When they exchanged papers and graded them at the end of class, Sophie's came back to her from Darbie with a D on it and a tiny sad face.

She was ready to cry, especially when Miss Imes stopped her after class. "Sophie, you were doing so well again, and now lately you've slacked off."

"I'll be okay," Sophie said.

"You're distracted." Miss Imes pointed her eyebrows up to her hairline. "That's one reason why students shouldn't be dating so young."

Is there anybody in this whole school who isn't talking about me? Sophie thought on the way to the cafeteria. It felt like she was walking down the hall naked.

When she got to the Corn Flake table in the cafeteria, the Lucky Charms were there too. Sophie didn't let her eyes linger on Jimmy. There was still the question of whether he really thought she was mental.

Vincent, it seemed, was in the middle of clearing that up.

"That so-called quote from Jimmy was obviously taken out of context," he said.

Maggie frowned. "What does—"

"It means he said it," Fiona told her, "but not about Sophie." She didn't look all that convinced to Sophie.

"I would never say that about Sophie!" Jimmy said. She sneaked a glance. His face was blotchy.

"If you can remember when you did say it," Vincent said, "we could probably figure out who recorded you."

"We already know it was Julia and them," Maggie said. "Who else?"

"But I don't even talk to them," Jimmy said. "Except in groups in class."

"All right then." Darbie's voice was brisk. "When did you say somebody had serious mental problems?"

Jimmy frowned, then snapped his fingers. "It was when we were talking about that book we're reading. Y'know, the one where the guy stands the woman up on their wedding day and she won't let anybody touch anything, and it's like forty years later and the cake is still sitting there."

"Yeah," Willoughby said. "She *did* have some serious mental problems."

"And you said that in group," Vincent said.

Jimmy nodded.

"There you have it."

"But how did they get my screen name on there?" Sophie said. "Because I did *not* say what it says I said."

Vincent put out his hands as if that were obvious. "It's so easy for somebody to copy your screen name when you're IMing. They just erase what you did say and put in whatever they want."

"But she doesn't IM with the Pops," Darbie said.

"I did once," Sophie said. Her brain was finally thawing out, and things were pinging in there. "Anne-Stuart IM'd me to say she was sorry about what Julia said about me that day."

"Did you answer?" Vincent said.

"All I said was *hi* and *thanks*."

"That's all it takes." Vincent popped a whole Oreo into his mouth and added, "Like I said, there you have it."

Just then Girl #1 and Girl #2 appeared and stood at the end of the Corn Flakes' table. They looked at Sophie, looked at each other, and became hysterical. They had to help each other stay upright as they moved away howling.

"Do you believe that?" Sophie said to Fiona.

Fiona just cocked an eyebrow.

"What does that mean?" Sophie said.

"It means what I said before. It isn't just the getting-together website that's making people think this stuff about you and Jimmy."

Sophie stared at her.

"I'm just saying they see you two together all the time." Fiona shrugged. "So what else are they supposed to think?"

As much as that ate at Sophie, for the rest of the week it seemed Fiona might be at least a little bit right. It didn't matter what Sophie and Jimmy did. Whether they were working on the website in the computer room, walking to a Round Table meeting together, or practicing their scenes for the Christmas movie, there always seemed to be at least two people there, pointing and whispering and snickering behind their hands. It was never the Corn Pops or the Fruit Loops, but Sophie constantly looked for camera lenses and tape recorders.

When she went to bed every night she tried to confess her sins, but it seemed like it was everybody else who was doing the sinning.

I know I'm supposed to forgive them, she thought more than once. *But I don't know how!* When Dr. Peter canceled Bible study at the last minute on Wednesday, she thought she might actually *develop* some serious mental problems.

Sophie was also spending every evening trying to bring her grades back up. That meant spending less and less time with the Corn Flakes, and Fiona was complaining right out in the open about that. Sophie hardly even had a chance to read and send emails, much less go to the Corn Flakes' chat room. The subject line on Fiona's email Friday night was: *Are You Still Alive?*

You BETTER make some time for me after rehearsal tomorrow, she'd written. *I'm going into Sophie withdrawal.*

I'm all yours tomorrow, Sophie wrote back.

But it didn't quite turn out that way.

Nine

The whole group, even Kitty in a wheelchair, met at the skating rink at Hampton Coliseum Saturday morning to practice the ice-skating scene for the movie. Boppa took a seat in the stands to watch.

"I don't remember any ice skating in 'Twas the Night Before Christmas,'" Maggie said for about the twentieth time.

"Whoever wrote it put it in there because you have to have action in a movie," Sophie told her patiently. She finished lacing her skates and stood up. She'd learned to skate when she was little, but it had been a while since she'd been on the ice. She put out one foot and slid into an almost split.

"That's perfect!" Vincent said. "If this scene is gonna be funny, you're gonna have to fall down a lot."

"It won't be funny if she breaks a leg," Maggie said.

Vincent blinked at her. "Are you, like, forty years old only you're disguised as a kid?"

"You ready, Sophie?" Jimmy said.

"Ready for what?" Fiona spun around on her skates and faced them both.

"The script says Mr. and Mrs. Linkhart skate together," Darbie said.

"We need to change that," Fiona said. "It won't be funny."

"Yeah, it will be," Jimmy said. "Watch this."

He grabbed both of Sophie's hands and pulled her toward him as he skated backward. She lunged forward, legs marching out stiffly behind her.

"That *is* funny!" Kitty squealed from her wheelchair.

Willoughby let out a series of poodle shrieks as Jimmy hauled Sophie all over the ice. He whipped her back and forth, held her up by the back of her sweater while her feet kicked in the air, and did a jump over her while she crouched on the ice. It was like doing gymnastics, only on skates. Sophie felt like a limp spaghetti noodle, and she could hardly catch her breath from laughing.

"It doesn't even look close to Victorian," Fiona said when Jimmy skated Sophie back over to the group.

Maggie waved the costume sketches. "You can't do all that in a corset."

"Bummer," Nathan said. "I liked it."

"I say we cut the ice-skating scene," Fiona said.

Sophie stared at her, but Fiona wouldn't meet her gaze.

"We can do the funny stuff *and* be Victorian," Jimmy said. "We'll just go along all serious and proper, and then Sophie'll fall and I'll catch her. We'll do one of those moves we were just doing, and then we'll go back to proper."

"But we haven't seen you do anything 'proper,'" Darbie said.

"Sophie can't skate that good," Maggie said.

Sophie squirmed. *Is it just me*, she thought, *or are my best friends not being very nice to me right now?*

She looked at Willoughby and Kitty, who were watching Fiona like they were waiting for a cue. Neither of them said anything.

"Let's see what you got," Vincent said.

Fiona rolled her eyes, but Jimmy grabbed Sophie's hand again and pulled her back out into the rink.

"Just relax and do whatever I tell you," he murmured. "I won't let you fall."

Sophie gave one more glance to the doubtful group on the sidelines. Even Boppa was leaning forward in his chair.

"Okay," she whispered back.

Jimmy put one arm around Sophie's waist and stretched the other one across the front of him to hold her right hand. "Just put your left hand on my back," he whispered.

She did.

"Now relax and let me do all the work," he said.

Relax? How could she do that when she knew she was turning red all the way to her toes? Getting slung around was one thing, but this was more like dancing.

With a boy.

I don't want to do this! she thought.

She glanced toward the sidelines. Fiona was already shaking her head, an I-told-you-so scrawled across her face. Kitty appeared to be biting her nails.

"Ready?" Jimmy whispered.

Louisa Linkhart looked into her husband's eyes. She knew how much he wanted to skate with her, even though she was terribly clumsy on the ice. What could it hurt? After all, it was Christmas Eve—and he'd said he wouldn't let her fall. He was a superb skater—

So Louisa breathed, "Ready," and let Lincoln Linkhart guide her smoothly across the lake, his hands solid and safe, holding her up. Little by little she relaxed, and she even leaned when he leaned and laughed when he laughed. It was as if they were one person, sailing past the other skaters under the moonlight. It was magic—

"Okay," Jimmy said, "when we go into the next turn, I'm gonna let go. You pretend you're falling and go all spastic. I promise I'll catch you."

"It won't take much pretending!" Sophie said—and then suddenly she was free on the ice. She flung out her arms and churned her legs to keep her balance. Laughter erupted from the sidelines.

Just as she was sure Jimmy was going to back out on his promise, he swung her back into place, and they were skating like a mature Victorian couple again. It was so real, Sophie could almost feel the corset around her middle.

"Smile when we pass them," Jimmy said.

They both turned their heads and grinned as they floated past the Charms and Flakes. Boppa was standing up, clapping, and Darbie was filming, and the others were all smiling and waving.

All except Fiona.

When Jimmy and Sophie skated up to them, it was hard to sort out which "That was perfect!" and "You guys rock!" was coming from whom. While that was going on, Fiona pulled Sophie over to the bench. Her face was as stern as Miss Odetta's.

"I know you don't want to make a fool of yourself, Soph," she said as she untied Sophie's skates. "And I'm telling you this because I'm your best friend. That really isn't going to work for the movie."

Sophie slid her foot out of Fiona's reach. "Everybody said it was good."

"They just don't want to hurt your feelings."

You're doing enough of it for everybody, Sophie wanted to say. She bit her lip.

"And besides," Fiona said, "what about when your parents see the movie?"

"What about it?" Sophie said.

"Hello! You're all snuggled up to Jimmy, holding hands. He had his arm around you, for Pete's sake!"

"That's the way they skated back then!"

"Yeah, but this isn't back then." Fiona gave Sophie her I-know-more-than-you-do-about-this look. "Listen to me, for once. Aren't you having enough trouble with everybody accusing you of being practically engaged to the guy? Think what they'll do with this."

"Nobody at school's going to see our movie for church," Sophie said.

Fiona swept an arm in the air. "Look around. There are kids from Poquoson all over the place here. You and Jimmy looking like you're attached at the hip is Internet material, Soph."

For an instant, Sophie started to go cold. And then something pinged in her mind.

"You know what, Fiona?" Sophie said. "I'm going to keep the power to be myself. Jimmy and I were working on the movie out there. It was embarrassing, but I was *trying* to play my part."

Fiona knotted her lips. "Other people don't know that."

" 'Other people' can think what they want."

"And they will," Fiona said.

"Then let them."

Sophie looked at her until Fiona stood up. "Then don't come whining to me when it's all over that *getting together* website," Fiona said. She started back toward the group.

"Are you sleeping over at my house tonight?" Sophie said.

Fiona didn't look back. "I can't," she said.

Suddenly, Sophie was very cold.

Fiona sat in the front with Boppa on the way home and didn't say much to anyone. She barely said good-bye to Sophie when Boppa dropped her off. Everybody else looked like they would rather be having their teeth cleaned.

What just happened? Sophie thought as she trudged up the stairs to her room.

She was lying on her bed, trying to find an answer in the curtains above her head, when Lacie poked her head in.

"Good, you're not online," she said.

Sophie blinked and smiled vaguely.

Lacie squinted at her and crawled onto the bed. "Okay, what's going on? Tell me those little Popettes weren't at the skating rink."

Sophie shook her head. "They're everywhere else. They even have Fiona believing that I'm going out with Jimmy—and I'm *not!*" Sophie raked her fingers through her hair. "Sometimes I don't care what people think—but then I do!"

"Is it that website you were telling Daddy about?"

"That's part of it." She told Lacie about Fiona, and about the picture that had appeared on everybody's camera phones.

"Can you prove it was the Pops?" Lacie said.

"No. They're being really careful. I know I'm supposed to ignore it, but it's hard! I'm used to telling them to their faces that they're not getting to me."

Lacie rolled over onto her stomach and propped her chin in her hand. "This time they *are* getting to you. You know why, don't you?"

"Do you?"

Lacie put on her Wise Big Sister face. "Because you can't get away from it. You turn on your computer in your own house and there they are. And if you stay off the computer, you're out of the loop."

Sophie nodded for her to go on.

"Besides that, you can't really go up to them and say, 'Back off,' because you aren't absolutely sure it's them. And by now, so many people are involved, they're probably taking it and doing their own thing with it."

"This isn't making me feel better," Sophie said. "I don't even want to go back to school now. Maybe Kitty's mom can homeschool me with her."

Lacie rolled her eyes. "First of all, that isn't going to happen. And second of all, you still can't let them have control over you. Next thing you know, you'll be escaping into Dream Land again and messing up in school."

Sophie gulped.

"You already have," Lacie said.

"I have *two* characters I can run to now," Sophie said.

Lacie sat up. "Okay, Miss Multiple Personality Disorder, you can't let this happen. If it's affecting your grades and your best friendships, you have to stop it."

"I don't know how!"

"Hel-*lo*! You just put together a whole website on it. You don't have any evidence that could point to those little vixens?"

"No."

"Who told you about the Getting Together website in the first place?"

Sophie thought hard. "I don't know. I got an email from somebody I didn't know, and like a stupid head I opened it. It told me to check out the getting together thing."

"Did you delete it?"

"I don't think so."

Lacie headed for the door. "Then it's still in your old mail. Let's get it off and give it to Daddy. He can find out who sent it."

"What do I do about Fiona and the Flakes?" Sophie said as she followed Lacie downstairs.

"Whatever you do," Lacie said, "do it face-to-face."

They printed out the mystery email for Daddy, and he asked Sophie to forward it to his email. Then he told her he was going to buy some software that would allow him to monitor what went in and out of Sophie's computer.

"Dad-dy!" she said.

"It's not that I don't trust *you*, Baby Girl. It's these other kids that are running wild all over the Internet." He put his hand under her chin and tilted her head up. "Meanwhile, you stay strong. Don't let the other team intimidate you."

But Sophie didn't feel right then like she even had a team of her own. And there seemed to be only one thing she could do about that.

The next morning at church, she gathered the girls in the hall before Sunday school started.

"I want to know if you all believe me when I say I don't like Jimmy as a boyfriend," she said. "Tell me to my face."

Everybody looked at Fiona.

"What about it?" Sophie said to her. Her stomach was squirming.

"If he isn't your boyfriend," Fiona said, "then why do you spend more time with him than you do with me—us?"

"You spent four hours with just him last week," Maggie said, "and none with just us."

"You were keeping track?" Sophie said.

"I hardly even got an email from you," Kitty said.

"We're not trying to make you feel guilty, Sophie," Darbie said. "But you asked."

Willoughby tucked her arm through Sophie's. "We know he's cute and everything—"

"Would you stop?" Sophie pulled herself away. "What do I have to do to prove to you that—"

211

"Spend more time with us," Fiona said. "And less time with Jimmy." Her eyes narrowed. "That Round Table website has to be planned by now."

"It is," Sophie said. "Mrs. Britt's got it."

"Then you could be with us before school," Fiona said.

"Well, yeah," Sophie said.

"I told you she'd do it!" Willoughby all but did a backflip.

"Uh-oh," said a familiar voice down the hall. "I see trouble."

It was Dr. Peter, grinning and wearing a sling on his arm.

Sophie's heart turned over.

"What happened?" they all said in unison.

"I had a little fender bender Wednesday afternoon," Dr. Peter said. "That's why I had to cancel Bible study. But I'll be back this week."

"Does it hurt?" Maggie said.

Dr. Peter sucked in air. "Yeah, but I'm man enough to handle it. So what's going on here?"

"Sophie's just getting her priorities straight," Fiona said.

While Fiona launched into a definition of *priorities* for Maggie, Sophie closed her eyes.

I think that means I figured out what's important, she thought.

But she wasn't so sure that was what had just happened.

And she was even less sure later that day.

Ten

After church, Sophie sat down in the family room and wrote Jimmy an email:

Now that we're done with the website, I won't be meeting you before school anymore. I'm not mad at you or anything. My friends just want me to spend more time with them. You're my friend too, but they're like my best BEST friends — and they decide who I can hang out with.

"No, that isn't right," Sophie muttered to herself. Her finger poked at the delete key. A message popped up on the screen:

Your Mail Has Been Sent

"No!" Sophie cried. "Not send! Delete!"

But there was no getting it back — and suddenly she wanted that more than anything. She confessed to Jesus right on the spot. And she added to it, *Please don't let Jimmy hate me.*

Then she sat staring at the monitor, shoulders sagging. Maybe if she let the Flakes know what she'd done to keep their friendship, she would feel better. At least they would believe her now.

Nobody seemed to be available for instant messaging, and an email meant waiting too long for an answer, so Sophie logged into the Corn Flakes' chat room. The screen names were popping up like snapping fingers.

CHEER: She said she would be with us more now.

WORDGRL: She didn't WANT to say it.

IRISH: She didn't promise.

MEOW: Sophie keeps her word!!!!!! She luvs us!!!!!!

WORDGRL: I think she luvs J more.

CHEER: No way.

WORDGRL: You saw them skating.

IRISH: She was acting.

WORDGRL: Not when we were talking after. She's way serious about him.

MEOW: She's lying???!!!!!

IRISH: Maybe she doesn't know she's lying.

CHEER: Huh?

WORDGRL:She doesn't know WHAT she's doing. We have to set her straight.

DREAMGRL: Don't bother. I think I have it pretty straight already.

With tears in her eyes, Sophie logged off before any of her friends could respond.

Her former friends.

She didn't go near the Internet for the rest of the evening. In fact, she didn't go into the family room at all after supper. The computer was suddenly a cyber-monster, waiting to devour her.

But her room, her haven, was a lonely cave, and so was she. It was as if everything had been hollowed out and she was just a Sophie-shell. She groped around for an exit.

Cynthia Cyber was more determined than ever to clean up the Internet. When friends turned against friends, the Web was no longer a healthy place to be. If only Dot Com and the others had not gossiped about her in the chat room as if she were some silly, boy-crazy—

"But they did!" Sophie said out loud. Especially Fiona. *She said I was lying. How could she THINK that?*

Louisa Linkhart smoothed her hands over her corseted waist and went to the library door, her gown swishing as she hesitated in the doorway. Lincoln was there, his head bent over the paper he was writing on. She hated to disturb her husband, but she so needed his advice about her friends. He was so wise and so good. It would only take a moment—

She tapped lightly on the door frame and waited for him to look up, waited for his straight-teeth smile. But there was no smile as he turned to her. There was only hurt in his very-blue eyes—

Sophie leaned against her closet door and scrunched her eyes closed. *I wish I could talk to Dr. Peter right now,* she thought. *I will on Wednesday.*

Right. At Bible study. Where all the girls she thought were her friends would be waiting to "straighten her out."

Sophie crawled onto her bed and let the tears come.

Monday was the hardest day ever. It was the week before Christmas vacation, but Sophie couldn't join in the gift-exchanging and the classroom-door decorating. She was too busy making herself invisible so she could avoid the Corn Flakes.

She hung out in Miss Imes' room before school, because she knew the Flakes would never guess she'd be anywhere close to math if she didn't have to be. Even when Miss Imes told her that as a Christmas present she was dropping everyone's lowest grade, it didn't help.

Sophie bolted out of first-second block when the bell rang and changed into her PE clothes in a bathroom stall. When she saw there was no getting away from the Flakes in the roll-check line, she told Coach Yates she had a stomachache and needed to go to the nurse. It was the truth. She had never felt sicker.

When she walked through the gym toward the locker room to change her clothes at the end of the period, Eddie Wornom was putting away the tumbling mats. Sophie pretended not to see him, but that became impossible when he said, "Hey. Sophie."

This is NOT the time to start showing your real self, Sophie thought. She said, "Hey," and kept walking. Eddie caught up with her.

"I know how you feel," he said.

That stopped Sophie with a squeal of her tennis shoes. *There is no way YOU know how I feel, Eddie Wornom*, she wanted to say. Instead, she just looked up at him and waited.

"I'm not hanging out with my old friends, either," he said.

And you're telling me this because—

"They do stuff I can't do anymore," Eddie went on. "So now they're doin' that stuff to *me*."

"They're bullying you?" Sophie said.

She almost added, *Serves you right*. But Eddie's eyes were drooping at the corners. She had seen other eyes look that same way, that very morning in her own mirror.

"Got those mats up, Mr. Wornom?" Coach Virile called from the doorway.

"I gotta go," Eddie said to Sophie. "If you need any help—"

He shrugged again and went back to the mats. Sophie broke into a run for the door, but Coach Virile didn't move.

"Big change in our man Eddie, huh?" he said.

Sophie swished her foot back and forth in front of her and watched it.

"I'll take that as an I-don't-think-so," Coach said. He waited until Sophie looked up at him. "Miracles do happen, Little Bit. You might want to hear what he has to say."

It occurred to Sophie as she hurried to the locker room that there was certainly no *other* kid she could talk to right now. But Eddie Wornom?

Lunch was the biggest challenge. Sophie escaped to the courtyard, but she didn't feel like eating. Toward the end of lunch, she heard an announcement over the intercom that the new Round Table website was now up and running, and everyone who planned to use a school computer from then on had to sign the AUP. Even that didn't lift her up.

When she got to Mr. Stires' class, there was a note on her desk, folded like a bird the way only Fiona did it.

She could feel Fiona watching her. *If I read it I'll start crying,* Sophie told herself. *And they'll know how much I miss them already.*

Sophie swallowed hard. She was probably going to cry even without reading it.

It wasn't hard to get a restroom pass out of Mr. Stires, although he did crinkle his mustache a little as he said, "Are you okay, Sophie?"

All she could do was nod, and in the restroom she slammed her way into a stall and sobbed. Only when she started to calm down did she realize she still had Fiona's note clutched in her hand. She fumbled it open.

We didn't do anything wrong. We're just trying to help you. Duh — we're your best FRIENDS!

Friends don't call you a liar! Sophie wanted to shout. Without reading the rest, she crumpled the note and pitched it into the trash can.

In sixth period there was no getting away from them because they all had seats together, the Flakes and the Charms. Sophie stood in the doorway, debating whether to ask for another pass to the nurse or just crawl under her desk, when Nathan was suddenly beside her. His face looked like the inside of a watermelon, minus the seeds.

"They want to know if you're rehearsing after school," he said. He spoke so low Sophie had to move her ear closer to his mouth.

"Excuse me," B.J. said behind them. "Other people need to get in."

Sophie moved, but B.J. still grazed her, knocking Sophie against Nathan. Sophie had to stay there until the rest of the Corn Pops strolled into the room. Julia flung a look over her shoulder at her.

"Can't make up your mind which boy you want, Soapy?"

Sophie looked frantically at Nathan, whose scalp had gone scarlet between his curls.

"So, are you gonna come?" Nathan managed to get out.

Julia and Anne-Stuart waited, as if he'd asked *them* the question.

"Yeah," Sophie said. "I'll be there."

Nathan skittered to his desk, but Julia didn't move. When Sophie tried to get around her, she said, "So, does this mean Jimmy is available again?"

All Sophie could do was stare at her.

"I'll take that as a 'yes,'" Julia said. She started to walk away, and then she stopped. "Oh, and by the way—that AUP

218

thing we're supposed to sign? Nobody's going to follow that."
With a victorious toss of her hair, she was gone.

"You still sick, LaCroix?" Coach Yates said. "You're looking a little green."

"Yes, ma'am," Sophie said. "Could I go to the nurse again?"

She spent all of sixth period lying on a cot, trying not to imagine what rehearsal was going to be like. She had been careful not to even look at Jimmy all day, and he hadn't talked to her, either. He'd even sent Nathan to ask her if she was coming.

How am I going to pretend I'm his wife? she thought.

Louisa Linkhart wiped the last of the tears from her eyes with her lace handkerchief. She had to do what a good Victorian wife did. She must go to Lincoln and beg his forgiveness, even if she had to get down on her knees—which was no easy feat in a corset and petticoats—

Sophie sat straight up on the cot. Of *course!* She could almost imagine Dr. Peter right there, saying, *Loodle, didn't we talk about forgiveness? Weren't you listening?*

The tears came again and there wasn't a lace handkerchief in sight. The nurse peeked in and then opened the door wide.

"Honey, do you want me to call your mom to come get you?" she said.

"No," Sophie said. "There's something I have to do after school."

As soon as the bell rang, Sophie dodged through the crowd in the hall to Jimmy's locker. To her relief he was there, but so were Nathan and Vincent. When he saw Sophie, Vincent poked Jimmy in the back and pointed. The very-blue eyes that looked at her came straight out of her daydream.

"I need to talk to Jimmy." Sophie's voice squeaked, but she didn't care. She had to get this out.

219

"Oh, so now you want to talk to him," Vincent said. His own voice matched hers, squeak for squeak.

"It's okay," Jimmy said. "I'll catch up with you guys."

Nathan tore out of there like he was being chased by a pack of dogs. Vincent shrugged as he passed. "I don't get girls," he said.

Jimmy stuffed some books into his locker, and then pulled the same ones out. Sophie was feeling smaller by the second, but she straightened her shoulders. This would be so much easier if she were wearing a corset.

"I was stupid," she blurted out. "Fiona and them were all complaining because I was spending all that time working on the website with you and I felt guilty and I didn't want to mess things up with them—only I like being friends with you but I didn't know what to do especially with all the stupid rumors and that website about us—I thought I needed my friends to help me—only I should have told them I could be friends with you *and* them and that's what I was going to do but I hit Send instead of Delete and I think I hate the Internet now—"

"Sophie," Jimmy said.

"What?" Sophie said.

"Take a breath."

Sophie took a huge one. "Will you forgive me? Because I'm *really* sorry."

"Sure," Jimmy said.

Sophie blinked. "That's it? You're just going to forgive me just like that?"

"Yeah. Why not?"

"Then—we're still friends?" Sophie said.

"We're cool," Jimmy said. "Only—"

Sophie held her breath again. Here it came.

220

"I'm not the one you gotta worry about," he said. "Fiona and the girls, they don't get why you're not speaking to them."

"They don't *get* it? They said I was a liar!"

"About what?"

"About—nothing." Sophie drove her fingers through her hair. "I don't think they're even sorry for what they wrote about me."

"Whatever it was, I don't think so," Jimmy said. "Fiona says they didn't do anything wrong." He shrugged. "I sure don't get why Fiona thinks I'm scum all of a sudden."

Sophie sank back against the lockers. "This is going to be a really weird rehearsal."

Jimmy shrugged. "We could just practice our scenes and they could do other stuff."

"You tell them that, then," Sophie said.

Sophie's stomach squirmed as she followed Jimmy to the courtyard. All of this felt so un-Corn Flake—not even being able to rehearse a film with her friends, when that was one of the main things that made them the Corn Flakes. It was heinous.

Am I making too big a deal out of this? she thought.

The aching emptiness told her no.

Am I supposed to just act like it never happened? They really hurt me, and they're not even sorry!

But maybe they were. Maybe Jimmy didn't get girls any more than Vincent did.

There was only one thing to do. Face-to-face, Lacie had told her.

When Sophie and Jimmy got to the courtyard, everybody was busy setting up. Willoughby did her poodle thing at the sight of Sophie, and then she looked at Fiona.

Fiona put down the baby Jesus doll she was carrying and put her hands on her hips.

"So are you going to rehearse with us?" she said.

"Can we talk first?" Sophie said.

"You mean about the fact that you've been ditching us all day?" Fiona looked at the Corn Flakes, who were all gathering nervously beside her. "We'd love to hear about that."

The little pink bow of a mouth was once again drawn into a knot. The magic gray eyes looked as hard as stones. There was no "I'm sorry" hinting around the edges of her voice.

"Never mind," Sophie said. "Let's just rehearse."

It was the worst. Everyone was so stiff and awkward, Vincent said there wasn't anything he'd caught on film that they could use. Sophie cut the rehearsal short early and ran like a bunny for the late bus. She was halfway there when a solid voice behind her said, "Sophie. Wait up."

Sophie turned to face Maggie and kept walking backward. "I can't miss the bus," she said. "My mom can't pick me up."

"Then I'll email you when I get home," Maggie said. Her face was still, like she was afraid if she moved it, it would show what was going on inside her.

"I don't think I'm ever going online again," Sophie said.

Maggie stopped. "I'm still gonna email you."

Sophie could only nod as she turned away. There was too much confusion in her head for anything to break free and make sense.

None of it got sorted out on the way home, not even when she tried to be Louisa Linkhart or Cynthia Cyber. Even imagining Jesus didn't give her any answers. When she got home, Mama was sound asleep on the couch in the family room, and there was a note saying Zeke was with Boppa. There was only Sophie and the monster computer, staring at her out of its one big monitor-eye.

Eleven

I'm still gonna email you, Maggie had said.

To tell me I'm a liar? Sophie thought. *I can't handle that!*

But the missing them, that was bigger than the being afraid. Palms sweating, she logged on with slippery fingers.

75 New Messages, the computer told her.

Seventy-five? Sophie thought. *I don't even know that many people!*

She scanned the list for familiar screen names. There were none. Maggie's email wasn't there, either. When the IM chime rang, Sophie twitched. It was from Anne-Stuart.

ANGELEYES: Everybody's been asking me for your email address. Going out with Jimmy made you popular. How come you broke up?

Sophie didn't answer. She went back to the email list. Were these all from people who had asked Anne-Stuart for her email address? Come to think of it, how did Anne-Stuart get her address? It didn't make sense.

Creeping the arrow to the Read icon, Sophie clicked it. An email written in a big purple font poked at her like an accusing finger.

```
You are a loser. Only losers go out with a cool
guy like Jimmy and then dump him. You are scum.
```

Almost as if the mouse had come to life, it clicked down the list, opening email after email.

```
You aren't even that cute. Who do you think
you are?
```

```
You're such a geek. You'll never get another
boyfriend.
```

```
You skinny little weirdo. I don't know why
Jimmy ever liked you in the first place.
```

Sophie didn't even realize she was sobbing until Mama's voice made its way across the room.

"Come here, Dream Girl," she said. "Don't look at that any-more. Come here."

Sophie ran to her and cried for so long with her face buried in Mama she forgot herself. Only when Lacie was suddenly there, saying, "Those hateful, evil little—freaks!" did Sophie lift her head. Her glasses were sideways on her face and salt-stained with tears, but she could see Lacie leaning over Sophie's computer, hand on the mouse.

"What are you doing?" Sophie said.

"I'm saving them and printing them out," Lacie said. "Daddy's going to want to see this."

"What is it?" Mama said.

"You don't even want to know," Lacie said.

But Mama did want to know, and when Daddy got home, they held a family conference at the coffee table.

"This has gone too far, Soph," Daddy said. "You know I have to do something."

Sophie didn't answer. It hurt too much to talk.

Daddy ran a hand over his head. "Of course, there may not be anything the school can do if none of this came from school computers. Not unless the effects of it have spilled over into school." He put a big hand on Sophie's shoulder. "Now tell me the truth, has this harassment started to affect your grades?"

"Yes," Sophie said. Her voice sounded like wood.

Mama stirred on the couch. "The school nurse called and said she saw you twice today, Dream Girl."

"This stuff would make me sick too," Lacie said. She scowled at the handful of emails she was holding. Her eyebrows puckered at the top one. "I know this address. Katie Schneider uses this one—does she have a sister or brother at the middle school?"

"There's B.J. Schneider," Sophie managed to say. "She's one of the Corn Pops."

"Hello!" Lacie said.

"It's a start anyway." Daddy smothered Sophie's shoulder with his hand again. "I'll see Mr. Bentley first thing in the morning. For right now, I want you to stay off the Internet completely."

"That's so not fair," Lacie said. "She's the victim and she gets the punishment."

"I'm not punishing, I'm protecting," Daddy said. "It's the same reason I had to cut down Zeke's giant yarn Spider-Man web—so he wouldn't get hurt." He let go of Sophie's shoulder. "I'm just shielding you from a different kind of web, Baby Girl."

That's me, all right, Sophie thought. *Baby Girl.*

But she nodded at Daddy. There was nobody to email anyway.

"Hey, look," Lacie said. "It's snowing!"

225

Suddenly it was all about the snow, which almost never happened in Poquoson. It put Mama in a Christmas mood, and within five minutes she had Lacie baking cookies and Sophie bringing her pen and paper to make lists.

"I'm going to direct Christmas right from this couch," Mama said. She patted her tummy. "You and me, little girlfriend."

Sophie didn't feel at all like Christmas. All she felt was sadness for her baby-sister-to-be. She was coming into a world where you couldn't even turn to your best friends when everybody else was ripping you apart.

There was no school the next day because of the snow. Although Mama tried to keep everybody focused on holiday preparations, Sophie spent most of her time upstairs wrapped in a blanket because she was cold from the inside out. She couldn't even stand to be in the same room with her computer.

When more snow came Tuesday night and the TV announced Wednesday morning that the roads were so bad school would be closed again, Sophie wasn't sure whether to cheer or cry. She decided it didn't matter. She was still going to feel like someone had kicked out her soul no matter where she was.

A little before lunchtime, Dr. Peter called.

"No Bible study class today, Loodle," he said. "Du-uh, huh?"

"That's okay," Sophie told him. "I wasn't going to come anyway."

"Oh?"

"I can't be around the Corn Flakes. I don't think we're friends anymore."

"Impossible!" Dr. Peter said.

"That's what *I* thought," Sophie said, and then she burst into tears.

"Are you up for a visitor?" he said in a husky-soft voice. "Let me talk to your mama."

Dr. Peter was there within half an hour, and Lacie set them up in Daddy's study so they could have privacy—since Zeke was home too.

Sophie wrapped up in the blanket she'd dragged from upstairs and curled up in Daddy's desk chair. But before he sat down, Dr. Peter said, "I realized on the way over here that I didn't even ask you if you wanted to talk to me about this."

"I do!" Sophie said. "I'm all tangled up in knots like I used to get, only Cynthia Cyber and Louisa Linkhart can't even help me. I have *two* dream characters, and I'm still confused." She took a breath. "And I *have* been talking to Jesus."

"I have no doubt."

"I've confessed every sin I ever committed."

Dr. Peter's eyes twinkled, but he didn't smile. At least *he* took her seriously.

"Then it's a sure thing you're forgiven, Loodle," he said. "Why don't you start from the top?"

Sophie told him everything, which took a while since there were so many parts to it. Her voice got higher and higher as she talked, so that by the time she got to the heinous emails, she could hardly hear herself. She pulled the blanket tighter, but she still felt like an ice cube.

Dr. Peter crossed one foot over the other knee and wiggled it. "This is huge for you, Loodle," he said. "I think we need to unpack it, like a suitcase. You want to start with the Corn Flakes?"

Sophie's stomach squirmed, but she nodded.

"The problem is, how are you going to be able to forgive them, right?" Dr. Peter said.

"How *can* I forgive them?"

"Like I said, God has forgiven you. Jimmy forgave you too, right?"

"But I told him I was sorry," Sophie said. "Fiona and the other girls, they don't even think they did anything wrong." She pulled at her hair. "Am I supposed to just pretend it didn't happen?"

Dr. Peter waggled his head back and forth. "Yes and no."

"How can it be both?"

"Okay, let's keep it simple. We have to try to handle forgiveness the way God does. We'll never get it totally right," he added as Sophie opened her mouth to protest. "But we have a responsibility to try."

"I'll never even get close," Sophie said. "But what do I have to lose?"

"That's my Loodle. Okay, think about the story we read last time. The master represented God, right?"

"Yes."

"And he forgave the servant. So there's your first step."

"But—"

"Even though it meant he wouldn't get paid back, the master let it go."

Sophie sat up and thought about that. "So, even if I don't get to hear them say they were wrong, I have to let it go."

"That's where the yes and the no come in." Dr. Peter rubbed his hands together. "Yes, the master forgave him, and the servant got off easy—but it didn't change him. So the next time the servant messed up, it was off to jail. When you forgive somebody, that doesn't mean she gets to escape her responsibilities."

"So—yes, I forgive the Corn Flakes. But—no, I don't just let them get away with hurting me." Sophie flopped back in the chair. "But I don't get how!"

228

"The whole reason for forgiveness isn't so people can just keep on doing stupid things," Dr. Peter said. "It's so people can have another chance to get it right."

Sophie considered that. "You mean, like a teacher dropping your lowest grade."

"Sure. And when somebody really feels like they've been forgiven, sometimes that changes something in them and they're better people." Dr. Peter wiggled his eyebrows. "Other times, you, the forgiver, have to help them."

Sophie looked down at her lap. "I want to forgive them—but it hurts so much."

"God never said it was going to be painless. But when you don't do it—well, what happened to the servant when he didn't forgive the guy who owed *him*?"

"He got thrown in jail for, like, six years."

"How did it feel when Jimmy forgave you?"

"Good!"

"And when a teacher drops that grade—"

"Relieved."

"And how about all the confessing you've been doing—does it help?"

"I think so."

Dr. Peter sat back, arms folded. "We'll only know that if you can find it in yourself to forgive your Corn Flakes."

Sophie felt the ping in her head. "So I forgive them, because that's what God does, and if they really get it they won't do that again, but I might have to help them."

Dr. Peter held up his palm. "That's it, Loodle," he said as Sophie high-fived him. "I think you can take it from here. You want to pray with me?"

After they talked to God together and Dr. Peter left, Sophie still wasn't completely sure what she was going to say. But she took the phone into her room. Her hand shook as she punched in Fiona's number.

"It's me," Sophie said when Fiona answered. Then, before she could chicken out, she plunged on. "I forgive you for not believing me about Jimmy—and for talking about me in the chat room. Even if you don't think you did anything wrong, I'm still gonna forgive you and I still want to be your friend because you're a good person and you'll figure it out and if you don't, I'll help you."

There was silence. Sophie's heart sagged.

Finally, Fiona said, "I'll send you an email."

"I can't—" Sophie started to say.

But the phone clicked in her ear. After that, she didn't even try to call the other girls. She just sat on her bed with the phone in her lap and closed her eyes.

I tried, Jesus, I really tried, she prayed. *It didn't work out the way it was supposed to.*

From the look in his kind eyes, she was pretty sure he knew exactly how she felt. He'd probably been there himself.

Sophie and Daddy got to GMMS early the next morning so Daddy could talk to Mr. Bentley. He had the emails in his briefcase.

"I can't make any promises, Soph," he said before they got out of the truck. "But I'll sure go to bat for you."

I don't think it's gonna do any good, Sophie thought. *It's probably going to make things worse.*

Daddy put his hand on her shoulder for about the fiftieth time since the night before. "I want you to be able to enjoy your computer the way it's meant to be used," he said. "I'm going to install some editing software on there so you and your team can do some killer stuff with your movies."

What team? Sophie thought.

"And I'm setting up a new email account for you."

"I don't think I'm ever going online again."

"You have the right to check your email without being afraid of what you're going to read. That's why I'm here."

Sophie swallowed a throat full of tears. "Thanks for trying, Daddy."

She went to her locker and was staring at her stack of books when somebody tall came up beside her. It was Eddie Wornom.

"Hey," he said.

It wasn't an I'm-about-to-make-your-life-a-waking-nightmare 'hey,' so she said "Hey" back. Besides, Coach Virile had told her to give it a chance.

"Coach Nanini says we have a lot in common," he said.

"Coach Nanini says *we* have something in common?" She didn't add, *Is he mental?*

"He said I should keep trying to talk to you, 'cause I've been getting cyber-bullied too."

Sophie let her locker slam shut and stared at him.

"I know," Eddie said. "It used to be, I woulda been the one doing it. That's probably why they're doing it to me now, because like I told you, I won't do that stuff anymore."

Half of Sophie wanted to say, *Do you think I'm a TOTAL moron?*

But the other half saw his eyes drooping again.

"Okay," she said with a heavy sigh. "We can talk—only not here."

"Coach Nanini said we could talk in the gym."

Why am I doing this? Sophie asked herself as they walked in silence to the gymnasium. *Don't I have enough problems?*

She was about to change her mind and bolt when Eddie held the gym door open for her. Since he didn't trip her on the way in, she sighed and sat down with him on the lowest row of bleachers.

"I didn't go to military school," he said. "My mom sent me to this boot camp run by a bunch of Christians. Nobody believes it, but it totally changed me."

Sophie squinted at him. "You do look different."

"I *am* different. I'm not a bully anymore, only the people I thought were my friends say I'm a loser now, and the people that always hated me look at me like, 'He's fakin' it. He's gonna do somethin' any minute.'"

"Yeah," Sophie said, "that's what we were thinking."

As soon as she said it, she was sorry. But Eddie just nodded.

"Coach said it was gonna take people a while to trust me. What am I supposed to do 'til then, though?" Eddie cracked a knuckle. "I almost helped Tod and them with some stuff, just so they wouldn't ditch me. I didn't, but it stinks being by yourself all the time."

"Tell me about it," Sophie said.

"It wouldn't be that bad if they would just leave me alone, but no—they gotta attack me on websites." His fists doubled in his lap. "It makes me wanna punch somebody—and I can't go there. I'm outta chances."

"They have a website about you?" Sophie said.

Eddie uncurled his hands and picked at a cuticle. "It's not just about me—it's about everybody they hate at GMMS." He looked at her sideways. "You're on there too."

Sophie covered her mouth with both hands. She was that sure she was going to throw up.

"Don't go to it," Eddie said. "I'm not even gonna tell you what it says. I just thought—maybe—" He sprawled back against the bleachers. "Coach says we could probably help

232

each other get through this. I don't know. If I bust those guys, I might as well just change schools."

The bell rang, and Coach Nanini appeared in the doorway. "You two need a couple of passes to class?"

Eddie didn't say anything else until Coach handed him a pass. Then he said to Sophie, "You probably have more guts than I do. I could maybe help—as long as you don't use my name."

Sophie squinted through her glasses as she watched him lope across the gym. *He's kind of being a coward*, she thought. *But, then, who could blame him?*

"You know," Coach Virile said as he scratched his signature on her pass, "the people who get forgiven for the most stuff usually change the most, Little Bit." Then he shook his head. "You might be just a smidgeon of a person on the outside, but you have a mighty spirit."

Feeling less than mighty, Sophie left the gym.

Twelve

✤ ⌂ ✺

Halfway through first period, Mrs. Clayton came to her desk and whispered,

"You're wanted in Mr. Bentley's office, Sophie."

"Busted," Colton said.

Before Sophie even got to the door, she saw Julia pass her phone to Colton.

I'm about to be a text message, she thought. She didn't see why Lacie even wanted a cell phone. Sophie didn't want any of it — ever.

Daddy was still there when she reached Mr. Bentley's office. They were sitting in chairs in front of the principal's desk, looking like old buddies.

"I'm impressed with your father, Sophie," Mr. Bentley said as Sophie sat down facing them. He rubbed his salt-and-pepper beard. "Most parents aren't paying attention to what's going on on the Internet."

Daddy smiled at her. "Sophie's taught me a lot about standing up for what's right."

Sophie stopped clutching the arms of her chair. Mr. Bentley shifted in his.

"I've told your dad," he said, "that I'll try to help, but unfortunately if nothing that's happened outside the school can be linked to anything here, my hands are tied. However, I am going to contact some parents, particularly Anne-Stuart Riggins' mother and B.J. Schneider's." Mr. Bentley held up two computer printouts. "They both sent you emails from their moms' work email accounts. That's why you didn't recognize them." He rubbed his beard again. "We have all the parents' email addresses in case of emergency."

"It's a start," Daddy said.

Sophie tried not to picture Anne-Stuart coming after her, sniffing and snorting like a bull, with B.J. and the rest of her mob behind her.

"Now," Mr. Bentley went on, "as for Anne-Stuart copying your screen name from an instant message, that's very likely. However, we can't prove it."

Sophie nodded. She pretty much already knew that.

Daddy leaned forward in his chair, toward Sophie. "But," he said, "there are some things we *can* prove."

"You can?" Sophie said. "What?"

"I'll tell you later." Daddy looked at Mr. Bentley. "I *will* get that website taken down. I'm willing to take legal action, although I hope it doesn't come to that."

Legal action? Sophie thought. She squirmed in the seat — until Daddy looked at her in a way he never had before. Almost like she was another grown-up.

"She's mature for her age," he said, "but I still have to do what I can to protect her."

Sophie heard a ping in her head. It seemed to say, right out loud, *Aren't you glad he's in your loop?*

"I admire that." Mr. Bentley leaned toward Sophie too. "But I do want to remind you that none of what's been said about you is true. Try not to let it get to you."

Daddy tilted his head. "Don't you remember being twelve years old, Mr. Bentley?" He looked at Sophie. "It's the most vulnerable time in your life. Words stab you, whether they're true or not."

Sophie smiled at him. It was *her* turn to be impressed with her father.

Daddy gave her a hug before she left Mrs. Bentley's office, and that made her feel safer than she had in days—until she reached the waiting area. They were all there—Julia, Anne-Stuart, Cassie, B.J., Tod, and Colton. Several other kids leaned against the wall, looking terrified. The faces of the Corn Pops and Fruit Loops had nothing to do with fear.

They were tight with pure hate.

Sophie tried to erase those looks from her mind as she somehow got through the rest of first-second block. Replacing them with Jesus' kind eyes helped, but she wished she had her Corn Flakes' faces sending her courage from across the room. She couldn't even glance their way.

But when the bell rang and she hurried down the hall, they were suddenly on her—Fiona, Maggie, and Darbie. Maggie gave Fiona a shove toward Sophie.

"Fiona has something to say to you," Maggie said.

Fiona looked like she would rather throw herself down the stairs than say a word. Her magic-gray eyes were actually frightened.

"Do it," Darbie said.

"I want to," Fiona said. "But it's hard! I said it perfect in the email."

"What email?" Sophie said.

"The one I sent you—saying I'm sorry and I'm a horrible friend and I should have believed you, only I was being possessive again and I hate it when I do that—but I could hardly help it this time because it was about a boy and I don't get that yet—" Fiona took a ragged breath. "I wish you would just read the email."

"I can't," Sophie said, tears welling up. "My dad took me off the Internet because people wrote me horrible things."

"I'm glad your dad did that," Darbie said. She jammed her hair behind her ears. "Talking on the Internet is what made a bags of everything to begin with."

"I'm sorry too, Sophie," Maggie said.

"You were hardly even part of it, Mags." Fiona looked at Sophie, eyes brimming. "Mags is the one who made me be halfway brave and come to you."

"I was part of it, though," Darbie said. "I'm so, so sorry, Sophie."

Sophie could see Fiona swallowing hard. "So, do you really forgive us?" Fiona said.

Sophie watched the tears trail down Fiona's cheeks. *You never, ever cry,* Sophie thought. That was what pinged in her mind. It wasn't the words Fiona said that convinced her. It was the look in her eyes, saying, *Please, Sophie.*

You couldn't see that on a computer.

"I already told you that I forgive you," Sophie said. "All of you."

Fiona just stood there until Sophie put her arms around her and squeezed.

"We should have done this in the first place," Maggie said.

"Soph, I didn't even know I was sorry," Fiona said into Sophie's hair, "until yesterday on the phone when you told me you forgave me."

Maggie gave them both a little push. "We gotta get to PE."

"Uh-oh." Darbie nodded toward the end of the hall. Julia and Colton were heading toward them.

"They're livid," Fiona said.

The Flakes tried to hurry past them, but Colton and Julia turned and walked right along with them, one on each side, eyes blazing.

You can't see THAT on the Internet, either, Sophie thought. But she felt some of the old Sophie-courage seeping back in. They couldn't hide behind their computers this time.

"Your father and his stupid program," Julia said, pointing at Sophie.

"What program?" Sophie said.

"The one that can track emails to the senders." Colton all but spit on the floor. "What is he, the Internet police?"

Sophie lifted her chin. "Somebody has to be."

"Huh." Julia tossed her hair, catching Sophie's cheek with it. "His little program can't prove that somebody didn't hack into our email accounts —"

"And steal our screen names," Colton put in.

"Here come the rest of them," Maggie muttered.

Sophie glanced back to see B.J., Cassie, and Tod charging their way.

"Let me get this straight." Fiona stopped in front of the locker-room door. "*All* of you told Mr. Bentley somebody got into *all* your accounts and ripped off *everybody's* screen names?"

Julia looked at the group now joining them. They all nodded.

"It looks that way," Julia said.

"And not even your *daddy* can prove it didn't happen," Colton said.

"Besides." Tod pointed his whole face at Sophie. "We told them we were just messing around."

B.J. rolled her eyes. "It was just a big joke."

Darbie put her arm around Sophie. "Does it look like she's laughing?"

"It doesn't matter whether you go down for this or not," Fiona said. "We can email people and tell them it was all lies." She looked at Sophie. "Because it was."

"Whatever," Julia said.

When the Corn Pops were gone, Maggie frowned at Fiona. "I don't think we should do that email thing," she said.

"We're not," Sophie said. But she smiled at Fiona. She'd heard what she needed to hear.

Willoughby was already at the lockers when the girls got there.

"Where were you?" Sophie said.

Willoughby pulled her shirt over her head. "I'm sorry about what we said in the chat room," she said from inside it.

"I forgive everybody," Sophie said.

"Thanks." Willoughby picked up her tennis shoes and hurried out in her socks.

"What's up with her?" Fiona said.

"I know one thing," Sophie said. "I'm gonna find out. Face-to-face."

But when the Flakes got to the gym, Vincent, Nathan, and Jimmy practically knocked them down getting to them. Willoughby was with them. So was Eddie Wornom.

"What are the Fruit Loops doing with *him*?" Fiona muttered to Sophie.

Coach Yates blew her whistle. "LaCroix?" she yelled. "You kids go up in the bleachers. You have ten minutes." She glanced at Coach Virile, who was standing beside her. "Make that fifteen."

As she turned away, Coach Virile flashed ten fingers twice and grinned at Sophie.

When they were gathered on the top two rows in the corner, Jimmy nodded at Eddie. "He's got something to tell us," he said. "Coach Nanini says we can trust him."

Nobody said anything. Finally, Sophie said, "Okay, so what is it?"

Eddie blew air out of his cheeks. "I was with Tod when he stole the school email list for the whole seventh grade. He used it to tell everybody about the Getting Together website and the hate one."

"And you helped him," Fiona said. "Which is why you haven't told on him."

Eddie's forehead folded into rows as he shook his head. "I didn't help him. I just didn't tell because all of them hate me enough as it is." He blinked his eyes as if they were full of sand. "I knew if I told and they found out, Tod and Colton would wanna fight me—and it would be too hard to say no. I had to stay away from them so I wouldn't blow my last chance."

"So why tell *us*?" Vincent said. "You're the one who has to turn him in." His voice cracked like an earthquake fault.

Eddie looked at Sophie. "I want to now. But it's like, man, who's gonna back me up when they come after me?"

"I will," Sophie heard herself say.

Corn Flakes poked her from every direction. She even heard Willoughby gasp. Vincent and Nathan gave Jimmy can-you-*believe*-this-chick? looks.

But Jimmy was watching Sophie. She could almost hear the ping going off in his head.

"I'm in," he said.

Fiona sighed loudly. "Like I'm gonna let you two do it alone and get massacred. I'm in too."

Slowly the rest of the group nodded. Sophie thought Eddie might actually cry.

"Will you back me up too?" said a tiny voice.

They all looked at Willoughby, who seemed to be trying to get as small as her voice.

"Okay, *what* is going on with you?" Fiona said. "You've been acting weird all day."

Willoughby just looked at Vincent, who pulled Willoughby's cell phone out of his pocket. "I figured out how to pull up that picture of Sophie putting her pants on. Willoughby only thought she'd erased it."

Sophie had to let that sink in.

"Hello!" Vincent said. "It was taken in the locker room. This is how we link all the outside stuff to school."

Eddie gave his knuckles a crack. "That picture was on the hate website," he said.

"What hate website?" Fiona said.

Cynthia Cyber leaped from her chair at the computer desk and made a victory lap around her office. "Yes!" she shouted to Dot Com and Maga Byte and anyone else who would listen. "I've got those cyber bullies now! Their Internet harassment days are over!" She stopped and smiled broadly. "In fact, their LIVES are as much as over!"

But Louisa Linkhart smoothed the skirt of her gown and looked at her dear friends. "That is not the proper attitude," she told them. "They must be punished, yes, but their only chance for change is if we forgive them." She looked lovingly at her husband and added, "Just as we have been forgiven."

"Okay," Eddie said, "you're still the weirdest person I know." And then he shrugged and added, "But who cares?"

Coach Nanini whistled through his teeth and waved his arm.

"You ready?" Eddie said to Willoughby.

Willoughby looked at Sophie as if she were about to be dragged by the hair.

"It's okay," Sophie told her.

She was glad that Coach Nanini escorted Willoughby and Eddie, though. It was still a little hard to get used to trusting Eddie Wornom.

As the rest of them picked their way down from the bleachers, Fiona said, "If we forgive those heinous little—the Pops and the Loops—does that mean we have to hang out with them? Because I am *not*—"

"No," Sophie said. "If they change, then—"

"They're not gonna change," Maggie said.

Sophie jumped from the bottom row to the floor. "I don't know if they will," she said. "But if forgiving can change Eddie Wornom, it can change anybody."

Sophie straightened her shoulders and started toward Group Six. Julia and Colton nudged each other, nervously. But then they stared blankly at Sophie as if they had just put on masks.

"Can't you just email them and tell them?" Fiona said as they got closer.

Sophie, Darbie, and Maggie just looked at her.

"Okay, okay," Fiona said.

Sophie had the urge to walk like she was wearing a corset. Cynthia Cyber's proof was forming accusing words in her head. But the kind eyes pushed all of that away. The kind, forgiving eyes.

Sophie and the Flakes stopped at the edge of the mat.

"Aren't you supposed to be at your own stations?" the student aide said.

Julia ignored her and stood up. "Why did Coach Nanini take Eddie and Willoughby to the office?"

"They can't prove anything," Tod said. He didn't bother to get up from the floor.

"Really?" Fiona said. "Then why are you two so nervous?"

Sophie nudged her, and Fiona sucked in her lips.

"The thing is," Sophie said to Julia and Tod, "*I* know you did it—and it was heinous—and you need to stop treating

people like that. You ought to take the consequences. But—"
Sophie stopped and took a deep breath. The whole gym was
suddenly silent. Although Coach Yates moved in close, she
didn't touch her whistle.

"But *what*?" Julia said.

"But—" Sophie breathed deeply, and with it came the old
power to be who she was. "But as for me, I forgive you."

She wasn't sure she'd ever seen shock before, but she saw it
now in Julia's and Tod's faces.

Any second now, they're going to laugh at me, Sophie thought.

But it didn't matter. With the Flakes and Jimmy and even
Nathan behind her—and the kind eyes in her mind—she
was ready.

She was ready for anything.

Glossary

appalled (a-PAWld) being really shocked, and almost disgusted, when something happens

class (klas) not a group of students, but a word that means something's really cool

embellished (em-BEL-isht) really tricky lying, like when you take the truth and add little details to make it sound better

furtively (FUR-tiv-lee) being really sneaky and not at all obvious, like an undercover spy who can't get caught

glean (gleen) to gather little bits of information to use them later

guffaw (guf-FAWW) a kind of laugh that happens when you find something really funny and can't help but laugh really loud

heinous (HEY-nus) unbelievably mean and cruel

livid (li-vid) becoming incredibly angry, and turning so red you feel like you're going to have a volcanic eruption

massacred (MAH-si-curd) to be defeated so badly that you feel absolutely destroyed

obnoxious (ub-KNOCK-shus) a person who is offensive and a complete pain in the butt, driving everyone crazy

out of context (owt of con-text) when you take something a person actually said, but make it sound completely different by repeating it in a different situation

priorities (pry-OR-uh-tees) what you think are the most important things in your life; what you give the most attention to

ravage (RA-vij) destroying something so completely that there doesn't seem to be any way to fix it

rehabilitate (re-hah-BIL-i-tate) going through a series of treatments that are meant to fix what's wrong with a person

spectacular (spek-TACK-yoo-lar) absolutely amazing, with breathtaking possibilities

vigilant (VI-jah-lent) keeping your eyes wide open and being on guard for anything bad that could happen

virile (VEER-il) the definition of manly; muscular, strong, and really hunky. Think cute movie star meets not-so-icky body builder

vulnerable (VULL-ner-uh-bull) being easily hurt or wounded; very delicate

Sophie and Friends

Nancy Rue

Meet Sophie LaCroix, a creative soul with a desire to become a great film director someday, and she definitely has a flair for drama! Her overactive imagination frequently lands her in trouble, but her faith and friends always save the day. This bindup includes two-books-in-one.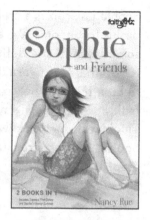

Sophie's First Dance: Sophie and her friends, the Corn Flakes, are in a tizzy over the end-of-school dance – especially when invitations start coming – from boys! Will the Flakes break up, or can Sophie direct a happy ending?

Sophie's Stormy Summer: One of the Flakes is struck with cancer, and Sophie severely struggles with the shocking news, until she finds that friends – and faith – show the way to a new adventure called growing up.

Sophie Steps Up

Nancy Rue

Sophie LaCroix is a creative soul with a desire to become a great film director someday, and she definitely has a flair for drama! Her overactive imagination frequently lands her in trouble, but her faith and friends always save the day. This bindup includes two-books-in-one, Sophie Under Pressure and Sophie Steps Up.

Sophie's Drama

Nancy Rue

Sophie LaCroix is a creative soul with a desire to become a great film director someday, and she definitely has a flair for drama! Her overactive imagination frequently lands her in trouble, but her faith and friends always save the day. This bindup includes two-books-in-one, Sophie's Drama and Sophie Gets Real.

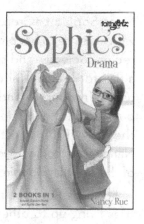

Available in stores and online!

Sophie's Friendship Fiasco

Nancy Rue

Meet Sophie LaCroix, a creative soul with a desire to become a great film director someday, and she definitely has a flair for drama! Her overactive imagination frequently lands her in trouble, but her faith and friends always save the day. From best-selling author, Nancy Rue, comes two-in-one bindups of the popular Sophie series.

Sophie's Friendship Fiasco: Sophie tries living up to other's expectations, but lately she's letting everyone down. When she misrepresents the Flakes - with good intentions - she loses their friendship. Will they ever forgive her?

Sophie and the New Girl: Sophie likes the new girl who joins the film club. She's witty and unique, even if she is a bit bizarre. When the camera goes missing, the other Flakes are quick to accuse. Will Sophie be able to identify the real thief?

Available in stores and online!

Faithgirlz Journal

My Doodles, Dreams and Devotion

Looking for a place to dream, doodle, and record your innermost questions and secrets? You will find what you seek within the pages of the Faithgirlz Journal, which has plenty of space for you to discover who you are, explore who God is shaping you to be, or write down whatever inspires you. Each journal page has awesome quotes and powerful Bible verses to encourage you on  your walk with God! So grab a pen, colored pencils, or even a handful of markers. Whatever you write is just between you and God.

NIV Faithgirlz! Backpack Bible, Revised Edition

Small enough to fit into a backpack or bag, this Bible can go anywhere a girl does.

Features include:

- Fun Italian Duo-Tone™ design
- Twelve full-color pages of Faithgirlz fun that helps girls learn the "Beauty of Believing!"
- Words of Christ in red
- Ribbon marker
- Complete text of the bestselling NIV translation

NIV Faithgirlz! Bible, Revised Edition

Nancy Rue

Every girl wants to know she's totally unique and special. This Bible says that with Faithgirlz! sparkle. Through the many in-text features found only in the Faithgirlz! Bible, girls will grow closer to God as they discover the journey of a lifetime.

Features include:

- Book introductions—Read about the who, when, where, and what of each book.

- Dream Girl—Use your imagination to put yourself in the story.

- Bring It On!—Take quizzes to really get to know yourself.

- Is There a Little (Eve, Ruth, Isaiah) in You?—See for yourself what you have in common.

- Words to Live By—Check out these Bible verses that are great for memorizing.

- What Happens Next?—Create a list of events to tell a Bible story in your own words.

- Oh, I Get It!—Find answers to Bible questions you've wondered about.

- The complete NIV translation

- Features written by bestselling author Nancy Rue

Available in stores and online!

ZONDERVAN
.com